On The Right Path

THE TRADIE LADY SERIES
BOOK TWO

RIAN BIRCH

Slow Sunday press

Edited by Alex Oldfield, The Editing Room

First Edition: August 2025

eBook ISBN: 9781763884021

Paperback ISBN: 9781763884038

Thanks Dad, for teaching me how to hammer that very first nail as a kid.

Australian Language and Slang

On The Right Path is set in Australia, and has Australian English throughout.

This is a book about tradies, so there's going to be some Aussie slang to keep an eye out for:

Brekkie - Breakfast

Bunnings - Aussie hardware store, similar to Home Depot

Butterfish - Battered takeaway fish

Chips - Thick cut fries

Dim Sims - Fried dumplings (usually with *a lot* of salt)

Hoodie - Hooded sweatshirt

Jumper - Sweater / pullover

Pineapple Fritter - Fried pineapple in batter

Smoko - Morning tea / coffee break

Snag - Sausage

TAFE - Similar to community colleges or vocational-technical schools

Takeaway - Takeout

Thongs - Flip flops

Toasties - Grilled cheese
Trackies - Sweats / joggers
Tradie - Blue collar worker
Ute - Pickup truck
Weet-Bix - Shredded wheat biscuits
Yeah, Nah - No (Nah, Yeah - Yes)

ONE

Jess

Jess eyed the amount, doing the math in her head.

It didn't add up.

Ricciardo had undercut her—again.

"Reasonable overtime, my arse," she grumbled, stuffing the payslip into her back pocket as she slumped into his office chair. Fifty-two-hour weeks were the new norm, replacing the forty-five that had already stomped all over her original thirty-eight-hour contract. This was getting ridiculous. The argument wasn't new, but it was time to step up and have a serious conversation with him. She needed more money, or she'd never save for a house with Adam at this rate. What was the point of busting her arse for the same amount? Time to bring it up again, threaten to leave and see if that would make him listen.

The rickety chair groaned as she leaned on the armrest, staring blankly at the front-of-house monthly roster on the wall. Her fifty-two-hour schedule stared back, mocking her. As one of Ricciardo's longest-standing employees, Jess knew she'd be missed—and that was the sore point she could push on to try and get things to change. Otherwise, unemployment didn't look so bad. She could totally live off two-minute noodles for a while.

Jess couldn't pinpoint the exact moment she'd started to hate her job. At first, she'd loved it, the bustling energy and late nights; fresh out of uni, it was a fun job that was secure, and Ricciardo paid her well. Eight years later, as the hours snuck up and the money remained the same, her patience had thinned to non-existence. Late nights and long days left her with little energy at home to just—be Jess.

Resting her hand on her chin, she thought of her friends Taylor and Sam, newly engaged and sailing together along the coastline of another beautiful white beach. She tried not to envy them, but in moments like this, it wasn't easy.

Jess had a full day ahead of her, it loomed long and large, each one feeling like rinse and repeat. At least she only had an afternoon shift tomorrow, before two days of blissful nothing. Then she thought of the laundry she needed to do, the stack of dishes still left in (and around) the sink, and the fact that she really needed to call her mum for a check-in.

Jess stopped her internal to-do list, bringing her focus back to the here and now with a deep breath. She'd promised herself she'd do another meditation session tonight, to try and reel in those negative thoughts and keep herself in the moment rather than sulking about everything that wasn't going right in her life. She let her breath out slowly. Much better.

Ricciardo's drab office around her wasn't helping. The back end of a restaurant was usually the opposite of what diners saw out front. Everything was in disarray. While Ricciardo ran things smoothly, his office was messier than the snack table at games night with her friends. Stacks of paper lined the desk, and clipboards hung on the wall. Clearing her mind, she left the cluttered space behind and stepped into the frenzy of the kitchen at peak dinner time.

Jimmy was spooning hot garlic butter over a steak, the flames licking at the edge of the pan like they wanted a taste. Her stomach grumbled at the thought. There was no way she'd get a break now, even if she wanted to. She eyed the clock on the wall. Time for her next round of customers.

The front door swung open as a pile of women walked in, laughing and chattering. One after the other, they streamed through the doorway, the noise level cranking up as they raised their voices to hear each other. It felt like twenty conversations taking place at once. Jess narrowed her eyes at the tablet in front of her, trying to concentrate as she tapped in the family's order at table six.

Twelve women later, Ellie had efficiently settled them at Jess's final table of the evening. Jess gave her a grateful smile, scooped up a pile of menus, and headed over.

"Welcome to Limone Restaurant. I'm Jess, and I'll be your waitress tonight." Jess tried to make eye contact with each woman at the table as she talked them through the weekly specials. She loved making everyone feel welcome and relaxed. Warm hands brushed hers as Jess passed the last menu across, her eyes catching on the woman's patchwork tattoos. She followed them all the way up her arm until they disappeared beneath long, dark wavy hair. Sage-green eyes locked onto hers.

"Nice sleeve," Jess said, unable to help herself. She

loved tattoos, and while she only had one herself, she was nosy when it came to others, wanting to know the stories behind every one of them. Patchworks were her kryptonite. She twitched, wanting a closer look. "Love the turtle," she said instead, clasping her hands behind her back.

"Thanks," the woman replied, flicking her long black hair off of her shoulder so she could study her own arm, hitting Jess with a wave of fresh shampoo at the same time. Her eyes brightened as she smiled up at Jess. "That's Ninja—"

"Do *not* ask her about those, or she won't shut up," interrupted a woman with a stylish blonde pixie cut and fade sitting next to her.

Jess smiled. "Well, I happen to be a fan, so I wouldn't be mad about it." She gave both ladies a wink. "I'll be back shortly to take your orders."

While the table was a rowdy bunch, there were no upended pasta bowls and the drink orders kept flowing, keeping Jess on her toes between them and the bar.

"I've got a lasagne and a principessa?" Jess held up the last two dishes.

"Principessa's mine," said the blonde.

A tattooed arm flung up. "And the lasagne is for me."

"Here you go, *Donatello*." Jess smirked, setting the woman's plate down. Their eyes caught again, making Jess feel warm.

"Do you know how many people don't get the *Ninja Turtles* reference?" The woman leaned back, hooking her elbow over the back of the chair. "I'm impressed."

"I know, I'm awesome." Jess pretended to flick her hair.

"Nerds." The blonde ribbed them as she scooped up a forkful of her pasta.

"I'm not a nerd—it's nostalgic," the tattooed woman defended.

"Damn straight," Jess agreed. "You two enjoy your meals." She quickly extricated herself from the group. It was a fine line—some diners loved to chat, while others spoke out of politeness but preferred their space. She'd honed her skills over the years: once the food was on the table, it was best to get out of there.

Before Jess knew it, most of the patrons had cleared out, and she began her closing routine, hoping the stragglers would take the hint. Three women remained at the big table, huddled together like ducks in what looked to be a serious conversation. By this time, the place had quietened enough for Ricciardo's soft Italian jazz to float through the room, bringing the energy down to a relaxed hum.

She spied Ricciardo behind the bar and hurried to him, hoping for a chance to speak up.

"Ricciardo, do you have a minute?"

He sighed at the interruption, though it didn't look like he'd been doing anything important. "Hmm?" he said, looking at her expectantly. Her armpits started to sweat under his gaze.

"It's just... I saw my pay, and it still looks like it's coming through at my contract rate... but with the extra hours, and I know—" She held up a hand to stop his usual argument, raising her voice to speak over the top of his attempted interjection. "I *know*. Reasonable overtime. But I feel this is getting beyond that and I want to be paid for my time." There. She'd asked for what she wanted. She tried hard to control her breathing, keeping it even and not thinking about her heart beating in her ears.

"It's the busy season Jess, you know I appreciate all the work you do out the front. You're an asset to this business."

"Yes, but—"

"I'll take it into consideration. Don't forget to keep your eye on your tables." He gave her a condescending smile, patting her shoulder as he moved past her and into the kitchen.

"Oh, and Jess?" he said in the doorway.

"Mmm?"

"Can you start at twelve tomorrow instead of three? Rachel is sick, and I don't have anyone else."

Jess looked at the ground, chest flushing before meeting his eyes. "Yep, sure thing." She smiled weakly. He hadn't waited for her answer.

She looked around the dining area, eyes catching on the tattooed woman, who was staring right back at her. Great. She'd humiliated herself in front of her patrons as well. Her face heated further. Why did every conversation with him make her feel stupid? She'd gone in with confidence, stood her ground... and nothing. "I *am* watching my tables," she mumbled. He was so good at complimenting then reprimanding her in the same breath, offering no change to her situation. How did she always find herself in the same situation no matter how much she tried to speak up?

Her thoughts spiralled as she went over the conversation repeatedly, until she stopped herself, refocusing on her clean up routine. At least she was no longer frantic between ten different tasks, with diners beckoning her left and right. Instead, she took her time. Methodically wiping down tables, laying out fresh, crisp white tablecloths, neatening their edges just so. Perfection. But time dragged like quicksand. The wall clock seemed to inch forward a minute every hour. Maybe the clock was broken. Or she was.

Time to make herself busy.

Jess approached the last lingering table.

"I can't just pluck someone out of thin air!" The tattooed woman sat rubbing at her temple.

"Ladies, final call for drinks if any of you would like a top up?"

"Can you find me an apprentice instead?"

Jess made a show of checking her pockets. "Looks like I am fresh out of those tonight unfortunately," she replied, playing along.

"Come on, Remi, leave the poor girl alone," the blonde butted in.

"I'm serious." Tattoo lady—*Remi*, it seemed—ignored the blonde and reached into her back pocket, taking out her wallet. "Here." She held up a crumpled business card. The third woman at the table eyed it with a pained look.

"Remi, the least you could do is give her one of our *clean* and *presentable* business cards!"

Out of the three women, the third was the most polished. Her hair was styled in a neat ponytail, and a slash of red lipstick made her blue eyes pop. Looking closer, Jess saw a resemblance between her and Remi.

Jess took the card. "*The Lady Builders*?"

"That's us," Remi said proudly. "I run it with my sister, Sophie." She gestured to the polished woman.

"We renovate homes, building kitchens, bathrooms and laundries," added Sophie.

The blonde piped up next, giving her a small wave. "And I'm JJ. The best painter you'll ever find—very unbiased opinion of course—I run my own business too."

"Awesome. Nice to meet you all." Jess eyed the card again. "And you're after an apprentice?"

"Yep," Remi replied. She looked over Jess's shoulder, then lowered her voice as she leaned forward. "I couldn't help but overhear earlier, so... you want a new job?"

Jess was momentarily fixated on the woman's face, distracted by the way her hair framed it just so. Free of makeup, and refreshingly beautiful. Then the question registered.

"Me?!" Jess let out an unhinged cackle, covering her own mouth at the outburst. "Yeah, right. I could ask some of the guys in my games crew if they'd be keen or know someone who might be?"

"We're The *Lady* Builders for a reason. *Women*-owned. We're wanting to train up the next generation of tradeswomen," Remi stated proudly.

"Right. I shouldn't have assumed."

Remi shrugged. "Most people do. We're here to, hopefully, change that misconception, one woman at a time."

"I love that." Jess slipped the card into her pocket. "While I don't think it's for me, I'll see if I know any *women* who might be interested."

"Please," Sophie chimed in, tucking a neat lock of escaped hair behind her ear and giving Jess an earnest smile. "We need someone, like, yesterday."

JJ chuckled to herself as she tilted back the last of her beer. "You two have some strange hiring techniques."

"Hey—you don't ask, you don't get," Remi replied, leaning back in her chair.

"She's got a point," Jess agreed, enjoying Remi's refreshing directness. "Speaking of—last drinks?" She checked the doorway to the kitchen, hoping Ricciardo wasn't listening in on this conversation.

"Sorry. Right. You have work to do," said Remi.

"—at her current job," JJ pointed out.

Remi cut her a look.

"I do work here, yes." Jess laughed lightly. "I don't think I'd be a good fit for a tradie anyway. You haven't seen me working with tools... I don't even own any *and* I wouldn't have the first clue about what you do with them."

Remi held out her palm. "Hence... apprenticeship. We'd teach you all that."

"I'll think about it. And I'll ask around. Promise."

"Thank you." Remi looked relieved. "Ladies, another round?" Remi checked in with the others.

"I'm done." JJ slid her empty bottle towards Jess.

"Me too. I have to be up early with Hudson anyway, I don't need a crazy hangover on top of it," Sophie replied as she took the last sip of her wine.

Remi looked back to Jess. "Looks like we're good."

"No worries. Head up to the bar when you're ready to settle your bill." Jess gathered their empties and left before they offered her another job.

She internally rolled her eyes at the absurdity. She had to give the women kudos for trying. Taylor would've been perfect, if she wasn't in the middle of the ocean. Jess was always impressed—and a little jealous—of her best friend's handywoman skills. When they moved in together, Taylor had spent the entire weekend fixing it up for them. The squeak on the door hinge of her bedroom disappeared with a quick spray out of a can, the cutlery drawer adjusted with a screwdriver, so it shut properly and stopped hitting the one below it...

Now that she thought about it, she really had relied on her housemate's skills to fix things for her. She didn't realise how much she missed it since Adam moved in a year ago.

When she'd asked him to replace the lightbulb in the laundry, he'd given an empty promise to "look at it later." Months passed, no matter how many times she reminded him or dropped the hint. Every time she flipped the switch, she felt the tension in her neck spring back and her teeth clench.

She sprayed the bar down and began wiping it with more force than necessary.

With Taylor gone, and Adam the least handy guy she knew, maybe it was time she stepped up. Learn how to handle a screwdriver. Watch a video or two. Though... she'd probably electrocute herself somehow.

She looked up to see Remi at the till.

"Thinking over my offer?" Remi leaned on the bar, eyes bright, following Jess as she cleaned.

"Do you need a screwdriver to change a lightbulb?"

Remi smirked, tilting her head as if checking to see if Jess was serious. Jess held her breath.

"No," Remi replied after a moment, realising she was. "You only need to know what type of bulb it is and either unscrew it or push it up and rotate it out of the socket."

Jess's eyebrows flew up. "That's it?" There had to be more of an explanation or difficulty for Adam to have left it for so long. It had been *months*. "But what if you don't know what type it is?"

"You take out the old one," Remi said, as if it was obvious.

Of course. Jess felt her cheeks warm at the stupidity of her question. "Right. That makes sense."

"Can I... pay the bill?" Remi held up her card, humour written over her face.

"Yes! Gosh, sorry." Jess brought up their tab. "Are you settling everything or just your portion?"

"All on the one card."

"Done. Tap here."

As Jess waited for the transaction to complete, she stared at Remi again, unable to help herself. She was mesmerising. She stood with confidence, the long loose curls of her dark hair sitting over her shoulders, not styled but just barely tamed. It suited her. Her short-sleeved white shirt enhanced her tanned skin, making her tattoos stand out even more.

Remi looked around then leaned over the bar. Jess was so confused at first, her eyes automatically going to Remi's chest as her shirt lowered with the movement. Flushing at the realisation, she quickly cut her eyes back up as Remi started whispering.

"—none of my business, but are you okay? I'm assuming that was your boss?"

God why were her eyes so... so caring. Concerned. She didn't even know this person. Jess tried to brush it off, feeling put on the spot with the reminder of her earlier conversation with Ricciardo. "Yeah, no... just... usual work politics. You know how it is." Jess tore off Remi's receipt and handed it to her, smiling as much as she could muster.

Remi's eyebrows drew together as she took the receipt, straightening up. She gave Jess another look, almost waiting for her to open up more. When Jess picked up her cleaning cloth to dismiss her, Remi tapped her card on the bar and made a move to go, pausing at the last moment. "Just know, I'm serious about my offer."

"You don't let up do you?" Jess sighed with a quirk of her lips. She dropped the rag she was using. "Honestly. I would be terrible. Before, when you asked, I was thinking about who I knew who'd be a better fit than me."

"Don't discount yourself," Remi replied, striding off with confidence in every step of her black jeans. "Just think about it."

Remi threw a final smile over her shoulder as the front door swung shut behind her, disappearing into the night.

Jess pictured working with someone like Remi as a boss instead of Ricciardo. They were both confident and direct, though Remi's motives seemed to come from a place of positivity rather than Ricciardo's constant push on their bottom line. It could be nice to have an employer who cared and listened.

This chance at a new job both thrilled and terrified her. If she *did* have another job lined up, it could give her the confidence she needed to finally stick it to Ricciardo.

Jess had a lot to think about—but she couldn't deny it.

This woman had her attention.

TWO

Remi

Remi thought hiring Jackie as their apprentice had been the turning point in their business. This was her dream coming true: helping shift the needle on tradeswomen in the industry. Hell, the whole country.

Less than five percent.

That was the current number of women in trades in Australia. Every single woman Remi inspired, taught or otherwise encouraged to take on a trade helped bump that number up, starting with Jackie.

Remi wanted the women she took on to have a different experience from her own apprenticeship. With some of the boys on her team, and especially her boss, she'd always felt like the eyes were on her and her work. Was she doing it right? Did she even know what she was talking about? She'd felt belittled, frustrated and furious.

So, Remi and Sophie spent months mentoring Jackie. It had been everything Remi wanted. Jackie was switched on, reliable and keen to learn, soaking everything up like a sponge.

Then, Jackie quit.

Blindsiding them, she'd dropped everything to move interstate for her internet boyfriend. And that's how Remi found herself at one of the most important meetings of her career with just the two of them. If only she could've signed up that sassy blonde waitress on the spot...

Seeing the woman dismissed by her manager on Saturday night had been hard to watch. It took Remi straight back to those early days of being talked over, told what was best for her and not yet having the courage to truly stand up for herself, even when she tried. She'd meant it when she offered the woman the apprenticeship. Her service was impeccable. The skills? Remi could teach. But really, it came down to the look in her eyes when Remi had asked the question. The waitress may have laughed it off, but Remi saw the curiosity there. Her body language read unsure, but at the bar, Remi knew she'd piqued her interest. She was hanging on to that glimmer of hope. Apprentices were hard to come by as it was. Throw in the fact that she wanted a woman, *and* someone available right now, and Remi was heading into needle-in-a-haystack territory. Maybe even flea-in-a-haystack.

Read: Desperate.

With Jackie gone and no new apprentice lined up, this could cost them the job. She had to believe it would all work out—that the right person would come along.

The waitress's blue eyes and friendly smile flashed through her mind again, before returning to the present, she and Sophie re-reading the proposal notes for the meeting.

If, by some miracle, they did win this job with Flinders Homes today...

The thought made her giddy. Butterflies erupted in her stomach, and she instantly regretted chugging down her entire iced coffee carton out of nerves. This project would mean solid work for The Lady Builders for *at least* one to two years, and possibly more if everything went well. With that amount of guaranteed income *and* work, Remi had a vision to expand the team to six women within that time frame. Here's hoping she'd have a signed contract in a few hours' time.

Remi and Sophie left the carpark, making their way to the front stairs of the sleek office building.

"Ladies."

Oh, no.

"Declan," Remi greeted coolly.

Dickhead Declan. The epitome of everything Remi hated about the trade industry, a walking stereotype of what she was trying so hard to change. Men like him still managed to get under her skin. Her neck flushed hot with anger just under the surface. She hated how much men like him still affected her. She made no effort to hide her disgust. Sophie stood next to her in a power suit, looking more like an attorney than a tradeswoman this morning, arms folded and unimpressed.

"Don't tell me Flinders are considering you two?" He didn't give them a chance to respond. "I expect to hear back shortly with a signed contract, so don't worry yourselves too much. Leave it to my guys to handle. You stick to designing your pretty things."

His jokes were getting old. Fat chance they'd ever stick themselves in an office to design all day. They loved getting on the tools, building each design from paper plan all the way through to the final screw in the cupboard or last bead of caulk around the tiles. He flashed a smile in his suit, brown hair catching the light, slicked back like a sleazy salesman. What a schmuck. His face reminded her of a weasel as he squinted into the sunlight. Maybe Sleazy Weasel should be his new nickname? Though Dickhead Declan did have punch. She smirked—*if only*.

She tilted her head. "Funny, Javier hasn't mentioned you during our talks. On the other hand, The Lady Builders being a front-runner for the project has *definitely* been discussed in our emails. All the best, Declan. We have pretty things to design *and build*."

She didn't wait for his response, but caught his smarmy smile sliding right off his face. Satisfied, she pushed past him on the footpath towards the stairs to Flinders Homes, the click-clack of her sister's heels right behind her.

They entered reception and let out a huge breath, then laughed.

"He is *such* a dick," said Sophie.

"I feel like I need to wash my hands just being near him." She eyed Sophie. "We need to win this job, Soph. It's non-negotiable now. I am not letting *him* get this work."

"Take a seat."

Remi took in the boardroom as she sat on one of the grey, high-backed swivel chairs. The fancy kind with all the ridges and the slightest curve to fit your lower back just so. The ones that made you sit up straighter than you usually did. Her back already twinged at the rigidity of it all. She'd rather be hunched over a cabinet with a hole saw any day.

The expansive dark walnut table brought some warmth to the room, offsetting the bland grey carpet, white walls and harsh downlights. If Sophie ever got her hands on this space, she'd redesign the shit out of it.

"Thanks for coming to meet us. We'd rather chat in person, instead of more back and forth over email or video calls."

"I appreciate that," Remi replied. And she meant it. She wanted to make an impression, and in person was their best bet to do just that. Wearing a long sleeve shirt to hide her tattoos, she smoothed down the front of her only pair of business slacks, hoping to look more presentable than usual. She hadn't come to play. Sophie sat next to her, looking stunning—effortlessly dressed as usual for the occasion. The most feminine of the two, Sophie was always the surprise on site when people saw her dressed down in her dirty, stain-splattered tradie gear. In contrast to her sister's full face of makeup and straightened dark hair, Remi was the opposite, but could scrub up when the moment called for it.

Today, they were meeting with Javier and Hadid, the CEO and CFO of Flinders Homes. Remi would do whatever it took to win this job. The Lady Builders were ready to start their next chapter in business.

"Water?" offered Hadid, pouring them a glass each, off to the side at a small refreshments cart.

"Please," both sisters said in unison. He placed their

glasses down and took a seat next to Javier, across from Remi and Sophie. The space between seemed far across the table, but the atmosphere was relaxed and jovial.

"We asked you to come in today because we love your work," said Javier, leaning forward and folding his hands on the table.

"So, you've seen our projects?" Sophie enquired.

"Yes. The Maylard's job in particular caught our interest. We loved the attention to detail, the use of subtle pattern and form to offset the neutral colour tones. It was beautiful tiling and cabinetry," said Javier.

"Thank you. That's one of our favourite projects to date," Remi replied, feeling proud to present their work.

"The herringbone splashback was time-consuming but really gave it the 'wow factor' when walking into the room against the marble benchtops, which is exactly what the client wanted," added Sophie.

Javier sat back in his chair, listening intently and nodding in agreement. "Fantastic. We pride ourselves not only on building beautiful houses here, but on making them homes for our clients. This is where they're going to raise their children, their grandchildren, celebrate milestones and sometimes spend the rest of their lives. So, when we look to work with new sub-contractors, we want to align with people who we know will bring that spark of life to the job."

Remi was perched on the edge of her uncomfortable corporate seat. She could feel the energy building inside her. She always got like this when she was excited and felt her values aligning with others.

"You're speaking our language. It's one of the reasons

we love our business. You need that passion and commitment in this industry, or you won't last long. I know it's competitive, but we take our work very seriously, and when we saw your callout, we hoped we'd be the right fit."

Remi was going in hard, she wanted this contract in her hot little hands, and she wanted it now. Her heart thumped in her chest at the thought, her underarms sweating as she concentrated on every micro expression and clung on to every word, hoping for affirmation that they had this job in the bag.

"That's great. Really great. I wanted to be upfront today and say The Lady Builders are still our front-runner, and to us, you're not just a diversity tick. I believe in your business, and we love to reward good work, regardless of gender. The fact that you're also advocating for women in trade is necessary and refreshing. It stood out when we first reviewed all the applications," replied Javier.

Yes, yes, *yes*. She could practically see their signatures drying on the paper already.

Hadid flipped through the paperwork they'd sent outlining their proposal and business. He frowned.

"I thought you had three on your team, but it says here it's currently just the two of you?" He met Remi's eyes. "Three is our preferred minimum."

Remi folded her lips in, nodding profusely. *Think Remi, think!* The contract was slipping through her fingers with every passing second.

"Sorry, typo! There's still three of us," Remi replied. *Bloody Jackie.* She felt, rather than saw, Sophie swivel to face her. "There's Sophie, myself and our apprentice."

Up against Declan's team of five, she needed to find

Jackie's replacement. *Whatever it took.* She'd sort it out. Sophie kicked her under the table, and Remi gritted her teeth into a smile that hopefully showed confidence without a hint of acute ankle pain.

"Good." Javier looked relieved, she had the feeling he really wanted them to have the job, and she couldn't agree more. "That was our only major concern at this stage. With the amount of work required, two people would be cutting it too fine to complete everything efficiently and on time. And as I'm sure you're well aware in this industry—time is money."

"I understand. It was one of the reasons we took her on. She's a fast learner—"

Kick.

"Loads of initiative—"

Another kick.

Remi's hand shot out under the table and squeezed Sophie's knee. Hard.

"Mmmph." Sophie clamped her mouth shut, hopefully sounding like she was agreeing with Remi to the men across the table.

"—and with her on the team, it should position us nicely to keep up with your timeline for the works."

A heel dug into the soft flesh of her calf. She cried out this time, turning it into a cough as she reached for her water. She still refused to look at her sister.

They *needed* this job. Her dreams depended on it.

"Sorry, dry throat." She dug her nails into her palm to distract from the pain.

"How are you planning to balance the project with your current work?" asked Hadid.

They were on fire with the questions today. Luckily, she'd planned for this. She rattled off everything she'd come up with just after midnight last night in the haze of inspiration that had struck. She could see how everything would line up, wrapping up all her current work just in time to start with Flinders. They could do this. She poured every ounce of confidence she had into the rest of the meeting, doing her best to get both men on board by the end of their session.

Javier buttoned his suit jacket as he stood and moved to let them out of the room, Hadid not far behind him.

"We'll be in touch." Javier reached out his hand with a genuine smile.

"Thank you, we look forward to hearing from you," Remi replied, shaking his hand.

She pushed through the office building doors and breathed in the fresh-*ish* city air.

They'd done it. *She'd* done it. Now they had to wait and see if it was enough for Javier and Hadid to take them on.

Her smile vanished as a hand whipped her around.

"What the *fuck* was that?!" Sophie screeched, as quietly as she could without making a scene. She was scary when she was dressed like such a badass. Remi almost cowered under her sister's glare. Almost.

Okay sure, there was the teeny tiny detail that they *technically* hadn't hired anyone yet... paired with the fact she'd just come up with that particular plan on the spot without Sophie's permission. But Remi had wanted to make sure they'd win the job. Her sister had to understand that.

Sophie stood there, almost huffing on the spot. *Oh, she was mad.*

Remi held up her hands. "All right, wait, hear me out. I knew once they asked about the two of us, we'd lose the job—"

"You can't just *lie*, Remi."

"It's not lying," Remi said through gritted teeth. "I have every confidence this person will be on our team in no time. It's only the end of November and we've got until next year to find her. I'm just putting it out to the universe."

"Oh come *on*, Rem." Sophie did stomp her foot this time. "The business world doesn't run on wishes and hopes."

Remi leaned close, using all four extra inches she had on her sister. The effect was somewhat diminished by the fact that Sophie was in heels... damn. She lowered her voice.

"Do you want someone like Dickhead Declan getting the job?" She knew that would help get Sophie on side.

"No." Sophie frowned, crossing her arms.

"Don't you want the opportunity to expand our team and bring on more women, like we've always dreamed?"

"Of course."

"Well then, it's settled." Remi straightened up with a grin.

"It's *not* settled," Sophie snapped, throwing her arms up.

Remi reached out and squeezed her sister's shoulder.

"Hey," she spoke softly. "We'll find someone, Soph. I promise."

"I'm the older sister. I should be reassuring you."

"Yeah, but I'm taller. And you know I'm the wild one most likely to get us into trouble." She raised a brow. "Life wouldn't be as fun without me in it."

Sophie tried to look grumpy, a small smile betraying her. "Fine. Just—" A sigh. "Don't make me regret this."

Remi bumped her sister's shoulder playfully, earning a real smile.

"C'mon then, we've got an apprentice to find and a contract to win."

THREE

Jess

Jess wrapped her hands around her mug, folding her legs underneath her on the outdoor bench. Tendrils of steam rose into the air, creating rolling wisps she tracked with her eyes until they disappeared into the morning sun.

Thankful for the day off, she sat in the stillness, soaking in five precious minutes of downtime before she tackled her long list of chores. Going in earlier yesterday had already cut into her meagre time off. Frustration had rolled through her with every customer nit-picking. From their Parmesan cheese being too sharp to the pasta portion being too large. Who complained about being given too *much* food? It felt like she was stuck on a hamster wheel, only now it was spinning faster, and she wasn't being fed any extra carrots. She was burned out, the exhaustion weighty on her shoulders. Even getting out of bed this morning was an effort, brain fog slowing the simplest of tasks.

She took a sip of tea, letting the heat warm her from the inside out, grounding her in the quiet morning. A cool breeze danced with the hair around her face, making her shiver. It wouldn't stay cold for long; she could already feel summer's breath ready to welcome the first day of December. And that meant Christmas was coming.

A pang of anxiety struck.

The silly season was the busiest time in hospitality. Brutal, unforgiving. This had to be her last Christmas at Limone. There was no way she was busting her arse for another year. Not with what little energy she had left in the tank. Why had she let it get this bad? Every time she'd tried to put boundaries in place with Ricciardo, he either redrew them or pushed them further. She'd had enough of his games. She was done. Done with him pushing her to her limit, done with being ignored and done with the same old shit.

If he wasn't going to change, she would.

She could do this. It was a new month, almost a new year, and definitely time for a new Jessica Greaves.

She nodded to the cloud of dancing bugs hovering just above the dewy lawn, their shadows cast in the sun's golden light. *Give me a sign.* Like glittering stardust, they shot up and over the backyard fence.

Wish granted, apparently.

Jess swallowed another mouthful of tea—piping hot, just the way she liked it. She adjusted her legs to the other side when something jabbed into her butt.

"Ow!" Frowning, she shoved her hand into her back pocket and pulled out the now-even-more-crumpled business card from Saturday night. In her tired weekend stupor, she'd completely forgotten about the tradie ladies.

"The Lady Builders, hey?" she muttered, flipping it

over before flicking the card onto the wooden outdoor table. She scoffed. Had they seriously offered her a job?

She didn't want to stay in hospitality, but she had no clue what she wanted to do next. As a little girl, she'd always wanted to be a firefighter. That ambition was squashed when her parents reminded her she was asthmatic... probably not the best combo.

Maybe a barista?

No. Still hospo, Jess.

An accountant?

God no. She hated doing her own basic tax return.

Perhaps it was time to become a mature-age student and head back to uni. Not that she'd done much with her BA. But she'd been young and stupid at eighteen, more focused on dating this girl or that guy, being "cool" and having no idea what to do with her future other than going to university and getting a degree. Mission accomplished. When she'd struggled to get a job afterward, she'd fallen into waitressing, and had been run off her feet ever since. She hadn't paused to take a breath, let alone consider what she might want to do next.

A buzzing noise caught her attention. A blue bee landed on her blooming catmint. The small shrub reminded her of lavender, less invasive, but just as loved by the bees. This one was already covered in pollen, diving loudly into each flower. It reminded her of the bee tattoo she'd spotted on Remi's arm, one of the many Jess had wanted to ask her about.

She grabbed the card again.

What was she doing?

She put it down, sighed... and picked it up once more.

Game over, Ricciardo.

She swapped her mug for her phone.

"Hello?" A loud vibrating hum reverberated through the speaker.

"Hi, Remi?"

"Hello? Can you hang on a minute?" Rustling. A bang. Then quiet. "Hi, sorry," Remi's voice came through, clear and direct.

"Hey, this is Jess." She toyed with the card, bending the tattered corner and dog-earing it further.

"Who?"

Jess closed her eyes. Of course. Remi didn't even remember her. So embarrassing. "It's Jess. Um, the waitress from Limone?"

This was a mistake. What if the job offer had been a joke? She should just hang up.

"Oh, the cu—" Remi coughed. "Blondie, right? Loves *Ninja Turtles*?"

"You're the one with the turtle tattoo, not me, *Donatello*."

"It's my pet, by the way."

"Your tattoo?"

"No. I mean, well *yes*. It's a tattoo *of* my pet turtle. His name's Ninja."

"Cute," Jess said, completely forgetting why she'd called in the first place.

"Don't judge me—I was nine." The laughter in Remi's voice made Jess grin. She liked her already. The tension eased from her shoulders.

"No judgement here," Jess placated.

"So... did you call to ask about my tattoos again? Or..."

Jess could already imagine the smirk on her face. She wanted to ask about that bee tattoo but— "I think I want to be an apprentice. I have no idea what I'm doing, but honestly, I need a new job, and this feels like a sign."

The blue bee buzzed past her face to the far end of the garden. She smiled.

"Are you serious?" Remi asked.

"I think so." Was she sure? No. Not at all. But what did she have to lose?

"When could you start?" Remi asked again quickly. Too quickly.

Jess was taken aback.

"What? Just like that? Don't I need to send you my resume or something?"

"Um." Remi blew out a breath and paused. "What are you doing today?"

"It's my day off."

"What if you visited our current renovation this afternoon? Spent a few hours with us? You could observe under my supervision and see what you think?"

Was she really doing this? Was there some sort of catch? It seemed too easy. You don't just make a wish on a cloud of bugs and get it granted five minutes later... do you?

"Okay."

"I've got your number, so I'll send you the details."

"Okay," Jess repeated, apparently unable to think of anything more useful.

"See you this afternoon."

"Bye." Her phone clattered onto the table. She couldn't believe she'd called. While the conversation had led to more questions than answers, excitement bloomed in her chest.

She might actually have a new job, one she might enjoy, with purpose and potential to grow. This was a chance at real change in her life and an opportunity to get away from Limone. The thought of never working for Ricciardo again... yeah, that would be nice.

Very nice indeed.

Footsteps and the creak of the screen door swinging shut told her Adam was coming out to say hi. Arms wrapped around her shoulders from behind, his cologne hitting her nose as he leaned down and placed a kiss on her cheek. Jess was hoping for five more minutes alone to process everything. She tried not to stiffen under his embrace.

"Morning babe, you wanna have breakfast soon?" he asked.

She gritted her teeth. Adam's stomach was the last thing on her mind right now.

"I may have just got a new job," she blurted, as he moved to sit beside her. "Well, potentially, anyway."

"What?! Where?" Food forgotten, Adam stared wide-eyed as he dropped onto the bench. His arm rested on the table as he searched her face.

"For a building company, I think."

"You think?"

Her face flushed under his incredulous gaze. But, then she remembered why she wanted the change in the first place. Sitting up straighter, she squared her shoulders. Taking a page from Remi's book, the new Jess needed more confidence. Starting now.

"I met these women on Saturday night who renovate homes. One of them asked if I wanted to work for them."

She gestured to the card, currently stuck under his arm. "Honestly, I wasn't sure they were serious, but I thought, what the heck, and gave them a call." She reached over and pulled the card out from under him.

"Huh. First I've heard of an all-female building company," he said, studying it. "So, what would you be doing exactly?"

"Well, I'm not sure yet. They've asked me to come and observe this afternoon. I know they build kitchens, bathrooms—that sort of thing."

"Oh. So you wouldn't be in an office, this would be on a work site with tools and stuff?"

"I believe so. We'll see what I find out today."

She caught his disappointed look. "What?" she asked, taking his hands in hers.

"I was kind of hoping we'd have the day together. I finally got the time off..."

"I know." She squeezed his hands. "But this opportunity might be just what we need. Ricciardo's been working me to the bone, and you already know how late I've been getting home. He underpaid me again, too."

"I don't get it. Wouldn't it be easier to talk to Ricciardo? Ask for better pay or shorter hours rather than jumping into a completely different career? I'm sure he'd understand."

"You know I've tried. Nothing changes. He just brushes me off every time. I'm working more hours than I ever have and getting the same pay I signed on for. He doesn't listen to me. I've told you that." She pulled her hands away, jaw clenching as the familiar tension settled between her shoulder blades.

"Is the pay better with this job?"

Jess grimaced. She hadn't even asked, too excited by the idea of change. "I'm not sure yet. I'll find out today."

Adam narrowed his eyes, brows furrowing. "Jess, make this make sense to me. Because right now, I don't know why you'd suddenly give up a stable job." He ran a hand through his curls.

This was *not* going the way she'd hoped.

"Because I'm not happy!" she burst out, ticking the reasons off on her fingers. "I'm sick of the late hours, of Ricciardo not listening to me, of doing the same thing. Every. Single. Day. Then this opportunity lands in my lap right as I'm thinking about making a change. It might not be my next career. Maybe it's a stepping stone to something else. Maybe it pays awesome and I love it. I don't know. This is new for me, too. So, we'll see."

Breathing heavy, she took a gulp of her tea, sitting in the swirl of emotions coming at her from all sides.

"Okay," Adam said with a sigh, looking out over the garden. "See how this afternoon goes, I guess." He wasn't happy, but he wasn't going to change her mind.

"Listen, how about you and I have dinner tomorrow night? I'm off at five. We could head to The Wharf for oyster night. Make up for missing time together today?" She poked his stomach, coaxing a smile from him.

"Fine. I can't say no to beers and oysters with the girl-friend." He stood to go, kissing her forehead. "I'll leave you to it. Oh, did you end up washing my blue shirt for tomorrow? I wanted to wear it for my meeting."

Sometimes...

Sometimes she really wished he would think for himself.

Jess thought back to all those times she'd ribbed him about his odd socks. Now she understood why. He never did his own laundry. Not unless she, or his mother did it. And Jess certainly hadn't signed up for that role.

"It's already in the machine. It'll be clean for tomorrow. I'll meet you inside soon, still going on my tea." She held up the mug with a tight smile.

As he walked away, she took in a deep breath, listening to the screen door click shut behind him. Mornings like this, Adam just got under her skin. She'd wanted to talk more about the job, but he made it hard, like she was bouncing between repeating herself and defending her decision. He could make his own bloody breakfast. It's not that hard to make Vegemite toast.

Jess took another breath, trying to diffuse the irritation that had crept in. Adam had been setting her moods off more and more lately. She could blame it on being tired or overworked. But it felt like more than that. She needed to talk to him. Tomorrow night. Be honest. Get him to help out more. Open up about how she was really feeling.

It had been over a year since Taylor had moved out and Adam took her place. She *should* be filled with joy, wrapped up in all the good feelings of finally living with her boyfriend of two years. So, why wasn't she?

She sipped her tea.

Stone cold. *Ugh.*

With a sigh, she meandered back to the house, going over her to-do list before she spent more time out of the house on her day off.

If this job worked out, and she really hoped it would, she'd have to tell her mum, too. Dread coiled in her gut. Her mum was guaranteed to find something about it she didn't like. Well, it wouldn't be the first person she'd disappointed today. She'd wanted Adam to understand. But it was clear he wasn't impressed.

Chewing at the inside of her lip, Jess pulled open the screen door.

She hoped she was doing the right thing.

FOUR

Remi

"Hello?"

Remi heard the front door open a crack.

"Come in!" she yelled back. "We're in the kitchen, down the hall and to the left."

They were halfway through attaching a corner cupboard to the wall. Sophie held it in place, while Remi lay flat on her stomach, adjusting the legs underneath to ensure they were flush at the back and everything was level.

"That'll do it," Sophie stated, stepping back and leaning the spirit level against the wall. Footsteps stopped nearby as Remi extracted her arm from under the cupboard. She turned her head and saw two long legs that seemed to go on forever. Jess stood smiling, looking a little unsure, dressed head-to-toe in athleisure: black leggings, a tight pink shirt and warm blonde hair pulled into a high ponytail. She looked like she was ready for a jog with the local fitness club.

And... wow. Out of her waitress uniform, their potential new apprentice was even more attractive. Remi blinked, clearing her head. No time for distractions. Her job was to make sure this woman was so intrigued by their work, she'd be knocking down doors to become their apprentice. *Hopefully*. Remi would make every minute count.

"Thanks for coming in at such short notice," said Remi, lifting herself up off the floor. She dusted off her hands and shirt, failing to make herself look more presentable. Jess looked her up and down, and Remi suddenly felt self-conscious in her dirty work gear.

"Should I be wearing a pair of those?" Jess pointed at their safety boots.

Sophie laughed. "You're completely fine. We won't have you using any tools. You need a white card to be within the work zone, so you'll just be observing from the family room today. Now, I know you said you don't own any tools, but do you have any knowledge about the building industry?"

"Soph, ease up. She's just walked in the door." Remi shot Jess a look that said *don't mind her*.

What Remi did know was that Jess was a proficient waitress with great social skills, an arsehole boss, and real potential. To be honest though, they needed an apprentice, and well... here she was. If this helped them land the Flinders job, Jess ticked all the boxes. Skills could be taught. That's what Remi excelled at... or wanted to.

She flashed back to day one of her own apprenticeship.

"You lost?"

"Funny looking kitchen."

A leer. A wolf whistle.

Remi didn't have the confidence she did now. Her knees had shaken so badly they almost knocked together.

Though her face, thankfully, gave nothing away. She'd wanted to learn, no matter what.

And "no matter what" turned out to be years of dealing with sexual harassment and micro aggressions on site. If she could buffer even one woman's apprenticeship, help her grow into something amazing without the sexist bullshit? That alone would be worth it.

In front of her, Jess stood bright-eyed, innocent and maybe a little nervous. A diamond in the rough, ready to be honed.

"We'll give you a run down of what we do, then you can hit us with all your questions. Make sure *we're* the right fit too."

"Sounds good to me," replied Jess, rocking back on her heels.

Remi clapped her hands. "So, in an absolute nutshell, we renovate and build kitchens," she made a show of the current space, "as well as bathrooms and laundries. We handle the demolition, design and construction of each space. While it's mostly cabinet-making, we also do tiling and some other aesthetic touches—patching gyprock, small paint touch-ups—that sort of thing. Everything else goes to electricians, plumbers or full home builders."

"Got it," said Jess.

Remi moved behind her sister and gave her shoulders a friendly squeeze. "This here is the design whizz and all-round guru. She makes everything look good and helps with all the installs. My job is to look after all the clients, suppliers and admin when I'm not on site."

Jess nodded as Sophie ducked away to unpack the next cabinet carcass.

"Do you only do residential houses like this?" Jess asked, following Remi to the open-plan family room to sit down.

"Yep, just residential clients for now. But, we're in talks to hopefully work with a home builder on an upcoming development project early to mid-next year."

"Cool. And what kind of things would I be doing?" Jess asked Remi.

"We'll get you on the table saw first—"

Jess's eyes bulged. Sophie turned, alarmed.

"She's kidding," she said quickly.

"Yeah, no way in hell you're touching a saw straight away." Remi grinned as Jess sagged with relief. "But in honour of tradies everywhere, I give thee, *the broom*."

Jess took it like it might be a prank. "I thought I'd be starting with some kind of tool."

"That there is a *very* important tool. Cleanliness is number one—no trip hazards, no lost parts or tools. And tidy sites make clients happy."

"Well, sweeping is one thing I do know how to do. Very well."

"Good." Remi took the broom back. "First thing you'll need, though, is a white card. They're essential for any trade job. If today goes well, you can book in to get your card in a day. Plenty of places do it around the city."

She kept the rest light, letting Jess guide the conversation as Remi went back to assembling the kitchen carcasses.

And ask questions, Jess did. At least *twenty* over the afternoon. All valid. Still, each one made her wonder how some people went through life being so... unhandy.

Remi had taught herself a lot of skills growing up, the

curiosity bug strong from a young age. She remembered her Dad giving her offcuts from his woodworking projects. She'd hammer away, building little creations while he guided her. Her favourite was a wooden guitar with an ice cream tub and rubber bands. What began as play turned into serious DIY.

"So how'd you get into this?" Jess asked next.

Remi answered first. "Our dad." Her grin widened, proud she had a dad who was so progressive with his daughters for the time. "He taught us how to use so many tools. He's amazing. I wanted to work for myself, leave a toxic job and work alongside Soph."

Sophie added, "I enjoyed renovating my own home, and wanted a job with flexibility around parenting. Working around my son, Hudson, has been a dream, and I guess working alongside my little sister isn't so bad."

"What about you? Why hospitality?" Remi asked, taking a break from the cabinets and sitting beside her.

Jess shrugged. "It was a uni job that never ended."

"You don't enjoy it?"

"I'm over the late nights, screaming kids and being underpaid—even if I still like the food."

"That's what you were talking to your boss about, right?" Remi checked, already feeling defensive on her behalf.

Jess retreated into herself, only slightly, but enough for Remi to notice.

"It's a whole thing. Loopholes and contracts... argh. The more I think about it, the more I want out."

"Well, while we *can* guarantee we'll pay you right, you'd

have to get used to early mornings, loud tools and gruelling physical labour if you do want in."

"I figured as much. I don't mind, though. I think finishing in the afternoon is great; you still get time to have a life with family and friends... and weekends—*god*, I miss weekends."

With the wistful way Jess spoke, Remi couldn't help but wonder just how unhappy she really was in her current line of work.

"Sorry to be the bearer of bad news, but we do work some Saturdays. Though, I try to keep that to tight deadlines, and you'll get paid for all the overtime. I promise."

"Right, I'm off to go pick up Hudson," Sophie interrupted them. "Rem, catch you later for pack-down?"

"Yep."

"Jess, it was so lovely spending time with you today. Sorry I can't stay longer—duty calls!" Sophie called over her shoulder as she left.

"I love how much flexibility you have here to juggle family and commitments." Jess watched wistfully as Sophie left.

Remi grinned. "It does make me proud. What we've created, and what we're planning to do." She noticed Jess eyeing her arm and held it out for a closer look at her patchwork sleeve.

"Sorry," Jess said sheepishly. "They're just so cool."

Jess was inquisitive, alarmingly so at times. She seemed to ask whatever came to mind, whether it was work-related, or in this case, tattoo related. The weight of her gaze felt like a caress down Remi's arm. Remi tried not to react as Jess's breath brushed across her skin as she concentrated on the detail.

"Tell me about the bee."

"Ah—my most painful tattoo to date." Remi tried to keep focus on her intricate black ink, doing her best to avoid those curious blue eyes.

"Really?"

"I wholly recommend never getting your elbow crease done if you can avoid it. It took a week before I could bend my arm properly again." She flexed it up and down, so the bee's wings appeared to flutter. "Worth it, though. It's one of my favourites."

"It's beautiful. At least you don't regret it. That'd be awkward after all that." Jess chuckled.

Remi almost reeled back. "I could never. It's a queen bee. A leader of women; small things, big changes and all that. It reminds me I can make a difference."

And it was a good reminder about the changes she'd hopefully be making to her business in the coming months.

Jess continued inspecting the rest of her arm. A strand of hair came loose as she leaned closer and Remi caught herself almost reaching to tuck it back. Thankfully, it was nothing more than a twitch in her hand. That would've been all kinds of awkward!

Then Jess touched her hand.

At first Remi had no idea what she was doing, until she realised Jess was nudging it to see the other side of her arm. *Duh, Remi—she's still looking at the tattoos.* She really hoped her face wasn't turning red. Even the fact she was heating up from a friendly touch was embarrassing. Remi dove into a few more stories from her patchwork collection,

Jess hanging on to each and every detail. It wasn't often she could talk about them in such depth.

To Remi's surprise, they'd been sitting there for almost an hour when Sophie walked back through the door, ready to start pack-down. Remi hadn't done any more work, or taught the poor woman anything else about their trade, which was the whole point of the day.

"I'll email through the details for the white card, the apprenticeship and the TAFE course tonight. You can deep dive into it all and see what you think," Remi promised as Jess got up to leave.

"Sounds great. Thanks for today. I appreciated getting to come and spend the time with you both."

Remi waved her off, having told Jess to think seriously about whether the apprenticeship was something she wanted to take on. She shut the front door and headed back to the kitchen. Sophie was neatly folding drop sheets as Remi picked up the other half to help. It was a practised dance between them as they worked in silence.

After a few minutes, Sophie spoke up, "I don't think she's the right fit, Rem. She's a lovely girl, but when it comes to experience, it would be good to have someone who knows more than how to sweep."

"I don't see any other female apprentices lining up to take the job," defended Remi.

"Why don't we take on someone more qualified then?"

"I wish, but our bank account says otherwise. Once we're established with Flinders, I'd love to. But for now, she's kind of all we've got. If Jess is on the books, we can do this."

"Are you sure?" Sophie asked as she hoisted up her toolbox.

"Hey, remember the first time I put a demo hammer in your hands? What did you say?" Remi smiled at her sister, hands on her hips.

"I couldn't do it."

"And I said—?"

"I believe in you. You just need to believe in you," Sophie finished.

Remi looked her sister in the eye. "I believe in Jess. Sure, she's not what we expected—"

"Or need right now," Sophie cut in, getting frustrated.

"Uh-uh. That's where you're wrong. We do need her, a lot. Sophie, this could be a game-changer. If we can get our foot in the door with Flinders, imagine where we'll be down the track with an entire team of women alongside us. Women *we've* trained up. Imagine Hudson growing up and saying, 'Look at the business my mum built'."

"Damn it. You'll always get me across the line playing the kid card."

"I want to offer her the apprenticeship," stated Remi.

"Okay," agreed Sophie.

"Okay? You're sure?"

"Don't make me change my mind now!"

"All right! I'm backing off."

Now Remi just needed to make sure Jess was on board.

FIVE

Jess

"Mum, hi," Jess answered the phone. She'd just got back from her observation afternoon with The Lady Builders and sat with her feet up on the couch. Now was as good a time as any to burst the bubble and tell her mum the news.

"I haven't heard from you."

Ugh, Jess hated it when her mum sulked.

"I've been busy doing late shifts, and you're usually in bed by nine. Plus, I was planning to call you today, anyway."

"How's Adam?"

"He's good."

"Work?"

Jess squinted, wondering how best to phrase it. She really hoped her mum would approve.

Hah. *Yeah, right.*

"I have some news, actually," Jess started, buying herself a little extra time. Why was this so hard? She just had to say it.

"I've just come back from an observation day for a new job."

"What's wrong with the current place? You've got good job security there."

There were two things that could be said about Suzanne Greaves: she always liked to make sure Jess was looked after, and she usually had something to say about Jess still working in hospitality instead of utilising her degree. So, Jess was surprised her mum was now defending the job.

"It feels like it might be time for a change," said Jess.

"Where's the new place? Is it a restaurant I know?" Her mother loved dining all over the city, dragging her father along to what seemed like a new cuisine every week. "Or have—" She gasped, cutting herself off. "—have you got an interview for project management?"

And there it was. Same old Mum.

"Not a restaurant, or project management." That career idea had faded into the background, just like her B.A. certificate, which now lived in a box at the back of the laundry cupboard. Her mother still couldn't let it go.

"It's a trade apprenticeship," she clarified, "with a renovating and building business."

"*Building!*"

Jess pulled a face at her mum's screech. Here we go…

"Jessica, that's a bit dangerous, isn't it? Working with tools. Do you even know how to use a drill?"

"That's the point of the apprenticeship, Mum. They'll teach me," Jess replied, echoing Remi's words. And if there was one thing Jess knew, it was that Remi would make an excellent mentor. From her passion for women and the industry to the meticulousness Jess had seen on site, her intrigue with Remi was growing by the day.

"This just seems so out of the blue. Like you're rushing into it." Her mum clicked her tongue, pulling Jess back into the conversation. "I'm not sure your father will like you doing that kind of work either."

Jess laughed. "You're so old school. Dad'll be fine. I don't even know what I'm doing yet. You make it sound like I'm starting some extreme bungee jumping course. It's just something new to try. I might not even like it."

"Well, don't quit your job yet. What about the house you two are saving for?" her mum asked. The conversation always circled back to building a future or starting a family with Adam… It was so… tiring.

"I literally got back five minutes ago; I haven't sorted anything out yet."

"Sounds like it." Jess could imagine her mum looking put out on the other end of the line. She rolled her eyes, glad her mum couldn't see her.

"Mum," Jess warned.

"Fine, I won't hold you up any longer. I only wanted to check in. Just… think about it before you make a rash decision you might regret. And say hi to Adam for me. Love you."

"Will do," Jess mumbled, the call already ended.

Two for two against her decision wasn't a great start. She pushed aside the thought, pulling up the list Remi had sent through of places that offered white card training. She clicked on the first one, read through it and booked herself in for the following Monday. A green *Booking Success* notification popped up on the screen. She smiled. Her life wasn't going to change unless she did, and even if she didn't end up with The Lady Builders, she was curious enough to get everything in place so she'd be ready for whatever came next.

Though, she hoped it would be with Remi. There was a pull there... something Jess couldn't quite put her finger on. Those green eyes were burned into her memory, lit with enthusiasm as Remi encouraged Jess to ask questions and feel comfortable on her first day learning the trade. It made Jess feel... nice. Warm. Welcome.

Jess sat across from Adam at The Wharf. They'd picked an outdoor table to be able to enjoy the sunset, overlooking the ocean on the edge of Karkalla Beach. It was a beautiful summer night. People were everywhere, walking dogs and prams, chatting at nearby tables. Behind them, a small boy whined endlessly about the lack of sauce on his chicken nuggets while his mother attempted to soothe a newborn baby's cries. Jess tried to tune it out, focusing instead on a man arguing with a waiter about his undercooked steak.

Adam sat with his phone propped up on the table, engrossed in a basketball game. Jess watched him, wondering how often they ate like this—together but disconnected.

This conversation was long overdue. Things had been... fine. Nothing was *technically* wrong. But she'd felt the space growing between them. She was confused. She loved Adam. He was a nice guy, made her laugh. But then she thought of Taylor and Sam. Exuberantly happy. That word, and others like it—ecstatic, enamoured—didn't come to mind when she thought about her and Adam. And that scared her.

So, they had tonight to talk. She wanted to try.

She knew her long hours weren't doing anything for her energy, her libido, or her ability to commit to deeper conversations. Adam had been busy too: project managing the engineering for a major stadium build, working late, or out with the boys, or his brother Heath. Their calendars never quite matching up.

Then on nights like tonight…

Adam adjusted his phone, getting more comfortable in his seat. Why did he make such a big deal about quality time if it only meant occupying the same space?

The waiter brought out their drinks and two trays of oysters—natural for Adam, Kilpatrick for Jess.

Jess nudged his legs under the table. "Hey."

"Hey, sorry." He gave a sheepish smile, picking up his first oyster and downing it in two seconds. "Man, they're fresh tonight."

"Really good," Jess agreed, picking up a stray piece of bacon from her plate. "I'm glad we made time to do this."

"Me too." His eyes snagged on the game again.

"I didn't get a chance to tell you about yesterday."

He hadn't even asked, too focused on his video games. She'd been hoping he'd bring it up so they could talk through her next steps together.

"Oh yeah, how'd that go?" His eyes slid to her.

"I enjoyed myself. Not sure I'll be any good,"—Jess laughed lightly—"but the two sisters were fun, and made me feel comfortable."

"That's too bad. At least you tried and still have Limone."

She paused. Not the response she expected.

"I'm not *not* taking the apprenticeship. I just haven't heard back yet. If given the chance, I wanna give it a go."

"You do?" Adam's eyebrows rose, an oyster shell halting at his lips.

"Yeah. I know the pay's been good for us with Limone, but I'm not happy there anymore, especially with the increase in hours. But I'm not just talking about the restaurant."

A pause.

"I think I'm done with hospitality."

Hearing it out loud, she *knew* it was true. "I was originally thinking about going back to uni—"

Adam snorted. "You didn't use the last bachelor's degree you got—your words, not mine." He held his hands up in defence.

While technically true, the statement still stung. "Well, Mum's words really." Jess didn't care that she hadn't used it. Her mum did.

Jess was glad she'd gone through all the information Remi had sent her, ready to talk about it with Adam. Or at least, talk him into it.

"Well, that's the thing. Instead of uni, which is expensive, apprenticeships are a form of study that *do* have a paycheck, at least. Sure, it'll be a steep cut the first few years, but we could make it work. And then I'll be earning more than I do at Limone anyway."

"How much is this gonna set us back with buying our house? Setting ourselves up for raising a family together?"

"A few years—"

"It kinda feels like a big risk, babe. You're telling me you're not good at something but also want to pursue it? It sounds like an oxymoron."

"That's the whole point, learning on the job. Trust me with this decision, Adam." Her heart started to pound, hands almost shaking as she scrunched the napkin. The baby behind them started wailing again. Jess ground her teeth.

"Seems like you're gonna do it anyway." His eyes slid back to his phone. Conversation over.

It wasn't the answer she was looking for, and now didn't feel like the right time to bring up their other issues. This was not how she'd envisioned the evening going.

Heat crept up her neck, and for some reason, she felt stupid. Or maybe it was shame? She'd never come up against a disagreement like this with Adam before. Usually, everything worked out and they were on the same page. Him moving in? Easy. She'd needed a new roommate when Taylor left. Boom. Done. End of story.

This felt the same, like she was making the right decision, so why did everyone around her think she was wrong?

The following night, Jess was still turning over the conversation with Adam in her head. The whole thing had her doubting herself. Maybe her mum and Adam were right. Limone *was* the safe option. She knew what she was doing and had a contract. If she could stick it out for a few more years... the thought made her sick. There was no word from Remi either, so this back and forth could all be for nothing.

No. She refused to believe that.

Even if the apprenticeship didn't come through, there was no way she'd stay in hospitality. That much she was sure of.

The observation afternoon had been an absolute blast. Watching the sisters' confidence and precision was so motivating. They'd encouraged her to ask questions, never making her feel silly, even when she thought the questions were. Perhaps bringing up Remi's tattoos got them a little too off-topic, but it was captivating hearing the meaningful stories behind them. Plus, Remi was easy to talk to, a nice contrast from some of the tense conversations she'd had lately.

She reread the line in her book for what felt like the twenty-fifth time before flipping it over onto the nightstand with a rough exhale. She couldn't concentrate. Sitting up in bed a little more, she readjusted the covers. Adam was in the lounge playing video games again. The rest of their dinner had been a silent disaster. The oysters and ocean views were nice at least, but she couldn't help but feel their talk was ruined by bringing up the apprenticeship. Still, if you couldn't talk to your partner about your goals over dinner, when could you?

Jess flicked Taylor a text, knowing full well she probably wouldn't get it straight away while out at sea. Sometimes it felt nice to send it regardless.

> I miss you. ☹ Can you two fly back to Adelaide already? Love your guts, loser! Ps. I may have a new job. Couldn't wait til our next call to tell you!!!

She went to shove the phone under her pillow when it vibrated.

"Hey loser, that was quick!" she answered brightly, excited Taylor was actually available for once.

"Hi, it's Remi."

Jess yanked the phone away from her ear, eyes blowing wide at the screen. *Oh, shit.*

"I'm so sorry. I thought you were someone else."

Remi chuckled. "It was still a very... energetic greeting. I'm not mad about it. Sorry for calling late, is now a good time?"

"Oh, sure. It's fine." Jess sat up straighter, readjusting her hair with her free hand, then caught herself. *It was just a phone call, Jess!* Her heart picked up as she played with the edge of her quilt, tracing the patterns with her finger. Was Remi calling to let her down gently? Or was this the start of something new?

"I wanted to touch base earlier," Remi said, "but today got away from us and I've been smashed with admin work all night. Daylight savings always tricks me into thinking I've got more time."

"Tell me about it. I had to shut my curtains so I wouldn't feel guilty for being in bed with a book while the sun is still up—even if only just."

"God, I wish I had time to read. What're you reading?"

"A thriller. I love my murder mysteries."

"Huh. Didn't pick you for that genre." Remi's smile came through in her voice.

"I'm full of surprises," Jess replied, noting that had become a theme between them. They'd call each other and start talking like old friends rather than business acquaintances.

"Speaking of surprises, I'm calling to offer you the apprenticeship."

Jess's hand stilled on the quilt, heart racing.

"Are you sure?"

Would she be good enough?

Remi laughed. "I mean, I'm sure, that's why I'm asking. I'd love to have you on our team."

"Oh, god. Am I really doing this?" Jess held her hand to her forehead. There were so many thoughts running through her mind, so many competing voices and choices. She remembered her promise to herself for a new year, new Jess. She wasn't about to turn down an offer just because Adam doubted her, or because her mum expected her to work somewhere else. At the end of the day, this was her decision.

"You tell me," Remi replied, waiting.

"Yes. I want to." She spoke the words and knew them to be true. Adam wasn't going to be happy. Neither would her mum. Or Ricciardo. She'd have to put in her notice. And it was coming up to—

"Christmas," Jess uttered.

"Christmas?" Remi asked, confused.

"Sorry, I'm getting ahead of myself. Just thinking about Limone, it's their busiest time of year. Me leaving would really put them out."

"We shut over the holidays anyway," Remi said, "and the apprenticeship wouldn't start until the new school year in January. If you get your white card now, though, you're welcome to shadow us for a few days—if you want to?"

"Oh, that works. It'll give me enough time to tie up loose ends." And get everyone on board.

"All right, I'll shoot the official paperwork through, and if you're up for it, you can hang with us next Tuesday if you like?"

"I'd love to. I'm booked in to get my card on Monday."

"Perfect. Well, welcome to the team, Newbie."

"Thanks, Remi. Have a good night."

"Hopefully... if I can get on top of all these emails. Enjoy your book. Hope you guess the right killer. Night!"

"Good luck!"

Jess threw the phone on her bed and stared at it, grinning. She had a new job. And she was going to be a student again—a mature age student at that. She let out a laugh, stunned she'd just said yes to Remi. Next year, she'd be a cabinet maker.

She had to tell *someone*. Adam's game blasted down the hallway. She cringed, knowing he should be the first person she told, running to him in excitement. A sick feeling sat low in her stomach as she remained frozen on the bed. She grabbed her phone again and hit call.

"Jess! What's up, lady of the hour?" Marie's exuberant voice answered, making Jess smile. She'd made the right decision.

"I have news, and thought you'd love to hear it."

"Hit me!" her friend squealed. Marie and Hayley were

her best friends, often hanging out together to play board games. "Oh, oh—wait! Is this for your 30th plans?"

Jess pictured Marie bouncing up and down on the spot. It made her smile.

"No, although I'll sort the details for that soon, promise." She paused. "I got a new job!"

"What! You sure I've got the right Jessica on the phone? Jess, who's been working at the one place since I've known her? That Jess? How? When? Why? All the details —now! Actually, wait. BABE!" she called straight into the phone, making Jess wince. "I'm putting you on loudspeaker."

"Hey, I'm here," came Hayley's voice. "What's up?"

"Jess here has a new job."

"You do?"

"You're both talking to a new cabinet maker apprentice. I start in January."

"Wow, back the truck up," said Marie. "An apprenticeship?"

"Yep, with a women-owned company called The Lady Builders. Seems I'll be building kitchens and renovating bathrooms in no time."

"No way!" her friends said at the same time.

"That's so amazing," said Hayley.

"And such an awesome surprise," added Marie.

"Thanks, you two. I needed this pep talk to feel like I'm doing the right thing."

"Why wouldn't it be?" asked Marie.

"Adam and Mum think I should stay at Limone."

"But you're forever bitching about that place," said Hayley, confused.

"I know, right? I'm sure I'll talk them around." She had to, though she wasn't convinced just yet.

"They better be on board or send us round to sort them out," said Marie.

Jess tried to picture her being anything but kind and excited. The only mean bone in Marie's body was her competitive streak on games night.

Jess laughed. "I love you guys. I'll have more details soon, but I wanted to let you know."

"Can't wait," replied Marie.

"Same," added Hayley. "Also, if you come across any painters on your building site, can you let us know? We're going to get the internals redone. Might have to hit you up if we end up wanting to renovate down the track too!"

"Huh, funny you ask. I'm pretty sure one of Remi's friends is a painter."

"Who's Remi?" Marie didn't miss a beat.

"Well, as of ten minutes ago, she's my new boss."

"She hot?" Marie whipped back. Jess pictured Remi standing in her tradie gear: all paint-splattered shirt, short shorts and safety boots.

"Babe!" Jess heard the dull thwack, what she assumed was Hayley slapping a thigh or an arm. Jess chuckled at their antics. She couldn't deny her boss was attractive, but it went deeper than that. It was her assertiveness with life, her care for others—especially when Remi spoke about her family or how she wanted to see women succeed in the trades. Jess could see herself working well with Remi. And a new friend could be just what she needed.

"Remi's cool. She looks badass in her work gear, with an awesome tattoo sleeve I'm kinda jealous of. Can't wait til

I get my own outfit. I'll rock the safety boots. Not sure my usual leggings and runners would cut it for the kind of work I'll be doing," said Jess.

"I'm trying so hard to picture you in baggy safety wear," said Marie.

"I'll be sure to snap a pic when I get it. The outfits aren't half bad!" Remi's tradie clothes flitted through her mind again. "Now, I got a hot date with my book, so I'm gonna love and leave you ladies."

"Bye!" they said in unison.

Now to tell Adam the news, if he even listened.

SIX

Remi

Jess was bent over the cabinetry, stretching to check the back holes were aligned with the water pipes before she pushed the sink cupboard against the wall. They were working on a galley laundry together today, and Remi was absolutely not looking at her soon-to-be apprentice's arse in those goddamn leggings. She really needed to stop objectifying her staff. And get Jess some work gear—because those leggings? They left *nothing* to the imagination.

The cupboard slotted in perfectly and Jess rounded to face Remi, her face the picture of absolute satisfaction.

This was why she did what she did.

Seeing women be proud of themselves, even with something as simple as lining up their first cupboard, was so rewarding. Remi held up her hand for a high five.

"Good work. Next, we need to attach the end panels for the washing machine space. Pass me that clamp over there."

It was only Jess and Remi on site today. Sophie had gone home earlier to collect Hudson from school, he'd come down sick, leaving Remi to finish off the laundry install. Jess was only meant to be shadowing again, but with Sophie out, it was nice to have an extra pair of hands to help fetch tools, hold levels and maybe even build her first cabinet carcass. The job was a cheap flat pack, making it a good starter for Jess compared to some of their custom kitchens, where everything was built from scratch.

"I'll get you to put that one together," said Remi, pointing at the smallest box on a stack across the room.

"Me?" Jess checked.

"Unless there's another wannabe apprentice in the room—yeah—you." Remi flashed a grin. "Go grab it."

Remi was enjoying Jess's presence, and even more relieved now knowing Jess had signed all the paperwork.

They had an apprentice.

And they had enough women on the team to satisfy Javier's terms and work with Flinders Homes next year, if selected as the winning sub-contractors. It felt good knowing there was truth sitting behind her words now. Remi had a few months to train Jess before Flinders began, so she'd have to hit the ground running come January when the apprenticeship officially started. Hopefully, Jess was a fast learner.

Jess brought the small box over, looking at it like it might bite her.

They had a long way to go.

"It'll be easy. Promise," Remi reassured her. "Now, see my toolbox over there? You want to grab out the Phillips head screwdriver."

Jess rummaged through it, longer than Remi expected, then returned with a flat head screwdriver.

When the woman said she didn't own tools, she hadn't been joking.

Remi bit back a smile, catching Jess's hopeful look as she held it out.

"Good try, but you want the one with the cross shaped tip, not flat. You could still technically use that, but they honestly suck. Flat heads are only good for when you absolutely have to use them—usually it's pulling out old cabinetry with old screws. Total nightmare!"

"Got it!" Jess raced back, eager to try again.

"This one?" she asked a minute later.

"It is... but I need the left-handed one."

Jess jumped up to look again, cracking Remi up until she had tears in her eyes.

"What?" Jess asked, looking around for the source of humour.

"There is no left-hand screwdriver."

"There's not?" Jess studied the tool in her hand.

"Nah. Classic newbie apprentice prank. Couldn't help myself."

"Oh," Jess replied, turning a light pink.

Remi finally calmed herself down. "All right, now we just need the piecost." She held her face as still as could be, laughter fighting its way out.

"What's a piecost?"

"About six dollars these days." She lasted another three more seconds before chuckling at herself again, Jess's unimpressed look doing her in.

"I'm so gullible. And now I feel like a pie," Jess replied, fighting a smile.

"Okay, no more jokes, promise. On the plus side, now

you know more about screwdrivers than you did half an hour ago." Remi pulled open the cabinet box. "Now, usually you'd put these carcasses together with drills, but we'll start you off old school with the screwdriver. That way it's harder to over-tighten the screws. Lay out all the pieces, read the instructions—twice, or even three times, then let me know once you've put it together."

"Throwing me in the deep end, huh?"

"It's the best way to learn." Remi winked.

Not even five minutes later, Remi could feel Jess behind her.

"What's up?" she asked without turning around.

"I got everything ready, but this instruction sheet is kind of confusing."

Remi turned, and copped a face full of chest. She looked up quickly, then moved back against the cupboard to give them some space. She hadn't planned to work in such close proximity with a beautiful woman today and tried to keep her head on the job. She held out her hand for the instruction booklet.

"Let's have a look then."

They moved over to Jess's setup.

"These all look the same," Jess said, pointing at the sides of the cabinet.

"Okay, the trick is to lay them out the same way they appear in the drawings. That way, you can double check all the holes line up exactly. Like... this one." Remi picked up the back panel. "This piece is upside down, so let's rotate it. Now look at the holes along the bottom."

Jess leaned in to compare the drawing to the now righted panel. Close enough that Remi caught her perfume. It was sweet, almost fruity, just like Jess's personality so far.

"Wow, that's so much easier. Sorry for bothering you."

"You can bother me as much as you need."

They worked well together, chatting the entire time. Jess was thrown in the deep end again as she learned how to help attach the laundry carcasses to the wall and to each other, while keeping everything level.

Remi handled most of the physical and tool-based work, but there were still a lot of hands-on skills to keep them busy all afternoon.

Later, Remi pushed a small cardboard box with her foot over to Jess who was sitting on the floor taking a break and chugging down her water. A drip made its way down Jess's neck. Remi licked her lips. *Wait, what was she doing?* She looked away, busying herself by rummaging through her toolbox.

"Door handles are in that box. And—" She found what she was looking for. "—here's the screws and a new tool. These are wire cutters. You'll use them to cut these snap off screws to the right width for the doors and drawers. Just be careful. And here." She handed Jess her own leather work gloves and plastic goggles. "Wear these. The screw ends fly when you cut them, and the last thing we need is metal in your eye."

"Thanks, boss." Jess saluted playfully as she adorned the gear. "How do I look?"

Remi turned from the toolbox.

Still hot. With a side of dork.

"Like a gym buff wannabe scientist?"

"Well pass me the Bunsen burner!" Jess joked back.

Remi kept watching as Jess set to work, then realised she was still standing there, staring like an idiot. Her cheeks heated, and she spun on her heel, trying to focus.

Jess, thankfully, got through all the handles while Remi finished off the cabinetry, more than she'd expected with one woman down.

"Right, c'mon, tools down. It's been a much bigger day than I'd originally intended. Can I shout you an early dinner?"

Jess leaned against the newly installed cabinetry. "I'd love that. Adam's out with the boys tonight, so I don't have to worry about feeding him. Plus, any excuse not to cook a meal for one at home. Which, let's be honest, was probably going to be toast or a slice of cheese."

"That sounds incredibly sad, and now I'm definitely taking you out for a good feed. I take it Adam is your... husband?"

"Partner. And thank you. I'm starving after you had me slaving away today." Jess winked.

Noted: possibly straight. Definitely unavailable. And, still *her apprentice*. Remi knew she'd be reminding herself of that frequently. Maybe she needed to go on a date again, get it out of her system and get Sophie off her back from asking her every other week. It had been... she thought back to the last girl she'd dated. Irene? Remi had been so busy back then, it hadn't lasted beyond a couple of months. Irene was sweet, and Remi had really liked her. But Irene wanted more—more time, more commitment. With her business still growing, Remi couldn't give her any more. Things ended not long after. That must've been at least three years ago now... and work sure didn't look to be slowing down anytime soon to allow for more dating in her future. At least she had Ninja for company.

Half an hour later, Remi leaned against the brick wall outside the restaurant, waiting for Jess to get out of her car.

"I *never* would've found this place if I hadn't followed you," Jess said, making her way over as she slid her sunglasses up into her hair.

Nyam Nyam was a Korean hole-in-the-wall restaurant, wedged between a laundromat and an Indian grocer in the suburbs. Luckily, it was only a ten-minute drive from their client's house.

Remi pushed open the door to the sound of K-pop beats floating out. She held it with a smile. "After you."

"Thanks," Jess murmured, shuffling past into the cosy space.

Even this early—just past five—half the seats were already taken. There were only six tables in the entire shoebox. A low buzz hummed through the room as plates clattered, chopsticks clinked and people spoke amongst themselves in relaxed chatter.

Jess squeezed herself into a corner table while Remi slid in opposite with a sigh and picked up the menu. The sun beat through the blinds, and the wall-mounted air con was working overtime. Soy sauce and spicy gochujang hung in the air.

"Aside from the Korean fried chicken, I've got no idea what to order," confessed Jess.

"Lucky for you, this is one of my all-time favourite establishments. It never disappoints! How about I order us a few dishes to share?"

"I'm down to try anything." A wicked grin spread across her face.

"You'll be sorry you said that," Remi warned. "I hope you like spice."

Before long, their table was covered in plates.

"Gosh. This looks incredible, Remi," Jess said, as the waitress brought over a pot of tea with two tiny mugs. "Aww, and these are so cute!"

Remi smiled at her excitement. It made the cleft in her chin more pronounced, and her blue eyes seem even brighter. "It's barley tea. It has a nutty, roasty flavour that goes so good with the spicy food." She poured it into their mugs. "Careful, it's hot."

Jess brought the mug to her nose and inhaled. "Wow. I can't wait to try it. So, what are we eating?"

"This is the sweet and spicy fried chicken, with daikon pickles on the side—those little cubes help cut through the heat. Then we've got tteokbokki—spicy rice cakes; japchae —sweet potato noodles with veggies and beef; and finally, a big bowl of bibimbap."

"Okay, I know bibimbap!"

"Good. Let's dig in!" Remi handed over a pair of chopsticks and a spoon.

Five minutes in, Jess was fanning her mouth. "That chicken is fucking amazing. I can't feel my mouth."

"Ah shit, I meant to warn you not to get the sauce on your lips. It's tasty but it stings. Here's a napkin, though it's probably a little late for that."

"Thanks." Jess took a moment for the heat to settle, then folded her napkin and slid it under her plate. "So, tell me about you. Who is Remi when you're not making strides leading women in trades?"

Remi snorted. "Trying to make strides. I haven't successfully taken on an apprentice yet."

"Sounds like there's a story there."

Remi took a moment, chewing a mouthful of japchae. "Soph and I tried training a girl earlier this year. We spent a few months with her. All of our time and energy."

"Oh no, did she quit?" Remi saw the pity in Jess's eyes.

"Not exactly. She transferred interstate to be with her boyfriend."

Jess frowned. "I wouldn't call that a waste of your time. Yeah, it sucks for your business. But Remi, that's still one more tradeswoman out there thanks to you."

Huh. She hadn't thought of it that way.

"I guess you're right." She hummed as she took a sip of her tea. "That does make it sting slightly less."

"Also, you wouldn't have this awesome apprentice on your team if she hadn't left. Even if I have, like, zero experience." Jess cringed.

"You sell yourself short. You've done fine with everything I've thrown at you so far. Once your formal training starts next year, you'll see your speed and skill really pick up."

"We'll see," replied Jess, looking unsure of herself again, which struck Remi as odd for someone who wasn't doing a terrible job at all. Then Jess brightened, "Right. I'm changing the topic away from work again. Don't think I didn't notice we skipped the question about us talking about you!"

"Can't get away with it that easily, can I?"

"So?"

Remi shrugged her shoulders. "What do you want to know?"

"Anything! What do you do for fun or on the weekends? What are your hobbies? All I know is that you have or had a turtle, you like tattoos and you work a lot."

"Ouch. You make me sound incredibly boring."

"I'm intrigued enough to want to know more," Jess pressed, struggling to pick up a piece of chicken with her chopsticks. Her nose scrunched in concentration in the cutest way. She gave up and switched to a fork, making Remi chuckle.

"Fine. Umm..." Remi's mind blanked. The heat crept up her chest. She wasn't often stuck for words or felt so put on the spot. Jess stared at her, waiting; it was unnerving having so much attention on her. She wasn't used to being under such personal scrutiny, and getting lost in those determined blue eyes wasn't going to give her the answers she needed to sell herself as a more appealing person either.

"I like fishing." Remi finally remembered. Was that lame? She wanted to be anything *but* lame in front of Jess.

"Now we're getting somewhere." Her face brightened at the tidbit of new information she'd been fed, it encouraged Remi to keep going.

"I live by myself—well with Ninja, who is still alive by the way. I named him when I was nine, and that was over thirty years ago now."

Jess almost spat out her mouthful of tea, covering her mouth at the last minute. "What!" she shrieked once she'd swallowed.

Remi startled at the outburst, quickly looking around

at the other patrons, who didn't seem disturbed. "Are you oka—"

"You're over forty?" Jess cut her off, albeit quietly this time, eyes disbelieving.

"Uh, yeah?" Remi replied, confused.

"Sorry, sorry, sorry." Jess waved her hands in front of her, words rushing out. "You just... you don't look forty. I thought you were my age."

"Thank you? I guess?" The compliment warmed her more than the fried chicken.

"Seriously though? How old are you?" Jess enquired, inspecting Remi's face as if trying to confirm Remi was telling the truth.

"I'm forty-one."

"I don't believe you. You look really good for forty-one."

Remi laughed off the statement but felt the heat spreading all the same. At least this time she was off kilter for a much better reason.

"Okay, I'll leave your age alone. Just know that I'm impressed," replied Jess, sensing Remi was uncomfortable with the line of enquiry. "Tell me about fishing."

"You're bossy for an apprentice." Remi quirked an eyebrow.

Jess smiled extra sweet, waiting. Remi enjoyed this woman's sass, the dinner more enjoyable than she'd anticipated.

She finally relented. "I don't have a boat or anything, but I sometimes head down to the very tip of Karkalla Beach to fish or crab off the rocks."

"Do you live in Karkalla?"

"Yeah, Soph and I grew up there. Sophie moved a few suburbs away, closer to the city, when she bought a house with her now-husband, Tomás."

"And she has a son, right?"

"Yeah, my nephew Hudson. He's amazing." Remi felt the warmth just thinking about him. He was such a great kid.

"Do you have any kids? Or a partner?"

"Nope, just me. My business is my baby."

Usually when Remi talked about The Lady Builders, she'd feel the energy build, ready to burst out so she could tell everyone and anyone about it. But right now? Jess's eyes bore into her once more, head tilted slightly to the side, assessing. Always so curious, this woman. People didn't usually *see* her like this. Aside from Sophie, but that was her sister. And maybe JJ... but this felt different. Like pushing on a bruise. It made her feel raw and seen all at once. She didn't usually have time to think about herself; the future *was* building her business for other women. Though it felt like Jess had an unspoken question aimed directly at her tonight—*but what about you?*

She wasn't sure she had the answers to that.

SEVEN

Jess

Her heart pounded, the printer taking its sweet time spitting out the paper. *Hurry up!* The back of her neck prickled as Jess swiped at it, looking around to double-check she was alone in Ricciardo's office. She quickly folded the paper in half. The irony of printing her resignation letter at work wasn't lost on her. She could have emailed it, but Ricciardo was old school, he'd appreciate a hard copy. He wasn't going to be happy though.

Well, join the club.

Adam hadn't been impressed with the news, unable to grapple with the fact she wanted to pursue something she had no experience in, *especially* for a pay cut. She'd tried to explain she'd be earning more once her apprenticeship was complete—delayed gratification and all that—but it didn't seem to land. It hurt, knowing he'd prefer her to stay at Limone.

Her second blow had been updating her mum, which went as poorly as with Adam. It was so frustrating when the both of them had looked at her like she was crazy over dinner. People changed careers all the time. If she was heading to the mines to earn four times her current wage, would it be a different story?

No, they probably wouldn't want her working in the mines either. Too dangerous for a woman. And who'd iron Adam's shirt's while she was gone? She rolled her eyes.

"Jessica?"

She tried not to jump as she folded the paper a second time, running her finger along the crease. Time to deal with the third thorn in her side.

"Ricciardo, hi."

She'd wanted more time to prepare a speech, but life had other plans. His eyes flicked to the paper in her hands, held tightly in front of her while she scrambled for words. She shoved it towards him. *God, this was awkward.*

Break ups and resignations: there was never a good time.

The small office felt too confined, thick with the heat from the kitchen. Jess stood backed up against the desk, Ricciardo blocking the doorway as he stared at the paper. She swallowed, waiting, wanting to snatch it back. The old fluorescent buzzed overhead, bathing him in an unappealing yellow hue.

"It's..." *Just rip that Band-Aid off, Jess!* "This, uh—" She stopped, took a breath, and started over. "This is my formal notice of resignation. I'm moving to a different industry in the new year, but I can stay on over the holidays. I don't want to leave you high and dry."

His jaw slackened an instant before snapping shut. "Well. I didn't expect this, Jess."

Checkmate, Ricciardo. She revelled in his surprise,

finally catching him off guard. It gave her the confidence she needed.

"To be honest, neither did I. An opportunity popped up I couldn't say no to. I'm training to become a cabinet-maker."

He opened and closed his mouth a few more times. "This seems so out of the blue."

He sounded like her mum. It only made her want to double down on her decision.

"What if we had a look at your hours? Maybe we could see about cutting them back like you'd mentioned?"

Of course, *now* he wanted to talk. Too little, too late.

He opened the letter, scanning the contents. "Could you at least stay on until the end of January?"

She clamped her mouth shut. This is where the guilt usually set in. She felt it almost like a physical pain, going against her usual *yes, whatever you need*, in these situations. Always for the benefit of others. She swallowed down the first response.

"It's a little late for changes. My new contracts are signed. The sixth of January will be my final day. That's still over your minimum two weeks' notice and will cover you through Christmas *and* New Years." She stood a little taller, thinking of the way Remi led her business.

"Right. Well. I appreciate you staying over the holidays. I'll work out your long service leave payment, and we can talk later about finalising your work here."

She knew a dismissal when she heard one, and she didn't want to spend any longer in his office anyway. Then it hit her. *Long service leave payment.* She'd completely forgotten she'd be owed a payout. Maybe the extra cash in hand would be enough to appease Adam and help smooth things over.

Leaving his office, she let out a big sigh. She'd quit. And on her own terms. She beamed, proud of herself for sticking to the final date. Time to celebrate!

Her excitement dimmed.

Even if it was a party for one.

Taylor's name flashed on Jess's phone. Surely, she was seeing things?

"Hello?" she answered tentatively.

"Surprise!" Taylor replied.

"This certainly is." Jess sat on a stool at the kitchen bench. She'd been mindlessly scrolling, avoiding making a decision about dinner. She couldn't stop smiling at hearing from her best friend so unexpectedly.

"To what do I owe this pleasure?" Jess said in her best British accent.

"Open your front door."

Jess couldn't get there fast enough. She almost knocked over the kitchen stool, catching herself at the last second on the back of the couch as she scooted through the lounge in her socks. She made the last few strides and swung the door open. There stood Taylor looking sun-kissed in shorts and a T-shirt with the biggest shit-eating grin.

"You fucking loser!" Jess choked on a sob, launching herself at Taylor, who whirled her around on the spot.

"I've missed you so much," she said into her neck.

They pulled apart, Taylor wiping at her eyes too. Jess

shoved her in her shoulder. "What are you even doing here! Shouldn't you guys still be in the tropics up North? I was only half-joking when I messaged you to fly down for a visit."

"Long story. Matt was coming back for a couple of months to catch up with friends and hired a house down here. He asked Sam and me if we wanted to pop down for Christmas, and I think it would mean a lot for Sam to spend the holiday season with her dad. Plus, it got me thinking about a certain someone's thirtieth, so we decided to come stay with him. Manny's up on the slip getting some work done—new anti-fouling and what not—so, here I am."

"Ho-ly shit. I'm just so happy to see you. You have no idea."

With everything that had been going on, she really needed her best friend right now. She felt tears brimming and blinked rapidly to hold them back.

"Hey, where's Sam? And Belle?"

"They're back at Matt's place. I thought we could catch up like old times tonight, I know you usually finish up earlier on Wednesdays. Adam home?"

"Nah, he's working late on a proposal, then catching the train back. Come in."

"So weird being back here," Taylor said, kicking her shoes off out of habit.

"I think you mean *awesome*! Have you eaten?"

"Not yet."

"Thai?"

"Done. The usual?"

"But of course."

Food ordered, they tucked up in their usual spots on the couch and Jess couldn't stop grinning. Everything felt so easy when it came to Taylor. Living together as long as they had, she'd really taken her friendship for granted. Until it wasn't there. Which was silly. Taylor had done a van trip around Australia before, and Jess hadn't struggled like she had this time. What was different? She felt for anyone in a long-distance relationship, she was struggling hard enough with just friendship!

Jess found herself staring at Taylor.

"What?" Taylor quizzed, throwing an arm over the back of the couch.

"I can't believe you're really here. You're you, and yet... there's something different that doesn't come across on video chats. You seem lighter and... glowy. I don't mean your tan. Though, I'm jealous of that too."

"It could be that I'm still riding the high from getting engaged, but I think I know what you mean. I do feel different inside. Taking the risk with Sam and living on the boat with her has been the best decision of my life."

Jess could see it. She'd never seen her friend so happy.

"Yeah, well, I believe you needed a little encouragement there." Jess remembered the pep talks she'd given Taylor when she'd let her past demons get the better of her.

"And I will be forever grateful for your support." Taylor looked at her in earnest.

A knock at the door interrupted the moment, and for a second Jess forgot what year it was, half-expecting an excited Belle to start barking and shoot off towards the door. Maybe she and Adam needed to look into getting a dog? Then she remembered how well *that* had worked out for Taylor and her ex, Liz.

"Yes! Food's here, and I'm starving." Taylor hopped up, grabbing their dinner and spreading it out on the coffee table.

"So," she added, digging into some green chicken curry.

"So," Jess parroted, tucking her legs underneath her as she got comfy again on the couch.

"How are we celebrating the big three-oh this year?"

If Jess was honest, she'd been avoiding thoughts of her birthday, let alone planning it. Everyone was so excited, especially with the weight of such a big milestone. She could still hear the anticipation in Marie's voice the other day, and now Taylor too. The pressure to be happy along with everyone else was exhausting. In reality, she didn't feel like she had the energy right now. Except for Remi. Spending time with her over dinner had been so fun and relaxed. Two things she hadn't realised she'd been missing. Her apprenticeship was one thing she *was* looking forward to in the new year. Ironic, considering how physically demanding the work would be.

"Your face just lit up," Taylor said, pointing her fork at Jess. "What *are* you planning for your birthday?"

Jess took a second, realising she'd stopped thinking about her birthday and started thinking about Remi instead. She was popping up in her thoughts more and more lately.

"I don't want a big party," Jess confessed. That was about as far as her planning had gone. "Something low-key and *fun*."

Because she needed more fun in her life. Everything had become so dull and grey.

"I'm listening. What were you thinking by 'something fun'?"

Jess tapped her chin with her spoon. "Good question. What if it's something with games? But something that works for a bigger group—like a board game, maybe?"

Taylor stared out the front window. "Hmm." She snapped her fingers and whirled back to Jess, her eyes alight. "How about a murder mystery party?"

"Oh. I've never done one of those."

"Neither have I."

They were both silent a moment, Jess slowly nodding as she considered the idea. She picked up her phone, looking up the game while Taylor refilled her plate with more food.

"These sound really good, Taylor. You could be onto something. It says here... da, da, da... up to twenty people... uh..." She kept scrolling through the information, a low buzz starting to build. "Just download the pack you want and self-host. It comes with a guide and everything, so you can host one even if you've never played it before."

The more she read, the more Jess could get behind the idea. It would be a night of celebration, but the focus wouldn't be all on her. She'd also get to celebrate with her favourite people.

A key turned in the door, and a tired Adam called out, "I'm home! God, dinner smells good babe—Taylor!"

"We had a surprise on the doorstep tonight," Jess said, grinning and flourishing her hand towards her friend.

Taylor hopped up off the couch to give Adam a hug.

"I'll say," he replied, letting Taylor go. "Let me get

changed, then fill me in." He flung his messenger bag on the end of the couch and disappeared towards the bedroom. A few minutes later, he reappeared, empty plate in hand.

"Load up," Jess encouraged. "I ordered plenty."

They caught him up on Taylor's return and finished up by sharing the new birthday idea.

"So... Taylor was asking about my thirtieth party, when she had the idea—"

"—to do a murder mystery party!" Taylor finished, bouncing on the couch. Her mop of brown hair flopped up and down with the movement.

"I'm so in!" Adam said around a mouth full of food. "That would be sick."

"Now to see if the fiancée is keen," Taylor added.

"I bet you love getting to say that," said Jess.

"Oh, I do. I really do. The only thing better will be when I get to say, 'my wife'."

"Congrats, by the way," said Adam, tipping his beer towards her.

"Thanks. Can't believe it's already been a month. But enough about me, how are *you* guys? Oh my god, Jess, I completely forgot to ask about your new job!"

Jess tried not to bristle with Adam in the room. She really would've preferred to have this conversation twenty minutes earlier. It was still an uncomfortable topic between them. But, maybe with Taylor here, another person could help get him on board. She gave Taylor the rundown, talking about Remi, her future business plans and that she'd officially resigned today from the restaurant.

"Wow. That's a lot of change," said Taylor.

"I think it's a rash decision, but she won't listen to me,"

replied Adam, downing the rest of his beer. He placed the empty bottle next to his dirty plate and got up to get another from the kitchen.

Jess gave a tight smile. "We're still working through the changes."

Taylor's face softened as she reached over and squeezed her knee. "Believe in yourself," she whispered with a wink.

"Thanks," Jess mouthed back. "Actually, there was one surprise today. I haven't even told you yet," Jess said to Adam, as he came back in with a new beer. "I'm getting a payout from Ricciardo for my remaining long service leave, so that'll help tide us over on my lower income."

"How much lower are we talking?" Taylor asked.

"My paycheck will be halved, but it will go up each year until I'm earning more than I am now."

"You guys will work it out." Taylor's eyes flitted between them. "Plus, Adam, don't you wanna see your girlfriend in a hot tradie outfit?" Taylor finished, trying to quell the awkward vibes.

"They are pretty hot," Jess added, thinking of Remi's outfit.

"I s'pose," Adam agreed. "I just can't see Jess on the tools."

Wow. Low blow.

Remi had said she'd done great with the cabinet. She hadn't broken anything, and she'd got the job done. Sure, she was learning, but it was nice to have someone actually believe in her potential.

"I've done all right with a Phillips screwdriver and a level. I even know the little 'lefty-loosey, righty-tighty' trick now, thanks to Remi."

"Anyone can learn a trade if they're keen enough. The amount Sam and I have taught each other since we've been together is incredible."

"I *bet* you've taught her a lot." Jess teased with a wink.

Taylor's face turned bright pink as she grinned. "Yeah, that too. Speaking of, I better get back to my girls. I'll call you once I've spoken to Sam about the party idea, but you can pretty much count us there with bells on."

"Give Belle a big squeezy hug from me. And Sam too," said Jess.

"Will do," replied Taylor, getting off the couch. "Thanks for dinner as well."

Jess waved her off. "Pfft, don't be silly. If my bestie shows up outta nowhere, she's getting dinner!"

"Night Taylor, good to see you again," said Adam, making no effort to get off the couch.

Jess saw her out, giving Taylor an extra squishy hug before she left. She paused at the door, hesitating. She didn't want to face Adam just yet.

Breathe in, breathe out.

When she finally returned to the lounge, Adam was already playing his game like nothing had happened. The whole night had felt off-kilter. His digs about her job change, the lack of curiosity, his shitty goodbye to Taylor...

"Well, that was awkward."

"What?" he replied, nonchalant.

The pain in her shoulder was back. She stood with her arms folded. "I get that you don't like me starting this new job, but you're right, I am doing it anyway. I promised you I'd make this work with the money. I also wanted the better hours so I could be home with you more on nights and weekends. It hurts when you put me down in front of my friends or say I can't do something. Just try to think about how it comes across when you talk like that."

She hadn't anticipated coming back inside to word vomit, but seeing him there playing games again, dirty dishes still sprawled on the coffee table—she'd had enough. The game's heavy main menu music thrummed between them, giving more gravity to the conversation than she'd intended. Lately, every talk left them more frustrated, more silent.

Adam scratched at the stubble on his chin. "I didn't mean to put you down, Jess. I was trying to be honest."

"Ouch. That doesn't make it any better." In fact, it was worse.

"What do you want me to say?" He threw his hands up, the controller discarded onto the couch.

Jess ran a hand through her hair. *Fuck.* For once. Just for once, she wished she didn't have to spell it out.

"I want you to say we can work through this together. That you're excited to see what I learn. That you'll clean up the dishes tonight," she bit out, hands flailing now.

Confusion washed across his face. "What do the dishes have to do with anything?"

"Everything apparently, Adam. I just..." She stopped, exhaled slowly, giving herself a moment. She pinched the bridge of her nose and leaned against the doorway. Why was this so difficult? Why couldn't he understand?

"I just feel like living together has been... hard lately." She focused on the couch's pattern, not quite able to look him in the eyes. "It's been a cycle of work, cook, wash, clean... and I've felt like a lot of that has fallen to me. That

wasn't what I expected when we first moved in together."
Her eyes flicked to him. He looked like a wounded puppy.
While she felt bad, this conversation was overdue. She
wanted him to take responsibility.

He gave a small nod, his eyes drifting to the coffee table.
"I'll clean all that up."

"Thank you."

"I didn't realise it was getting to you that much."

"I've mentioned it before. I know you've got a lot of
pressure with your work too, but we both live here."

He nodded again, face downturned as he picked up the
controller.

End of discussion. Again.

Even though he'd agreed to help, Jess doubted it would
last. The lack of energy in his response said everything. The
whole conversation felt more like a mother telling off a
teenage son rather than her partner. Why did it feel like she
couldn't fix this? She always tried to sort things out through
conversation, but recently, it felt like every talk only drove
them further apart.

The next few weeks were going to be anything but
"happy holidays". More work, awkward family conversations... her apprenticeship couldn't start soon enough.

EIGHT

Remi

It was a new year, and Remi had a good feeling.

The first day back was always filled with positive vibes for the work year ahead, and this year was no different. There was so much to look forward to, starting with her newest employee.

Remi pulled up to Jess's house. It was a quaint suburban home, kept neat with a small patch of grass out front. Before she could hop out, the front door swung open and Jess came bouncing down the steps. *Someone was excited to start work.* Adding another tradeswoman to the industry had Remi pretty excited too.

"Good morning!" Jess greeted brightly, getting in the car. "You seriously didn't have to pick me up. It feels like I'm going to school."

"Of course I did. Happy first official day of your apprenticeship, Newbie! You kinda are starting school, but this one's for kickass women." Remi grinned.

Jess had managed a few more days shadowing them last December, before work at Limone had ramped up for the holidays, and Remi had closed shop to reset. She spent her time planning the year ahead, catching up on admin—even taxes, finally—and squeezing in family time over Christmas. Her parents still hosted Christmas each year. Another scorcher in Adelaide meant long lunches, seafood, and hours in the pool. It had been bliss. But she was ready to get back to it.

She and Jess had mostly kept in touch by text, sorting out paperwork for her apprenticeship. Jess was so eager to start, it was rubbing off on Remi. She'd anticipated Jess's first day, wanting to make sure it was perfect. After the crap treatment she'd copped at Limone, Remi wanted this to be the opposite. There'd be no sneering remarks or bad-mouthing on her watch. Remi never wanted to see that bright grin wiped from Jess's face.

"I thought you said our first reno was down at Karkalla Beach?" Jess questioned as Remi swung the ute in the opposite direction.

"It is. But first I'm taking you to get proper clothing and tools."

Jess lit up like a kid on Christmas. "Seriously?"

"Uh, yeah, I'm serious. You've graduated from screw-driver and broom duty. Time to teach you some real skills, woman! And to do that, I wanna make sure you're kitted out correctly—and safely."

"Yes, boss."

Remi drove them to a hub of her favourite shops: a safety workwear place right next to a warehouse stocked with every trade tool imaginable. This morning was going to be fun!

She was really hoping to work on Jess's skill set in these

coming weeks, especially with Flinders Homes expected to announce their chosen sub-contractor soon. They were so close to potentially getting this job, to starting the next chapter of The Lady Builders. Their proposal had to be more promising than Dickhead Declan. Surely.

"What the hell. Remi, this place is huge!" Jess stood at the doorway, eyes wide. It really was like taking a kid to visit Santa.

"While this place is massive, our lovely ladies' section is squished *alllll* the way over in that tiny corner. Come on."

Jess followed, head swinging in so many different directions before going straight over to the work leggings.

"Nope. You'll need something more rugged. Here." Remi grabbed a pair of Zadie shorts—the ones with the extra pockets, and a long pair of their work pants. "I'm assuming you're around Sophie's fit. These are actually made for women, by women. And believe me, it makes all the difference with the fit!"

Remi could see it now: Jess in a toolbelt, standing in a demo zone, hair up, confidence growing. She was going to rock it.

Next, Remi picked up a few work shirts and jumpers. "Love a good hoodie in winter." With both their arms piled up, she ushered Jess into the changerooms.

A minute later, the door opened.

"How do I look?"

Remi looked up from her phone, and blinked, several times. Jess stood in her socks, biting her lip as she waited for Remi's response.

Wow.

Jess looked taller in the shorts. The fit was absolute

perfection, accentuating her hips and—suddenly Remi had no idea where to look. She hadn't expected Jess to pull off the whole tradie look so well.

Jess glanced down at herself, tugging at the hem. "Is it okay?" she asked, sounding almost nervous.

"Looks grood. GREAT. Sorry, went to say good, then great. At the same time." Remi over-explained, earning a chuckle from Jess. Remi's ears burned as she looked down at her phone again. She needed to stop acting like such a weirdo and get out of her head. This day wasn't going to go well if she couldn't even speak properly around her apprentice!

"Glad I look grood," Jess humoured her, drawing a smile from Remi. "I'll try on the pants next, but they should fit."

They did.

Everything looked amazing on her, like she'd been wearing workwear for years. Only problem was, it was all far too clean for a tradie.

Safety boots were next. Jess squealed, spying a pink pair on the bottom row. "Oh. My. God. These are so *cuuuute*." She picked one up, basically cuddling it on the floor. Remi couldn't help but shake her head at the display. She hadn't had this much fun when she'd taken Jackie to get kitted out. It was more of a quick transactional process, in and out.

"Don't tell me you love pink," ribbed Remi.

"It's one of my favourite colours."

Remi scrunched up her nose. "Ew."

"Well, we can't all look as good as you do in yellow

boots," said Jess, kicking off her sandshoes to try on the pink ones.

"Um, thank you," said Remi, taken aback. She felt her face heat, again. Jess was too busy lacing up her boots to notice her overreaction. *What is wrong with you? She literally just complimented your work shoes... Pull yourself together, Remi!* Jess just seemed like the kind of person who gave out compliments freely. Remi had to learn to accept them more gracefully... like a normal human being. Why did Jess affect her so much?

"They're perfect," Jess declared, clomping up and down the aisle rather inelegantly. Remi couldn't help but laugh.

"What?" Jess eyed her, perplexed.

"Like high heels, these shoes also take a little bit of getting used to."

With that, Jess straightened her shoulders, pushed her nose into the air and began walking like she was on a runway, hips swaying. Remi watched her with delight. If this was any indication, they were going to have so much fun on site together.

"Careful, you'll have all the boys coming to the yard if you keep that up," Remi joked.

"Ew, no thanks." Her booted heels dropped to the ground. "I struggle enough with the one boy in my yard." She let out a light laugh, though it didn't match the upbeat tone of the moment. Jess sat on the floor with a sigh and took off the boots.

"Everything okay?"

"Things between Adam and me have been... strained. Because I took this job. Among other things."

"Oh. Man, I'm sorry to hear that. I had no idea."

"It's okay. I'm trying to sort through it. Plus, I shouldn't be complaining to my boss on day one about my partner not wanting me to do this." She gave a tight-lipped smile, shutting the shoe box and standing up.

Remi frowned, reaching out to Jess's shoulder. "Hey. I'm sure you'll sort it, one way or another. I've known some women in the industry whose partners or husbands have tried to hold them back or undermine their careers when they've felt threatened by 'not being the man of the house'."

"I don't think it's that. Though, far out, that sounds like a crap situation for those women, and so unfair. One of his issues is that we're putting our life on hold so I can do this. He wants the house and kids now, or at least soon, and I... I..." She trailed off, eyes landing on a rack of marked down men's fleece jackets. "Shit. I guess, I want to put *me* first right now," she said finally, meeting Remi's eyes.

"That's a pretty valid reason. Have you told him that? Or are you just coming to that conclusion?"

"Both. But maybe not in those exact words. I'm happy to put our trajectory on hold for a time, and still make things work. But maybe he isn't."

"Well, talk to him. Hopefully that clarity you just found might help." Even as Remi offered the advice, she wondered what kind of a person wouldn't want Jess to be her best self. She stood before her, so full of energy. Her blue eyes gleamed at those damn pink boots like they were made of diamonds, and Remi made a promise to herself then and there to try and make this woman happy, however she could. She deserved it.

Next door, the tools acquisition went quicker. Remi

and Sophie were Makita fans, so that's what Jess would have too. Remi had a checklist of essentials, ticking them off swiftly as they made their way around the store. They stopped every so often so Remi could explain each piece as it went in the basket.

"This is going to be your new best friend." She passed Jess an impact driver.

Jess turned it over in her hands, eyes alight.

"Aww it's so tiny and cute. Is this seriously a drill?"

"Yep—and it packs a punch. It'll take apart an old cupboard in minutes and build new ones just as fast. Its small size is perfect for getting into those awkward spots. Like the ones you struggled with a couple of times last year."

"Oh, I'm so keen to test this now!"

"And I've already got the perfect project for you today."

"Fuck's sake!" bellowed down the hallway and into the bathroom they were working on.

"There's a different vibe working with other trades around," Jess commented. unscrewing the old vanity with her new drill. She'd changed into her new work gear and looked much more the part of a tradie lady.

"We've worked on a few projects alongside Karkalla Renovations. Let's just say we're not fans."

A loud crash echoed, followed by more cursing. Remi poked her head out the room. "You guys need a hand?" she called.

Declan appeared at the other end of the house, lugging

a large plasterboard with one of his tradies. "Bit heavy for you, love," he huffed out. "But you can grab us some coffees if you like?"

Remi flipped him off and returned to the architrave she was prying off. "Why do I even bother?" she muttered.

Karkalla Renovations were building the new kitchen extension for their client, Cole Donaldson, while The Lady Builders handled the bathroom and laundry reno. Today the insulation and internal walls were going in for the kitchen framework, and Remi was glad to be working at the opposite end of the house from the boys.

"Is that dick serious?" Jess said, eyes blown wide.

"Unfortunately, yes." Remi lowered her voice. "An appropriate choice of words too. We call him Dickhead Declan for a reason."

Jess snorted, setting the vanity door aside. "Love that for him."

Remi shoved the hammer into the next segment of wood, working through gritted teeth to loosen each nail. Finally, the long piece of wood popped off the edge of the doorway. She caught it and placed it against the wall, ready for the rubbish skip later. Wiping sweat from her brow, she moved to the other side of the door and caught Jess staring.

"What?"

"Sorry. You just make it look so effortless. I could watch you all day."

Ha. She wished it felt effortless. Her aching arms told another story. "Years of practise," she replied, starting to prise off the other architrave. A Radox bath tonight was definitely on the cards. While she couldn't work as quickly as she did in her twenties, she prided herself on eating well and being very fit for a forty-one-year-old. Who needed a gym when the job kept you moving all day?

Jess still paused, watching. May as well turn this into a lesson.

"Come give this bit a go."

Jess opened her mouth to protest, but Remi stopped her with a glare, the corners of her mouth upturned.

"All right," Jess said, laughing as she got to her feet and stood side-by-side with Remi. "What am I doing?"

"See here? I've started to loosen the panel and it's coming away from the wall."

Jess leaned in as Remi wedged the claw of her hammer into the slot. She tried not to think about the fact she could feel Jess's breath on her face.

"Watch where it's placed. You want the hammer's claw, or a crowbar, against a hard surface. If it's a brick wall or the thick hardwood it's been nailed into, you're fine. What you don't want is to have it pushing against gyprock, because if you put pressure on that, you'll end up with a hole in the wall."

"Got it."

"Next, come in front of me, grab the handle and bend your knees. That's it. Now pull to the right."

The wood creaked and groaned as Jess loosened it.

"Perfect. Now you have more room, keep moving up, wedging the hammer in as you go. Once you get near the top, give it a final tug."

Remi stood behind, observing. Jess had a lot more confidence in herself today, and it was great to see her trying new—

"Aah!"

Everything happened at once. The architrave flung off as Jess lost her balance in a flail of limbs, the hammer flying through the air and crashing to the tiled floor. Remi went into autopilot, grabbing the airborne wood with her left hand and wrapping an arm around Jess with her right.

"Gotcha."

She leaned the wood against the wall and righted Jess. "You okay?" Remi checked her face, making sure she hadn't hurt herself and copped a nail in the process. Up close she could see the dirt all over Jess's face. She resisted the urge to wipe it away.

"I'm fine." Jess straightened, wiping loose wisps of hair out of her eyes. "Only my ego. Think I'll stick to learning one new tool a day." Her cheeks burned bright red, as she turned back to the vanity.

"You didn't do anything wrong. Just over-balanced. But next time, I'll make sure you have safety glasses. Just in case." Remi bent over and picked up the hammer. The tile was chipped, but the flooring was being ripped up today anyway. Maybe practising tools on a demo site was a good idea?

"I've just realised we never got a coffee. Want to grab one on smoko?" Remi asked, hoping to give her new employee a reset before she went straight back into the tools.

"Oh, I don't smoke."

"Tradie slang, Newbie. Morning tea break." Remi slapped Jess on the back, making her smile, then grabbed the architraves and threw the hammer back in her toolbox. "Grab the doors you've pulled off the vanity, and we'll dump it on our way out."

They almost collided with Sophie in the hallway.

"Could've warned me Dickhead Declan was on site today," Sophie hissed. "He asked if we could clean the kitchen when we're done with the bathroom."

"What did you say?" asked Jess, intrigued.

"Nothing. He's not worth my time. I've got my Bluetooth earmuffs and Betty," she hoisted up a big blue box, "and I'm going to start going to town on those tiles."

"Betty's Soph's demolition hammer," Remi explained. "It's a good thing we're taking a break. It's gonna get *loud*."

"Hey, before you go. Did you end up ordering that sink for Mrs Williamson's kitchen for next week?" asked Sophie.

"Fuck. I completely forgot. I was in the middle of something and meant to write it down. I'll do it as soon as I'm back from break."

"You better. If it's not here by Tuesday, she's not going to be happy, and you're the one she's going to be calling."

"I know. I'll make sure it's ordered and delivered by COB Tuesday. Promise."

"All right. See you two later!" Sophie said, disappearing into the bathroom with a quick wave.

Remi tried to rush them through the rest of the house.

"Need me to carry those for you?" Declan appeared beside Jess, a look in his eyes that made Remi want to step in.

"No?" Jess frowned. "Do I look like I'm struggling?"

"Just offerin', love. Wouldn't want your clean outfit to get any dirt on it." The smarm on his face was sickening.

"Declan, fuck off and leave my trades alone. C'mon, Jess." Remi turned to let Jess pass by with the doors, knocking into Declan with the end of her architraves.

"Oops. My clumsy womanness didn't realise how long these were." She sauntered after Jess, a refreshing smile on her face as Declan scoffed and walked off.

Seatbelts clipped in, Jess turned to her. "How do you work on site with that guy?"

"With very little patience, and by giving him all the shit right back. Though I think he secretly likes that game too."

"Is there any way to avoid being on the same sites?"

"It depends. It's such a small area we currently cover; the crossovers are bound to happen. But if—no, *when*—we get the Flinders job, there'll be no more Dickhead Declan."

"I really hope so. For all our sakes."

Remi started the car and flicked through the radio stations, stopping as *G Flip*'s latest track belted out.

"Hey, have you been to the cafe by the marina?" Jess asked, foot tapping away.

Remi gave her a look. "Does the Pope shit in the woods?"

Jess barked out a laugh that echoed around the cab. Remi loved the sound.

"Pretty sure that's not the quote," said Jess, once she'd calmed down.

"Yeah, well, it is now," replied Remi, pulling away from the kerb, a smile on her lips she couldn't wipe off if she tried.

Toasties and take away coffees acquired, they sat at one of the outdoor tables to scarf down the food before heading back. While they had the shade of the umbrella, the heat of the day was already hitting hard. With no rain on the radar, the week ahead promised more sun and more heat. Working in it all day could be gruelling. Jess sat with her legs stretched out in the sun, toastie wrapper on her lap and her bright pink boots glinting in the light.

"Watch out, you'll have the feared tradie sock tan by the end of summer," Remi joked.

"Well, I've already got a thong tan."

Remi spluttered on her mouthful of coffee.

"On my *feet*, Donatello," Jess clarified with a chuckle.

Remi wiped her mouth with a napkin. "Right. Of course." Her face flamed. Of course Jess was talking about footwear, not underwear. What was wrong with her lately?

"Want to make a quick stop at Garner Marine?" Jess asked, pulling Remi out of her head.

"Never heard of it." She pushed out her bottom lip, thinking.

"Well then. We're making a pit stop on the way back. Though technically, it's five minutes that way." Jess pointed down the road.

"Why do we need to go to a marine shop? I don't have a boat."

"Two reasons. One: They sell hardware stuff, including a lot of things I've seen you use on site. Two: You said you like fishing, so I thought you might like it."

Remi finished her toastie, scrunching up the paper and throwing it in the nearby bin like a basketball. "Yes, score!" She checked the time on her phone. "All right, five-minute stop. Then we've got to get back." The fact Jess had remembered she liked fishing wasn't lost on her. It was nice. Thoughtful.

They grabbed their coffees and drove down the road, pulling into a little shop Remi must've driven past a hundred times. "Huh. Well, there you go."

A buzzer sounded as they walked in.

"Jess!" A scruffy-looking older gentleman lit up behind the counter, scrambling to his feet.

"Larry? What are you doing back there?" Jess leaned on the counter.

"Got bored and thought I'd help out Roy and Andrea. Plus, I get cheap boat parts." He winked. "So, eh, caught up with Sam and Taylor?"

"Sure have. So happy they're back in Adelaide for another month."

"Me too. They've already been in to catch up with the new owners. Though I guess Roy and Andrea are basically part of the furniture now. I really should see if Taylor is free to look at my boat again—"

Jess tugged on Remi's shirt, glancing toward the back of the shop. "Anyway, Larry, we've only got a few minutes today. I need to show my friend here some parts."

He waved them off, already muttering to himself about maintenance and masts.

"Don't mind him," Jess said once they'd made it to the back. "He's a good friend of a friend, but he loves a chat."

"Fair enough," Remi replied, taking in the shop. "Wow, you weren't wrong." The place had all sorts she could stock up on for the business. She'd have to bring Sophie back.

As they passed by the paints, Jess slapped her head. "I keep forgetting to ask you for your painter friend's details! My friend Marie wants to get her place done, and I told her about supporting women in trades, so she's holding off, waiting on me."

Remi was momentarily stunned by the thoughtfulness. "Wow, yes. Of course. I'll get you JJ's details. She should definitely be able to help them out. Thanks for remembering her. That's so nice."

They wandered through the rest of the shop, stopping when Remi eyed the bait fridge.

"Ooo." She lifted the lid, spying exactly what she was after. "I'll take one of these, thanks." Remi dumped the bait on the counter.

"I'll get you an extra bag for those," Larry said as she paid. "Hopefully that'll keep the smell down. And here's your receipt."

Remi grabbed the bait and docket as Larry waved them out.

"Great to see you, Jess. Say hi to the girls for me."

"I will."

Remi handed the bag to Jess on the way back to the ute. Jess looked inside, scrunching up her face. "Gross. Fish heads?"

"Whiting heads."

"To fish with?" Jess asked, confused.

Remi laughed. "To catch crabs with."

Jess raised an eyebrow.

"Not *those* crabs," she clarified, pulling the ute's tail down and sliding out the fridge. "Want to come tonight? I usually head down straight after work and eat fish and chips on the rocks for dinner."

"Sure. But I'm not touching these." Jess held out the bag to Remi with a look of pure disgust. Remi chuckled, throwing it in the fridge and closing everything up before hopping in the ute.

"I'll just let Adam know I won't be home for dinner," Jess said, climbing into the passenger side and typing on her phone. "Pretty sure there's an emergency pizza in the freezer he can heat up," she mumbled to herself.

"Hey, if it's too late notice, all good, we can go another time," Remi offered. Though she'd never say it aloud, she wondered why Jess had to worry about making sure a grown man could feed himself.

"No. I think it'd be good. I'd rather be out than home."

Remi frowned. Maybe tonight she could get Jess to open up and find out if she was okay.

NINE

Jess

Jess recoiled as Remi drove the wire through the eyes of the fish heads.

"Yuck. I can't look." The horizon was suddenly very interesting.

When Remi had asked her to come along, she'd meant it when she said she was happy to be here... but from a distance... away from the fish heads. Or the crabs. Especially the ones with big claws.

No thanks.

Being out of the house, on the other hand, was great. She'd never been to this area on the rocks before, even though she'd lived near Karkalla Beach her whole life. Sitting at the top of the rocks, she could see all the way to the tip of Karkalla. A few others were fishing or crabbing, but much further out. Remi had told her this was the best spot though, right near the edge of a dark seaweed patch where the crabs loved to feed.

The tide was up, water lapping lazily against the rocks where Remi was working. Like everything she did, even baiting the nets looked professional. Jess found it strangely captivating, watching her do the most mundane things with such quiet competence.

Since quitting Limone, she'd realised how little she did outside of work. This spontaneous adventure felt so fun and fresh. Literally. The sea air was amazing. She inhaled deep breaths, letting it fill her lungs and calm her with every exhale. She needed more slow moments like this.

"Done!" Remi took off her bait gloves. "You wanna do the honours?" She held up the crab net.

Jess shook her head, keeping her distance at the top of the rocks. "Oh, I'm good watching from up here."

"Suit yourself." Remi spun the net into the air, the rope chasing it like a dog with a toy. With a splash, it sank to the bottom. She tied the end of the rope around a rock. "Now, we wait."

"And eat?" Jess asked hopefully. Her stomach growled, loud enough for them to both hear.

"And eat." Remi laughed, washing her hands in the ocean and scrambling to the top of the rocks. From her bait box, she pulled out a bottle of sanitiser, squirted some on and gave her hands a sniff. "Much better."

Remi picked up a big paper bag and brought it over. Jess scooted over to make room on the rock "seat" she'd acquired, their sun-warmed thighs brushing as Remi settled beside her. She laid the big paper bag between them, the scent of hot salt hitting Jess's nose. Was that even a smell? It was now. Different from the salt air off the ocean. This was the smell of summer nights, beach days and those good nostalgic pangs that hit you right in the gut. She licked her lips as Remi carefully ripped open the bag and glanced around.

"I don't wanna drop one chip, or we'll have a whole host of seagulls descending on us."

One screamed overhead, like it was passing on the message to the rest of the scavengers in the area. There'd be no sharing tonight. Not even to the one-legged ones Jess usually felt sorry for. As soon as Remi ripped it open, Jess dove in, shoving two chips in her mouth.

"Wait!" Remi tried to stop her.

The searing heat hit. Jess's eyes burned as squished, hot potato stuck itself to the roof of her mouth.

"...it's hot," Remi finished weakly, wincing as Jess flapped at her mouth.

Remi pulled out a bottle of Coke from her little cooler bag. "Here." She uncapped it and handed it over.

"Sorry. Too keen," said Jess, after putting out the food fire in her mouth. She took another drink. "Ah. Those bubbles are good. I regret nothing." She dove in for another handful of hot chips, spying some other morsels under-neath. "Oh, what else have you got under there?"

"I wasn't sure what you liked, so I got my favourites— butterfish, dim sims and pineapple fritters for 'dessert'." Remi bit her lip. Her hair looked extra wild today, let loose from its ponytail as the wind whipped her black locks. "Hope that's okay?"

"What about the salads?"

Remi recoiled, nose scrunching in revulsion. "Seriously?"

"No. Not at all. Potato is a vegetable, right?" Jess grinned.

"Phew. I thought we might not be able to be friends if you were a salad girl."

"I like to eat healthy, but I'm also not averse to a good takeaway night."

"I'm the same," Remi agreed.

They ate in relative silence, watching boats head into the marina. A cargo ship's horn sounded from the local harbour. When only a few crumbs remained, Remi balled up the paper and shoved it into her bag.

"Necessary," said Jess, leaning back against the rock behind her and patting her—now very full—stomach. A burp escaped before she could stop it. Her hand flew to her mouth, eyes wide. "I'm *so* sorry. Excuse me. I blame the bubbles."

Remi let out a laugh, then an even bigger burp.

"No need to be sorry. You're officially a tradie now." She winked.

Jess felt herself smiling, the embarrassment fading under Remi's broad grin. It felt kind of... nice. Freeing. Adam hated it when she burped, always saying it was so unladylike. Secretly, when he wasn't home, she'd see just how loud she could make them. She smirked at the thought.

Remi suddenly jumped up, making Jess jolt.

"Time to check the net! Sure you don't wanna try pulling it in? You don't have to touch any fish heads or crabs. Promise."

Jess hesitated, assessing whether she wanted to move from her comfortable rock. Remi's face was open, ushering her down by the water.

"I'll give it one go." Jess tentatively climbed down. She

was thankful for her new boots, as scrambling over rocks wasn't part of the plan today, but these were super grippy! Remi held out her hand to help Jess down the last couple. Her grip was warm and sure. Jess almost forgot to let go, but Remi cut the contact first to reach for the rope.

"Okay. Trick is to reel this in as fast as you can. That way, any crabs get stuck in the net against the water pressure."

Jess blew out a breath. With a quick nod, she pulled on the rope like a complete lunatic. Bright green rope flung left and right while Remi cheered her on.

"Go, go, go! You've got one!"

Jess spotted the glint of blue. Then another. And another! Exhilaration hit her once she saw them, and she doubled down on her speed, desperate to say she'd caught her first crabs.

Water ran down her arms, dripping everywhere as more rope was pulled out. It was so close, the net almost breaking the surface.

Then it was in the air.

The pressure released and by the time Jess realised what was happening, it was too late.

The net smacked her square in the chest—fish heads and all—before flopping at her feet. The crabs scuttled out and plopped back into the water.

Water dripped from her eyelashes as she stood there stunned. She turned to Remi, gauging her reaction. Worry. Shock. Then her mouth clamped shut. She bent over, trying to hold it in. She failed and doubled over with laughter spraying out uncontrolled.

Jess felt it bubbling up. It rolled out as she threw her

head back into a total guffaw. She looked at the net still at her feet and started up all over again.

"Damn, Newbie," Remi said, wiping at her eyes and trying to calm down. "You didn't tell me I needed to bring your safety gear out here too."

"Oh, shut up." Jess smiled, pulling up her new work shirt and giving it a whiff. "Yuck. Pretty sure I got fish on me." She turned to Remi, whose eyes flicked quickly away. Was she checking her out? Nah, surely not. Jess let the shirt drop.

"Think I'll spectate for the rest of the night. I'd rather eat crabs than wear them."

"Probably a good idea." Remi threw the net back in. "I'm not too fussed about them escaping, they'll just walk back into the net now they know food is there. They're a bit dumb like that. Makes it frustrating when you catch a female that just won't quit."

"You can't catch females?"

"Not if they've got eggs. If they don't, technically... yes, but I usually let them go." Remi pulled a piece of blue plastic out of her pocket and showed Jess as she sat back down. "We'll measure them with this. Make sure they're big enough. But for now, we wait."

Jess watched the sparkle on the water as they sat in silence.

She turned to Remi. "So, where do you see yourself in five years?"

"You're so random." Remi's face pulled into a half-smile as Jess met her green eyes—they reminded her of the sea today. "You really like asking the big questions, huh?"

Jess shrugged. She'd always been inquisitive. She loved

knowing what made people tick, what problems she could help solve. Asking big questions up front told her what kind of person Remi was. Did their values align? Was this a company Jess could see herself staying in? Or was it a stepping stone to something else? Could she see Remi becoming a good friend, not just her boss? Not that she was trying to replace her current friends, but now that Taylor had Sam—plus the added distance between them—their friendship had changed. Marie and Hayley had each other already...

Jess could see, or hoped, Remi might fill this friendship gap she'd been missing. She hadn't done this many exciting new activities in... well, not since hanging out with Taylor. And she completely sucked at them! But she didn't care. And neither did Remi.

It was nice to be allowed to fail happily, without judgement. To learn from failure, not fear it. Not feel ashamed like Adam had made her feel. With Remi, she *wanted* to fail more. She wanted to study this new craft and new world of cabinet-making. Jess wanted to prove to herself she could do it.

Remi finally answered.

"In five years, I'd love to grow the team to five or six women. Each with an apprentice to train. We'd take on bigger projects, maybe work beyond residential into new home builds and what not. Hopefully starting this year." Remi smirked, her chin resting on her knee as she looked out to the ocean. "Eventually, I'd like to find more of a work-life balance. More office time or running workshops for tradeswomen... looking into the education side of things to help women enter the workforce as an apprentice. Yeah. That would be my five-year plan."

Jess was caught up in Remi's dream. She could feel the passion Remi had for the industry, for other women like her. If this job turned her life around, what doors could it open for others? It felt good to be a part of something that mattered.

"Any plans for a family?" she enquired next.

Remi's eyes slid to her. "All the questions."

"Yep," replied Jess, sweet as pie, her legs swinging off the side of the rock.

Remi shifted next to her, dropping one knee and sitting on her hands. She blew out a breath, staring at her scuffed boots next to Jess's shiny pink ones. "I don't think kids are for me. That time has passed. Being an aunty to Huds is enough. Major respect to my sister and Tomás. They've done a great job parenting him. What about you?"

"Me?"

"Yeah. If you're gonna ask it, I'm gonna throw it right back."

"Fair." Jess took another sip of her soft drink. "If you'd asked me six months ago, I would've given you a very different answer." She let her face fall into her hands, a soft growl escaping her lips. "Half of me feels like I'm completely fucking up my life, and the other half feels like I'm on the right path. How is that possible?"

"Because change is hard. And scary. I guess the key word is *change* though. When change is your choice, it doesn't make it any easier—*but*—it does make it yours. Your choice, your actions, your decision. There is power in that."

Jess nodded slowly. "What happens when it's not just about me, though? I have Adam. A year ago, I was dreaming about us moving in together. We've been saving for a house... planning to settle down..." She trailed off.

Remi listened intently. Taking in every word like it mattered, like Jess mattered. Her green eyes caught the sun, lighting up as she waited.

"Okay, it's like this." Jess held her hands out in front of her, concentrating. "I feel like I'm over here on this train. My life as it is, happily chugging along. And this new train has come up alongside me." She shifted her hands to demonstrate. "I can step onto this new one. But I feel like if I do, this new train is going to keep going, with the old train eventually disappearing out of sight."

"So, what I'm hearing is, you're wondering if Adam is going to take that step with you into your new self, your new life, or if he'll stay behind?"

"Exactly." Jess let her hands drop into her lap, exhaling slowly.

"Keep talking to him, like I suggested earlier. Finding out if you're on the same track, on the same path—whatever metaphor you want to use—is going to give you the answers you need."

"Thanks. For listening, and for the advice." Jess meant it. Being able to talk to someone on this level made such a difference. She felt better already, lighter, even without knowing what the future held.

"So, in answer to your original question..." Jess laughed, bringing them back to a lighter topic. "In five years, I want to be a kickass cabinet-maker, at a kickass women-owned business with a kickass new-friend-slash-boss. That's all I know for certain right now."

Jess glanced at Remi, hopeful.

"That sounds pretty good to me." Remi smiled warmly, matching Jess's energy, then her eyes grew comically wide. "Shit! Forgot about the net!"

The moment broken, Remi jumped up and hopped down the rocks to the water's edge. "Now watch how it's done!"

Thirteen crabs later, their bucket was full, and so was Jess's soul.

As corny as it sounded, nights like this relaxed her in a way nothing else could. The sun hung low on the horizon, the golden hue simmering on the water. She and Remi had found a comfortable rhythm between conversation and companionable silence. It reminded her of the mornings she'd sit outside with her tea, where usually she wanted solitude, but she didn't mind the presence of the person sitting alongside her right now. All in all, she couldn't have asked for a better first official day of her apprenticeship.

She sat up. "Hey, are you doing anything on the twenty-eighth of January?"

"Oddly specific." Remi pulled her phone out. "Uhh... Saturday... I'm free. What am I doing?" Remi's hand hovered over the screen.

"Would you and Sophie like to come to a murder mystery party? It's for my thirtieth. It'll be pretty chilled, but we'll be taking the game *very* seriously."

"Of *course* you'd have a murder mystery party."

"Huh?" How could Remi know that about her?

"You said you liked reading them, right?"

"Oh, yeah. I can't believe you remembered that."

Remi shrugged. "Well, I'm in." Her fingers flew over the screen. "Done. It's in the calendar, and I'll check with Sophie. Is there a theme?" she asked as she flicked off a text.

"Yep, I'll send you the details, but it's a 1920s speakeasy vibe. Think gangsters and flappers. Costumes are non-negotiable."

Jess had ironed out the details and got all of her friends on board. Now, they just needed the numbers confirmed to fill all the roles in the game. She loved the setup, where even as the host, she'd have no idea who the murderer was until the night. She couldn't wait to show off the outfit she'd put together!

"All right, I better get shopping then." Remi grinned.

Jess hadn't meant to stay out as long as she had, but once again, she'd lost track of time with Remi. The sky had put on a spectacular sunset she couldn't walk away from until it had completely slipped below the horizon. Her cheeks still ached from the constant smiling and laughing, a nice balm against the rest of her body that ached, sore and heavy from the strenuous first full day of physical work. A hot shower was calling to relieve her muscles and wash away the lingering fishy smell of her net-pulling mishap. She'd declined taking home any of their catch, having no idea how to cook crabs and little inclination to eat them. Adam was no chef either, so they'd be wasted in their household.

She slipped her boots off in the doorway, reminded of Taylor's old habit she'd now adopted. They were always far too dirty to trudge through the house. She padded into the lounge to find Adam in his usual spot on the couch, controller in hand, pizza crusts on the plate in front of him. The conversation she'd had about cleaning up after himself had well and truly worn off, lasting barely a week.

"Big day for you," he commented, not looking up from the game.

"Yeah, I'm stuffed. Going to grab a shower. I stink. From work and from crabbing." She passed through the lounge and into the kitchen, spying the pizza box on the bench, and yesterday's dishes still in the sink. She ignored it all, beelining for the bathroom.

As the steaming water hit her skin, she sighed in relief. Nights like tonight were the norm now. He played his games, she read her books, two ships passing in the night under the same roof. He felt more like a roommate than anything else. The strain and extra demand of her holiday work had only exacerbated things between them. And now... sure, she'd be getting home earlier, but she already worried about how little energy she'd have left after being on site all day.

She could see herself doing less around the house, hoping Adam might pick up the slack after their discussion, especially now that he could see how hard she was working. But, so far, nothing. He only noticed what wasn't being done *for him*: dinners cooked less often, washing left on the line an extra day, dishes waiting to be put in the dishwasher. Everything just waited for her to pick up the pieces.

It begged the question: Did she want to pick them up anymore?

TEN

Remi

Somehow, late January had already arrived. Work wasn't slowing down, but thankfully Jess was keeping up with everything Remi threw at her. Nothing was fast or perfect, but Remi could see the confidence growing in Jess each day. She tried to keep a good balance between observing and learning while on the job. On top of that, Jess also had off-site TAFE training to complete her certificate. As much as Remi hated being down a person on those days, she managed. She had to.

"Remi speaking." Phone wedged between her head and shoulder, she kept adjusting the door's alignment on their current laundry cupboard install.

"Remi. It's Javier from Flinders."

She nearly dropped her phone, fumbling before gripping it tight as she stood. She always felt she could hear better if she was standing.

"Javier, hi! Great to hear from you... I hope." Remi was too nervous for pleasantries. If they'd won the project, she wanted to know. Sophie jumped at the name drop, coming over to listen in.

Javier chuckled. "I think we've kept you in limbo long enough. You've got the job, girls. We'd love to have you on the Flinders team."

Sophie shook Remi by the shoulders, grinning like a mad woman. Jess had downed tools too, now watching them in earnest excitement.

"Wow. Thank you, Javier. We won't let you down."

"I'd hope not. Now, we'll need you to come in and make it official with paperwork, then we'll get Sophie started on the designs in the next few weeks."

Fuck. That was earlier than expected. Remi tried to mentally calculate their current jobs in the pipeline. She'd make it work. Somehow.

"No problem. Let us know when and where and we'll be there," she replied.

"Done. Thanks, Remi. Looking forward to working together."

Remi hung up and flung her hands in the air. "We got the project!"

The three of them broke into a celebration dance of questionable taste in the half-renovated laundry.

"Today is a good day." Remi couldn't wipe the smile off her face as she took a moment to catch her breath. Her cheeks hurt and she didn't care. She'd done it. They'd done it. The next stage of their business was happening, and she couldn't be prouder.

"Celebratory dinner at mine tonight, ladies. Soph, bring Tom and Huds. I'm thinking pizza."

"To The Lady Builders!" Remi raised her beer to the table. Everyone clinked their glasses, orange juice sloshing onto the table.

"Careful Hudson, too keen there buddy," said Remi.

"Sorry Aunt Rem." He jumped up from the table, grabbing a washcloth from the kitchen sink and wiped down the table himself. He was such a good kid.

The doorbell rang just as Remi took her first celebratory sip.

"Pizza!" Hudson yelled, rushing to the door.

"Money is on the table!" she called.

He raced back to the dining table and back up to the door.

"Does he need a hand?" Jess asked, not quite believing the six-year-old could manage.

"Oh yeah, he *loves* being the 'adult'," replied Tomás.

A couple minutes later, the front door slammed. Hudson's little legs raced down the hall. "Here's the drink and garlic bread." Hudson hefted them up onto the table like they were the heaviest things on earth, then ran back to the door.

"Slow down!" Sophie yelled after him.

Hudson soon reappeared with three big boxes almost swallowing his head.

"Watch where you're going, hunny." Sophie winced as he almost hit Jess in the shoulder with the boxes.

"'Scuse me," Hudson said, sliding the boxes onto the table and handing Remi her change.

She gave him back two dollars. "That's for your good work—make sure it goes into your savings."

His eyes lit up like stars. "Wow, thank you! Mum! Dad! Aunt Rem gave me money!"

"Yeah, Kiddo, now come sit and let's eat," replied Tomás, pulling out Hudson's chair.

They opened up the boxes, spreading them out across the table. Remi leaned over to grab the end piece of the garlic bread, hitting Jess who dived in at the same time.

"Sorry. After you." Remi laughed, pulling her hand back.

"You like GB crust too?"

"My favourite piece."

"You're both weirdos," Tomás interjected, picking up a slice of pepperoni pizza and taking a huge bite.

Jess grinned and broke off the other end, handing it to Remi. "There you go, we both get the best parts." She winked.

Remi couldn't help being drawn into Jess's vortex. She took in the way Jess gave a little snort if she laughed too much, the way she'd light up talking about the new tools she'd tried (their table saw) or just then—when she looked at Remi like that. There was a sparkle in those cobalt eyes—ones that spoke of mischief and joy, as if you were the only person that mattered in the moment she shared with you.

"Sorry to interrupt your little garlic bread bonding session ladies. I just remembered Luka called earlier today and said his tiles arrived, but they were gloss and not matte. Do you remember what you asked for?"

"I swear I said matte." Remi opened her emails on her phone and checked. Her chest prickled with heat. She'd written gloss. She could've sworn she'd said matte. "Uh..." She cleared her throat. "Looks like I stuffed that one up. I'll get it sorted tomorrow."

"You're lucky it's the 600 by 300 standard, so they should have enough to swap at the warehouse." Sophie's face was full of concern. "You sure you're going okay with everything?"

"It's just an oversight, Soph. I've just been sorting out the jobs pipeline and clearly got it mixed up with another. Sorry. I promise I'll fix it tomorrow. Let's keep it about the celebration."

Remi forced a smile as Tomás looked between them. She hated work talk at family dinners. There had to be a boundary, or it wouldn't stop. Plus, she didn't want to bring down the mood over such small issues.

The rest of dinner was exactly what she needed—a fun meal shared with family and her newest recruit. Jess slotted in like she'd been there a hundred times. She and Hudson ended up on the living room floor, surrounded by Lego, building forts and waging epic battles that Hudson, of course, won. Later, Remi let him carefully feed Ninja a cricket or two as Jess watched on in abject horror. Hudson had no such qualms.

The best part of the night was Jess's hug. She held on extra tight, whispering her congratulations and goodnight. Remi hadn't wanted to let go.

❀

Three nights later, it was Jess's birthday. Sophie would be

here to pick her up any minute and Remi was still racing around like a maniac.

"Shit—Ninja!" She skidded into the lounge in her socks and ran to his tank. "Hey, lil' dude. Here's your food for the night."

He clambered at the corner of the glass, trying desperately to get out, ignoring his food completely.

"I know. I'm a terrible turtle mum. I haven't taken you out in ages. Things have been so busy. But! Tomorrow is Sunday, and I'm home. I promise I'll get you out for a run around." He stretched his neck out as she reached in to give him a quick head pat.

A car pulled up in the driveway with a quick *beep beep*. Sophie was here already. Time to go!

Standing on the lawn of a very nice Hamptons style two-storey home, Remi handed her plastic gun to Sophie. With her hands freed up, she adjusted her fedora, re-tucked her shirt into her black slacks, and adjusted the straps on her suspenders. Dirt still lingered under her fingernails, seemingly caked in from the frantic work pace this week. She'd scrubbed as best she could. Now she wished she'd got Sophie to paint her nails. Actually, no, painted nails would be worse. She'd have them picked off in a day or two.

"Better?" Sophie asked, standing in a gold flapper dress complete with a faux fur shawl and her signature bright red lipstick. The plastic gun looked very out of place against her outfit.

"Hang on." Remi looked down and undid two more buttons. She wanted to look good, but also add a touch of femininity to the gangster costume she'd put together. Plus, she had to look at least a little sexy, otherwise why else go to the effort of dressing up? The edges of her black lace-trimmed bra peeked out just a touch. Perfect. She'd kept her long hair down, styled into loose dark curls that fell over her shoulders. It had been some time since she'd dressed up this much, but Jess had asked for commitment to the theme, so here she was.

"We look good!" Sophie declared, looking them both up and down before handing the gun back to Remi. "The Pearce sisters know how to turn it out."

"Let's hope this isn't one of those parties where we go all out and everyone else is just wearing a headpiece or scarf." She took in a deep breath, trying to calm her sudden nerves. Why was she nervous? It was just a party. Perhaps, deep down, she wished for Jess's approval, to see her light up knowing Remi had dressed up to impress her.

"Don't be silly. Either way, we look amazing," replied Sophie.

Remi threw her an appreciative smile, blew out a breath and pressed the doorbell. The party was being held at one of Jess's friends' houses, a sleek modern place in various shades of white, grey, and cream, with a landscaped yard and palm trees swaying in the breeze. She heard voices inside, but no footsteps. Two balloons, gold and black, hovered nearby, tied off on a verandah post.

Remi knocked on the door this time, loud enough to hopefully be heard over the chatter.

No movement.

She lifted her hand about to knock again when the door swung open.

She froze.

A black-gloved hand held the door open.

Fu—cking—*hell* and a nutcracker.

She swallowed. Her mind turned to solid white noise. Static. Blank. Nada.

Jess stood in a slim black beaded dress that barely brushed her thighs.

And it only got worse from there.

Black sheer stockings hugged her long legs down to black stilettos. The look was completed with a red feathered headband, her long golden waves styled into a fancy updo, a few loose curls left to frame her face.

Remi resisted the urge to bite her lip as her eyes caught on the suspenders holding up said stockings on Jess's thighs.

She is my apprentice. She is my apprentice. She has an effing boyfriend. What. Are. You. Doing?!

"Wow," she breathed, then quickly cleared her throat, ready to apologise. But Jess's eyes were focused right at her chest. *This was a dangerous dance.*

"Happy birthday, Jess!" Sophie squealed behind her, breaking them out of their moment. She nudged Remi.

"Yeah!" Remi joined in with way too much enthusiasm. "Happy birthday." She handed over an envelope. Jess eyed it with a raised brow. Remi couldn't look away from her quirked red lips. They looked fuller. Shinier. She forced herself to say something. "You can open it later. It's just something little. I hate having to open presents in front of people."

They'd got her a voucher for the local tool shop so Jess could buy her own toolbag. It was an item that had made Remi feel cemented in her career, making her a real tradeswoman once she started hauling it around. She hoped Jess would get as much satisfaction from it as she did.

"Me too. Thank you both." Jess launched into a hug, squeezing Sophie first, then Remi. Her bare arms wrapped around Remi in a warm embrace, her sweet scent lingering, this time with an edge of spice—vanilla? Cinnamon? They were ushered inside before Remi had a chance to decide.

"Come in, come in. Everyone is out in the family room," Jess said, guiding them down the hallway.

"Wow." All other words had apparently left her vocabulary. It really did feel like walking into a 1920s speakeasy. Rich dark fabrics draped over surfaces, golden balloons floated on the ceiling and tall vases were scattered about, overflowing with white fluffy feathers. Jess and her friends had gone all out. Gangsters and flappers flitted about, dressed so impeccably, it looked like a film set. One corner held platters of food, another featured special menu boards along the back with different cocktails and mocktails available for the evening, served in coupe glasses, of course.

A tall, blonde woman in a beautiful emerald and black flapper dress made a beeline for them.

"Hi, you must be Remi and Sophie—sorry, *Detective Joey Maloney* and *Estelle Montgomery*." She winked, reading the name tags they'd stuck on. "Welcome to The Blue Velvet Lounge. The bar's to the right, and please help yourself to any refreshments along the wall. I'm Hayley— ahem, *Mae Belle*, and I'm one of the waitresses this evening."

"Thanks for having us," said Remi.

"Your home is so lovely!" gushed Sophie, still taking in the scene before them.

"Thank you. Make sure to grab a drink now, we'll start the game as soon as everyone's arrived," Hayley finished with a smile, floating off amongst the crowd.

"Right, I'm off to check out the bar," said Remi.

"And I'm checking out that *kitchen*. Look at those benchtops!"

The last thing Remi wanted to think about right now was work. After all, she was "*Detective Joey Maloney*", and she had a murder to solve!

ELEVEN

Jess

Jess couldn't think straight. She'd already had a couple of champagnes. *Whoopsie.* But trying to set this game up had taken much longer than anticipated, even with everyone helping with the setup, food and decorations.

Then, she'd opened the door.

Since when was her boss that fucking hot? She had no right rocking up to Jess's birthday looking that good. That patchwork sleeve. The white shirt folded at the elbows. The hint of bra. Nobody had ever rocked a gangster outfit so well. Jess wasn't sure if she was jealous of her, or wanted to be her... or...

She winced, her stomach dropping with guilt. She shouldn't even be *having* these thoughts. The alcohol was clearly going straight to her head. What was wrong with her? She needed food. Stat. She legged it to the table Hayley and Marie had laid out. It was a smorgasbord of easy finger food so everyone could eat, drink and figure out whodunit.

She picked up some bread, plunging it into the spinach cob loaf and stuffing it in her face. Necessary. Next came a twiggy stick. Two cheese cubes. A mini sausage roll. A party pie—dipped into tomato sauce, of course. She was careful not to burn the crap out of her chin as she bit into it.

"Hey."

Jess whirled around at the sound, meat pie and sauce squishing into something soft right in front of her face.

Cleavage.

Remi's cleavage.

Now covered in smushed pie and red sauce.

Oh shit.

"*Fuck*, that's hot," Remi yelped, looking downward.

Jess's eyes blew wide. "Oh my god, I'm so sorry." She whirled back around, eyes frantic for a cloth, a tissue—

"Napkins! Here." She grabbed one and started dabbing at the mess, then realised what she was touching. *Who* she was touching. She scrunched her eyes shut. "Sorry! I'll let you—uh..." She spun again, suddenly dizzy from all the turning. Her face burned. Jeez, did Marie need to turn on the air con?

"It's fine, Jess. See? Clean," Remi said a minute later.

It was—surprisingly—fine.

Having to look at her chest again? Not fine. Though, thankfully, the pie had mostly landed on her skin, with just a touch of sauce left on the very edge of her shirt. It reminded Jess of the white tablecloths at Limone splattered in pasta sauce. She shuddered at the memory, then realised she was staring again. Jess blamed the height difference, never more obvious than in this moment. *Eyes up, Jess!* Honestly, what had gotten into her tonight?

"Actually, if you dab your napkin in some soda water, or even Champagne, that should get the last of the stain out. Old hospo trick," Jess said, as Remi gave her thanks and disappeared into the crowd in search of some bubbly.

Hands landed on Jess's shoulders. "Happy birthday, bestie!"

"Taylor!" Jess whirled again, the room spinning. She almost threw both of them into the food as she went in too strong for the hug.

Jess righted them, then stepped back to take in Taylor's costume and settle her dizzy head. "Loving this!" she said, gesturing up and down. Taylor stood looking dashing in a white zoot suit and black shirt. Sam came up alongside her, Belle on a leash.

"Hey Jess, long time no see!" Sam said, eyes sparkling.

Jess went to greet her back, then saw Belle and absolutely lost it. They'd dressed the damn dog in a black and gold flapper dress, complete with sequined headband. Belle looked like she'd never been happier, tongue lolling to the side in what looked like a huge smile. She jumped at Jess, eager to give her kisses.

"Hey Sam, you'll get a hug after princess here gets her cuddles."

Sam laughed. "Oh, I know all too well about the petting order when it comes to Belle."

Jess gave Sam a huge hug when she stood up, squeezing her tight. "Great to see you again. I hope Taylor has been on her best behaviour?"

"Of course." You could fry eggs with the heated look Sam gave her fiancée; Jess almost felt the need to look away.

"Though maybe I don't mind her bad behaviour either," Sam said, smacking Taylor's butt.

Jess couldn't help but smile at them, though the

familiar prickle of envy still reared its head. *Why didn't she have that? Why didn't she feel what those two seemed to share? Was it just a rough patch with Adam? Or was it a different type of love altogether? Was it love at all?* She didn't even know where he was right now. And she wasn't sure if she'd ever looked at Adam that way. Laughing at his jokes? Sure. Cute cuddle game nights on the couch together? Yes. But firing hot, smoking lasers into each other's eyes? Couldn't say she'd experienced that. *Way to have an existential crisis on your birthday, Jess.* Maybe it was a mid-life crisis? Surely thirty was too young for that?

"Hey, you good?" Taylor checked in.

"Yep. Later."

She wasn't usually a crier, but all bets were off when it came to Taylor and their D&Ms. She didn't want to ruin her glitzy makeup. Plus, it felt nice to be clean and dolled up after being so dirty at work.

"Did Matt make it?" she asked Sam, changing the subject.

"Dad's with your parents, I believe." Sam nodded towards the other side of the room.

Jess looked over her shoulder and spotted all three of them, along with Adam.

"Perfect. I haven't said hi to any of them yet. I'll be back." If there was anyone else who'd felt the loss of Sam and Taylor taking off, it was Sam's Dad. Jess had a real soft spot for Matt. They'd struck up a surprising friendship when her friends had first left.

Adam and her mum seemed to be chatting quite animatedly, her dad and Matt off to the side.

"—right, I agree. She didn't want to talk about it at

Christmas and hasn't spoken to me since," her mum was saying.

"If she spoke to Ricciardo, he'd take her back in an instant," replied Adam.

Jess blinked. "Why would I want to go back to Limone?"

They hadn't seen her approach. They looked at each other in silent conversation, then her mum finally spoke. "I was just telling Adam, it's always good to have a backup plan. In case things don't last."

"Or, if you're not cut out for the job. Which is completely fine if you change your mind," Adam rushed to add, his eyes soft, like he thought he was being supportive. She swallowed down the sudden sour taste in her mouth.

"Why are you both talking about me like I can't do this?"

"You said yourself you've been so tired since you started. You've had hardly any energy at home. I wasn't sure you could keep it up," replied Adam.

"You could talk to me about it first." And preferably not at her birthday, and in front of her mother.

She'd lost track of the amount of conversations her mum had brought up over the years about her unused university degree. And now, all of a sudden, hospitality was the better option? When would people stop telling her what to do? Or what was best for her? She wanted to throw herself on the floor in a complete toddler tantrum, drumming her fists until someone stopped to listen to what *she* had to say.

"And I am happy. I love learning the job; yes, it's hard; yes, I'm tired. But I choose to do this. Why can't you two accept that already?" She didn't have the time nor the inclination to work this out tonight. They got along so well, they could sort themselves out. "Whatever," she huffed, spinning on her heel and heading to the drinks table.

Remi caught her eye as she made herself an old fashioned, dropping in two cherries for herself.

"Classy choice," Jess said, sliding alongside her, trying to push her family to the back of her mind.

"Thank you." Remi tipped her drink towards Jess, then took a sip and let out a satisfied sigh. "I make a good drink." She turned to Jess and leaned in, concerned eyes searching her face. "Things looked a little intense over there. Everything okay with your friends?"

"That would be Adam, my boyfriend, and my mum, Suzanne."

"Right." Remi dragged the word out, squinting. "I see the resemblance now. It's harder to spot in costume."

"That, and Mum loves to dye her hair a copper blonde for some reason. Please don't ever let me do that."

Remi snorted. "Wouldn't dream of it. Everything's okay though?" she asked again.

"Let's just say it wasn't the conversation I wanted to walk in on, nor do I want to see either of them for the rest of the night." Jess forced a smile, speaking through her teeth. "But as they say, the show must go on!"

It was right on seven according to the oversized clock on the wall. She didn't give Remi a chance to respond, catching Marie's eye instead, who gave her the nod to begin.

Jess stepped up onto the makeshift stage, tapping the microphone—thankfully it gave a dull thud and no ear-piercing feedback. All attention turned to her.

"Thank you, everyone, for being here tonight. A thirtieth is a big milestone, one where I didn't think I'd be starting a new career, but here I am. You're looking at a new apprentice cabinet maker, and I'm so looking forward to seeing where this takes me and becoming a tradie extraordinaire by the end of it." She grinned at the crowd, her focus snagging on Remi, in the corner, a smile smothered behind her glass as she took a sip.

"Now, we're here for *two* very important things. The most important being, my birthday." She gave a curtsy, prompting cheers and laughter around the room. "And second, we're all here to solve a murder," she finished in her most sinister voice. "So, putting our real names aside, it's time to don our aliases' for the evening. The game is about to begin!"

The room fell silent. Jess dropped her head, squared her shoulders, and a brilliant smile bloomed across her face—

"Good evening, ladies and gentlemen. I am your host, *Ruby Hydewell*, singer and entertainer extraordinaire! Welcome," she paused, "to The Blue Velvet Lounge!" She swept her arm across the crowd, landing on the real blue velvet couch, placed in the middle of the room. It was no secret the blue sofa was Jess's seat of choice on games nights, and when the girls suggested it as the speakeasy's namesake, she couldn't have picked better herself.

"Tonight is a night like no other. Let us razzle, dazzle, *dazzle* you with the sultry jazz tunes of the beautiful, the one, the only—*Estelle Montgomery*!" She gestured to Sophie, now standing alongside Remi. "Or sit back, relax and let our waitress, *Mae Belle*, shake and pour you one of our finest gins." She pointed at Hayley, who waved to the crowd. "Remember, keep your eyes everywhere. You never know what might unfold at The Blue Velvet. Mingle, drink up and enjoy!" Jess threw her head back with a laugh that edged on manic, playing up her character's flair as *Ruby Hydewell*.

Right on cue, the lights cut out. The room plunged into darkness. Soft cries echoed around.

A scream. A thump. The clink of glass.

Gasps.

The lights returned. People blinked against the brightness. Jess's heart was racing, even knowing it was just a game. The energy in the room was electrified.

Another scream.

No—a wail.

"She's dead!" *Estelle Montgomery* (Sophie) sobbed over the body of *Mae Belle* (Hayley). *Estelle* held up a glass. "She's been poisoned!"

"That can't be!" cried *Isaac Hydewell* (Adam), crouching next to *Estelle*.

More gasps.

"And there's a note!" she continued, unscrunching it from the pocket of the waitress.

*Keep quiet if you know
what's good for you.*

With the murder in motion, everyone began to talk, playing up their characters with precision and absolute commitment. Hayley vanished to get changed into a gangster outfit to match Remi's, now playing her second role as

Officer Elizabeth Elroy, ready to kick butt alongside *Detective Joey Maloney* (Remi). Thankfully Jess's character, *Ruby*, required her to talk with *Vincent "Mad Eye" Maloney* (Sam's Dad, Matt), who was *Joey's* (Remi's) mobster brother, and *Dorothy "Shiny" Rimes* (Marie), who appeared squeaky clean on the surface but had darker motives to uncover.

As the night went on, clues emerged, alibis were questioned and accusations flew. When it came time to fill out the suspect cards, only one person had guessed everything correctly.

"*Detective Joey Maloney*, would you like to come up on stage and give your statement?"

"Gladly." Remi sauntered up and took hold of the microphone. "Tonight, we have witnessed a terrible crime. A poisoned drink is a coward's choice. A snake among us, closer than we think. They certainly thought they hid it well. Let's start with *Mae Belle*. She overheard the entire conversation between *Dorothy* and my brother, *Vincent*, trying to get rid of *Isaac Hydewell* (Adam). Famed rumrunner and *Ruby's* (Jess) husband."

Jess clutched her chest, mock horror written over her face.

"*Mae Belle* became an unfortunate liability and had to be eliminated. Though *Vincent* and *Dorothy* had nothing to do with this death. No. Remember, friends, this death was hidden well. Some might even say, *Hydewell*... That's right —it was... *Ruby*!"

Remi shot a finger at Jess, towering over her in all her white shirt-suspender glory. Jess tried her best to stay in character.

Look shocked, woman! Not distracted!

"How, you ask?" Remi turned back to the crowd. "Simple. Running the speakeasy wasn't enough. *Ruby* wanted it all. The fame. The fortune. She'd used *Vincent* to catalogue the rumrunner operations, ready to handover everything to *Ruby*. *Dorothy* was to become *Ruby's* new offsider to run the entire business. So, there's to be a few arrests tonight. Starting with you."

Remi produced a pair of fluffy pink handcuffs. Laughter rang out as Jess held up her hands. Without breaking character, Remi spun her around, pulled her hands behind her back like a real cop and cuffed her. Then, she marched her right off the stage, to cheers and whistles.

They stopped at the end of the hallway, Remi now grinning wide. "Well, that was fun."

"I didn't think anyone would guess me for a minute there."

Remi pulled a key from her slacks. "Shall I let the murderer go?"

"The cuffs are kind of comfy... maybe I should keep them on?" Jess teased with a smirk, then realised how that could come across. A look passed over Remi's face, one Jess couldn't quite decipher, before it went as fast as it came. Jess spun around, breaking the awkward moment and lifted her arms for Remi to release her.

As Jess faced the wall, warm hands encircled her wrists. Calloused and rough from years of labour, but her touch was the opposite. Soft. Precise.

The cuffs released quickly.

The moment was oddly mesmerising. Jess forgot where she was for a second.

"Thanks," she uttered, rubbing at her wrists as she turned around.

"Did I hurt you?" Remi looked at her arms with concern. She hesitated like she might move closer but stayed frozen.

"What? No." Jess dropped her arms, mortification growing. Had she really just been thinking about Remi's touch? "I'm just ticklish."

Jess needed to put some space between them. She was overwhelmed and confused by her reactions, and her thoughts, about her boss tonight. "We should get back, or they'll be wondering if I was murdered next! Plus, I owe *Detective Joey* a very official certificate for guessing the correct murderer." She threw Remi a smile over her shoulder as she joined her friends, it didn't reach her eyes as a looming feeling of unease filled her gut. With her thoughts swirling, it seemed she'd stumbled upon one more revelation this evening, one that had been growing clearer over time.

She knew what she had to do.

TWELVE

Remi

Remi dropped the angle grinder and looked at the edge of the tile. Perfect. They were back on the Donaldsons' project today, tiling the bathroom walls, and she was taking her time with every measurement and cut. The mitred edge around the main window was going to be schmick. Unfortunately, that meant constant trips in and out to cut tiles out the front, bringing her into close vicinity with Declan, who was still working on the kitchen extension. If she had to hear one more thing come out of that wanker's mouth, she was going to lose it.

They were running a day behind, something Remi was trying to put out of her mind, but she physically couldn't go any faster. Her mind felt overloaded by the mounting list of jobs, like she was trying to wade through mud. Still, the end was in sight. Flinders was happening, the contracts were signed, and Sophie was deep in design mode today with Javier and one of his project managers.

It had been two weeks since the party. Two weeks of noticing Jess retreat into herself a little more each day. She'd also spent a few days off-site at TAFE, and between that and their work commitments, Remi hadn't had a chance to check in. She could admit she was a little worried. What Jess had been saying recently stuck with her. The job was hard enough on its own; Remi couldn't imagine doing it without support at home too. Jess's skills were improving. While she wasn't yet working at the pace Remi needed for Flinders, if they could just push through this project backlog, Jess would be ready in two months' time.

"Hey, Remi." Declan jogged down the front steps, squatting next to Remi's cut tile. For once, there wasn't snark in his voice.

"Yeah?" she replied warily.

"Just wondering what the new apprentice's name is?"

"Go ask her yourself. Actually, on second thought— don't." She never knew what was going to come out of his mouth.

"Aww c'mon. I just wanna see if she's maybe free Friday night. Hook a brother up?"

Why? Why did she even entertain this waste of space?

"Declan." She composed herself, opening her eyes to see his gross puppy-dog-weasel face eagerly waiting. She leaned in closer. He did the same.

"Fuck. Off." She grabbed her tile and headed inside. "How many times do I have to tell you—stay the fuck away from my staff," she threw over her shoulder.

No matter how many times she tried to get him to stay away, he just... kept... talking. Their interaction played on repeat until her heart pounded and her teeth clenched. By the time she laid the tile, her frown was so intense, she could feel the pressure building at her temples.

Forget headache, Declan was a walking migraine.

Why had she even responded to him? It was like he knew exactly how to push her buttons and get under her skin like a parasite.

"You good?" Jess checked in as she pushed a wedge spacer on for the tile.

Remi tried to clear her head. "I could ask the same about you."

"Me?"

"Yeah." Declan didn't deserve any more airtime. "I don't mean right now, I mean lately. Overall. How's things at home?"

"Oh." Jess picked up another wedge, flipping it between her fingers. "Complicated."

"Do you want to talk about it?"

Jess blew out a breath, now picking at the edge of the red plastic spacer. "No..." She pushed the wedge in, then paused, staring at the wall. "Yeah," she confessed quietly. "I probably need to talk to someone."

"What if we aim to try and finish this wall early today, then we go for a walk along the beach before heading home? You can't say no when this house is literally beach-front." Remi went to squeeze Jess's shoulder but she held back. *It wouldn't be appropriate.* Instead, she gave a reassuring smile. While they were behind on work, she wasn't going to catch up by pushing her employees into the ground. Mental health came first, and Remi could see the relief in Jess at her suggestion.

"Looks like we better finish this job then. I think there's gonna be a lot to unpack."

"Okay, this is nice."

Remi stood at the shoreline, Jess pressing her feet into the sand next to her, the water washing over them like a soft caress. It felt good to have their work boots off, shoved into the back of the ute so they could walk down barefoot. It had been another scorcher. After being trapped in the bath-room all day, getting hot and dirty from laying tiles, the beach walk was necessary in more ways than just getting Jess to open up.

"Can't believe it's been a month since you started," Remi commented as they began walking slowly along the coastline.

"I want to break up with Adam."

Remi's eyes widened. "Okay. We're jumping straight in." She faced Jess. "I'm listening."

"That's the first time I've admitted that out loud. To you, and... to myself. God, that feels good."

The relief on Jess's face was instant. She really *had* needed to talk. She was quiet for a moment as they kept moving. This is why Remi brought her here. Walking had a way of untangling the mind. No pressure, no forced eye contact. Just time to allow thoughts to form, words to flow and in this case, perhaps, realisations to crystallise.

It had certainly been the case for her.

Remi still remembered the day Sophie had brought her to the beach when she was sixteen; her older sister was twenty at the time. Remi had been struggling with bullying, staying home two days in a row, too scared to go back to school. Sophie had got them chocolate thickshakes—

Remi's favourite—and she'd practically marched Remi down to the jetty, then onto the beach. Remi had been a brat, grumbling into her drink the entire way down, but then they'd started walking... and it had all poured out.

"I think I like girls," she'd confessed, staring straight at the water. She was unable to look her sister in the eye. Sophie had pried the cup from her hands, setting both drinks on the sand, and bundled Remi in the biggest hug she could remember. She'd sobbed uncontrollably into her sister's shoulder until their drinks turned into milkshakes and were nearly swept away by the tide.

Remi snapped back to the present as Jess started talking again.

"This is something I've been sitting on for longer than I care to admit. At first, it was just a feeling I couldn't name. I think it's because my mind and heart were in two different places. My mind was checking off a to-do list: Have a boyfriend. Check. Move in together. Check. Save for a house. Check. Think about starting a family. I was going through the motions of what I'm 'supposed' to do. What people like my parents—especially my mum—encouraged me to do. Even friends. And I don't blame them. The only problem was, I stopped listening to the most important part of the equation—me. How did I feel?"

Jess looked at Remi, and Remi was sure to keep her mouth shut. Adding any more voices to what Jess was already wrestling with would only complicate things. Instead, Remi held the eye contact, taking in every word and allowing space for Jess to gather her thoughts.

"Starting to listen to my heart was when the questions began to emerge. Quiet at first, then louder over time.

Why did I still feel unsettled when Adam moved in? Why did I miss living with Taylor? Why didn't I enjoy my work anymore? When had I begun to loathe it? When did it become so obvious that Adam and I wanted such different things in a partner? Why was it that when I thought about no longer being with him, I felt happier? Lighter?"

"When did you first notice that gap between what you wanted versus the life you were living?" Remi gently pushed.

"Late last year. There was a particular day when it all just... clicked. I'd had a busy day at work, feeling worn out and done. I'd got home to Adam playing games with his brother, the house an absolute mess, and I had a video call with Taylor. She looked so at ease with her life, I felt this raw jealousy brimming to the surface that I'd never felt before. The whole '*I want what she has*' thing. Not Sam or the sailing life specifically, just her happiness. That sense of contentment. I didn't have that. I felt like I was living the opposite."

"Kind of like your epiphany moment."

"Exactly!" Jess replied, visibly brightening. "Then, the bloody next day, you walk through the restaurant doors and drop this opportunity in my lap, and I thought—*what if this was my sign*? Try something new. See where it takes me. Shake up my whole life."

"And?"

"And everything is so thoroughly shaken, so damn obvious, that I can't in good conscience stay with Adam one more day, not feeling the way I do. It's not fair to him. And it's not fair to me."

"So, you think things have reached the point of irreconcilable differences?"

"I don't want to be with someone who doesn't want to stand by my side and help me grow into the best version of myself. Someone waving tiny flags, yelling '*Go team!*' as we work together to bring out the best in each other, and be the best *for* each other. I want that. And in the meantime, until I find that person, I want to support *me*. Back *my*self. Because... because I am so damn tired..." she huffed out. "I'm tired of defending myself and my choices to the one person who should be in my *fucking* corner." She spat the last words with such fury, Remi almost recoiled.

They'd stopped walking and now stood face-to-face.

Jess was heaving, gulping down air. Remi had never seen her eyes flash so blue, burning with intensity, like the hottest flame. They were wild. Something had unlocked in her tonight, Remi could see it unravelling and knitting itself back together with every word.

Remi swallowed, taking it all in.

"Wow. That's a lot," she spoke softly.

"Yeah," Jess said after a beat, giving a sheepish smile as her breath slowed. She looked out to the water for a moment, then back to Remi. "Sorry. I don't even know where that came from." She laughed lightly. "Apparently, I needed to get that out more than I thought."

"So then... what now?" Remi kept her voice even, careful not to add her own opinions. Jess had to work through this on her own. Remi would be there to support her as she came to these conclusions. She'd let her feel without judgement or suppression.

"The million-dollar question." Jess nodded. "This was a

good start. I think I needed to talk to someone who doesn't know Adam, someone who won't judge this decision."

"Why would I judge your decision? It's your life. Your relationship."

"Yeah, well, that's exactly what it's felt like lately." Jess sighed, stopping herself. "Okay, I know that's overreacting. Not everyone. Mainly, Mum. And Adam."

They'd reached the other jetty and turned back, heading towards the house.

"So, if you do this, is there anywhere you can go? Could you stay with your parents? Or would you ask him to move out?"

"Not my parents. That's... complicated. And they live in the hills. For now, I think I'll ask the girls—Marie and Hayley—if I can stay with them. That way I can get some space, work it out from there, and not put Adam out of a place to live."

"Seems like you have it all sorted out."

"In theory. I still have to actually *do* it."

The beach walk had been the right call. The change in Jess was obvious, her strides more sure and her shoulders back as she took in their surroundings. She was more in the present moment. Now that she'd let it all out, she could enjoy the late sunny afternoon for what it was. As they walked on, Remi changed the topic to lighter things, entertaining Jess with her favourite '90s and early 2000s movies she loved to watch when she had the chance, earning her a smile or two along the way.

Still, Remi couldn't help feeling protective of Jess. She wanted to do more. But it wasn't her place. Even this, spending so much time outside of work as friends, was probably crossing a multitude of employer-slash-employee rules. Yet somehow, Remi couldn't stop herself. And that was an issue. Somehow, she needed to put more space between them while still being supportive—in a completely professional way, of course. The small glimmer of hope she'd felt at the possibility of Jess being single soon didn't help her situation. At all. She needed to place those *feelings* that kept trying to surface into a box. Locked up tight and pushed into the dark depths of her mind.

THIRTEEN

Jess

Jess felt sick. Her plan to speak to Adam on the weekend seemed like a good idea at the time, giving them the space to deal with things without work hanging over them. But now that Saturday morning had rolled around...

She could just not do it—and try to talk to him again instead.

No. This had to happen.

Her toast sat untouched on the plate, staring back at her. She couldn't bring herself to take a bite, her stomach retaliating just thinking about it. She sipped her tea instead, the warmth easing her discomfort, if only a little. She focused on her breathing, counting to ten, her heart slowing with the rhythm.

She'd made a pros and cons list in her head, going over it again and again. Though, making said pros and cons list was probably *not* what someone did when they wanted to be with a person. Jess had to face the facts—she was not her best self with Adam.

Remi entered her mind next.

Ever since her birthday, she'd been a mess.

Who was she kidding, it had been long before that. But, her party stood out most clearly. Remi was attractive. And she was attracted to Remi. Attracted to her *boss*. And while nothing would, or could, ever eventuate from that thought, she knew she couldn't be with Adam any longer. Not when she'd started even entertaining those thoughts. She should be obsessing over him, not questioning how to break up with him.

There would never be a good time.

"Hey."

Adam looked up from his cereal bowl at the dining table and her stomach dropped. *Ugh, fuck this was hard.* Jess leaned on the kitchen bench, hugging her tea mug close, its warmth grounding her.

"Can we talk?"

"Uh, sure?" He looked at her quizzically.

"This... isn't working for me anymore. Us."

"Yeah, okay," he said with a smirk, scooping another spoonful of Weet-Bix into his mouth. Even from across the room, she could see the milk collecting at the corner of his mouth with every chew. She couldn't help but feel repulsed.

"I'm serious, Adam." She gripped her mug tighter to steady her hands.

The smirk dropped. "Oh."

She pressed on. "I've been thinking a lot. And I know we've talked a lot too—about my work, our future—but every conversation feels like there's a wedge driving us further apart. Ultimately, I think we want different things. *I* want different things."

She could see him slipping into that place. That quiet

place where his mind went into overdrive and he spiralled, his communication in shutdown mode. This was why their conversations never went anywhere. She tried to volley, but the ball always hit the net.

"Okay," he replied, eyes downcast toward his bowl.

Just like when he told her to give up on her job, she saw in real time as he gave up on their relationship. Or at least on fighting for it. This was why they were at this point. It couldn't be on her this time to fix everything. She was done. A relationship went both ways, and this was where they always went wrong. Adam didn't get it. His answers lived in his silence.

"Did you want to talk about this? Or..." She left the word hanging in the space between them. He stared at the bowl, shoulders slumped. Defeated. His dark shaggy hair now covered his eyes, hiding them from her view. Her heart hammered in her chest as she struggled to keep her breathing calm.

"Adam."

He looked up, eyes shining. "Jess, I love you." Like those four words could fix everything. With an internal sigh, she crossed the room and knelt down, taking his hand.

"Hey," she said softly. "I know this isn't what you wanted to hear, and I'm sorry. I'm guessing this also shouldn't be a complete surprise with how things have been between us."

He turned, pleading with his eyes as he squeezed her hands. "But... you are my happiness."

Still, he pinned everything on Jess.

"Adam. This is for the best. Your happiness should be

yours, not something I have to give you." She squeezed his hand back then let go.

Unsure what else to do, she leaned in and kissed the top of his head goodbye, a gesture he usually gave her. Grabbing her keys from the hook on the way into the lounge, she made her way out, refusing to look back. She swore she heard a sob as the door shut behind her. Her hand stayed on the handle, squeezing it, unable to let go.

Fuck.

She had to remain strong. This was the right thing to do, no matter how hard it felt. Her stomach still rolled. Not easing exactly, just shifting. Shifting with the weight of her unknown future, the pain she'd just caused Adam and the ripple effects this would create.

She rushed to her car, driving around the block and pulling over. Closing her eyes, she took a deep breath and released it shakily.

Remi's words came back to her, *"When change is your choice, it doesn't make it any easier—but—it does make it yours."*

This was her choice. Doing hard things was okay. *She'd* be okay.

She pulled away from the kerb, calling Marie on loud-speaker as she drove around with no particular destination in mind.

"I broke up with Adam," she said the moment Marie answered.

"What the fuck, Jess? What is with you dropping life-altering phone bombs on your friends?"

Jess let out a laugh-sob as the emotion hit her all at

once. Voicing it made it real. All the emotion was so unlike her. She roughly wiped at her eyes with her arm.

"Aww honey. Okay, listen, where are you? I'm about... fifteen minutes from finishing up with something. How about we meet at The Wharf?"

Jess sniffed, pulling herself together. "That... that would be great, I'm not far away. See you soon."

She sat at the same table where she and Adam had been almost three months ago. Had it really been that long?

She mindlessly stirred her cappuccino with her spoon, stopping to eat a mouthful or two of the froth.

"I'm here!" Marie's voice called out as she raced around the corner of the pub, impeccably dressed as always and not a minute late. Her short bob bounced with her little strides. Jess stood with her arms out, catching Marie as she smashed into her with a hug so fierce it nearly knocked Jess back down onto the bench seat. God, Marie's hugs were everything.

"Sorry, I got here as fast as I could." Marie was still puffing as she took a seat across from Jess and smoothed down her hair. But Marie's Singaporean roots meant there was never a hair out of place. It was always silky, black, glossy perfection. Jess hadn't even brushed her hair this morning, her messy bun a beautiful metaphor for her life right now.

"Marie, I literally called you exactly fifteen minutes ago with a surprise emergency. Why the hell are you apologising to me?"

"True. When you put it that way. Now, what the hell is going on?" She levelled Jess with a look so caring it hurt.

Jess let it all out. She'd always been able to open up to

Marie. While she loved Hayley, too, Marie was the one who'd been there when Taylor left, when Adam moved in and through every little check-in. She'd met Taylor in primary school, but Marie didn't come into her life until university. They didn't have the same classes but caught the train together, and often had lunch in the cafeteria. Marie had spoken to Jess first, she'd just come out and asked what Jess was studying and if she wanted to join her for lunch. They'd got along like a house on fire ever since.

"Sounds like you made the right decision. How do you feel?" Marie asked carefully.

"Right now?" Jess drained the last mouthful of her now cold coffee, her insides still churning with a storm of emotions. "Relieved. Nervous. Like, what happens now?" A seagull flew overhead, and she paused to watch it.

"I also feel free." She laughed lightly. "So, so damn free... and that makes me feel so selfish. But..." Jess held her friend's gaze. "God. In the end, he felt like my roommate; a friend. Not the love of my life."

They sat in silence for a moment.

"It doesn't make you selfish. You can't force love or help how you feel. It's called being human." Marie shrugged, pulling her mouth to the side.

"Thanks Marie. I feel like you always know what to say."

Marie reached over and gave her hand a gentle squeeze. "Anytime."

"There is one other thing, and I know it's a huge favour, but... could I crash at yours for a little while?"

"Shit, Jess." Marie's face crumpled. "Far out... the timing." Her head shook in disbelief, looking skyward before meeting Jess's again. "You're not going to believe this, but Brooke's staying with us."

"Brookie? She's back?" Of all the names she expected, Brooke's wasn't one of them.

"Yep, and my super wife—golden child that she is—Hayley, is taking her in. She rocked up out of the blue on Thursday night. We were just about to get your painter to start too..." She threw up her arms. "It's all happening at the Mayfield household."

Jess's heart sank, she hadn't accounted for a spanner in her plan, and it sounded like Marie already had enough going on without worrying about Jess too. She plastered on a smile. "That's totally fine. Don't worry about me! I've still got the guest bedroom." Though she really needed more space away from Adam than a single bedroom wall could provide.

"I'll ask around. What about your parents?" Marie cringed even as she asked. "Yeah, maybe not," she added quickly, answering her own question.

"You don't need to do that, honestly. I'll sort myself out. I'm having dinner with Mum and Dad tonight, so that's gonna be fun."

"You could just... not tell them?" Marie suggested, knowing full well how upset her mum would be. Adam was her favourite...

"Adam usually comes with me. He's not great at fending for himself." Jess rolled her eyes. "So, him not being there would be a red flag. Plus, I can't lie to Mum. She always knows. Better to deal with it head on and throw myself in the shit with everyone. Get it over and done with."

"That sounds horrible."

"I agree. I don't know why I do this to myself."

Dinner was as good as Jess thought it would be.

"Can't you make things work with Adam? Have you tried couple's counselling?"

Jess pushed three beans onto her fork and tried to relax her jaw enough to chew them.

"Mum," she warned.

"Honey, this just seems so out of character for you. Like you're throwing your life away. First your career, and now your boyfriend." Her mum's eyes held hers, worry creasing her forehead.

Jess snorted. She couldn't help it.

"Mum, you're the one who was on my back the *entire* time I was at Limone's because, and I quote, 'I hadn't used my degree.' Now I'm back at school, completing an apprenticeship through TAFE, working for a reputable building company and *that's* throwing my life away?"

More beans. More chewing.

Her mum made a sound of indignation, lips forming a thin line. Her dad, as always, remained silent, head down, focused on his food. Typical.

"And with Adam," Jess powered on, scooping some mashed potato. "We wanted different things. I want someone who will support me. I want *parents* who will support me." She eyed her mum in challenge.

"Honey, we do support you. We want what's best for

you." Her mum placed her cutlery down, her face full of misguided sympathy.

"Then listen to me. Let me make my own choices!" Jess couldn't help raising her voice. This conversation was going around in circles.

"I just think—"

"*What*, Mum?"

"I just don't want you to throw it all away," she pressed.

Jess closed her eyes and blew a loud breath out her nose to give herself a moment.

"I'm not!" she cried, almost hysterical now. Her mum always pushed until she cracked like this every single time. Why wouldn't she just *listen*?

"Well, you can stay with us as long as you need," her dad interjected, trying to keep the peace.

"Thanks, Dad," she replied at a lower volume, cutting her eyes away from her mum. "But I'll stay at my place for now, in the spare bedroom. It's closer to work. Speaking of, I should head back, I've got a few things to sort out tomorrow. Thanks for dinner." Her chair scraped loudly, she'd had enough. She'd said her piece. She'd been honest. With more time, hopefully they'd come around, but she wasn't going to wait to find out.

"Jessica, just wait and talk to us," her mum pleaded, trying for a warmer tone.

"There's not much of a conversation happening right now, so I think we'll leave it there. I'll talk to you both soon."

The heavy feeling returned to her stomach. Her mind screamed to sit back down, to try and work everything out. *But, doing hard things was okay.* She didn't look back.

The long drive home gave her time to think, and she was thankful for no company in the car. She rolled the windows down, letting the warm summer breeze rush in. She took in a lungful of fresh air, the eucalyptus strong as she whipped through the windy roads that led back down to town, and finally to home by the beach. She hadn't been back since this morning. With any luck, Adam would already be in bed or out.

When her mother got an idea in her head, it was her way or the highway. Stubborn to a fault, something Jess had inherited, meant conversations often ended up like tonight; a crossfire of opposing opinions, her dad on the sidelines waving his white flag. What frustrated Jess most was feeling like her mum wasn't seeing her. Instead, her mum was seeing her as who she *wanted* Jess to be: Jessica Reaves, star daughter, project manager for a swanky business in the city putting her degree to use, homeowner and mum to two perfect grandchildren alongside Adam, her perfect husband.

Her mum was so deep into delusion land, she couldn't understand any other path Jess chose, other than the one her mum picked out for her. Even if those opposing paths made Jess happy. Sometimes Jess wanted to shake her and say, "Look at me, here I am. Right here. This is your daughter, your *real* daughter, over here living my life."

She held her arm out the window, making wave shapes through the air as it whipped past the car.

One day, you'll see me for who I really am.

FOURTEEN

Remi

Eight. That was how many projects stood between Remi and starting the Flinders job. And she only had six weeks to squeeze it all in. How was it almost mid-Feb already? April would be here before she knew it.

Sophie was currently dropping Hudson off to school and would be on site soon so they could finish the laundry install by lunchtime. That way, they'd be ahead on this job, and could start demoing a little kitchenette reno around the corner in a granny flat.

Remi finally felt like she was catching up.

"Hey, Remi?"

"Yo," she called out as Jess appeared in the doorway.

"I've finished the last two overheads. You ready for them?" Jess wiped her forehead, already sweaty from the heat, and it wasn't even lunchtime. February was kicking their butt with the dry weather.

"Bring 'em in," Remi replied.

Jess was getting faster. Remi hadn't expected her to

finish everything so quickly. At least now she had an extra pair of hands.

They were installing a galley laundry today. The floor cabinets were done; now it was time for the overheads. Jess carried in her two cupboards. They set them up on cabinet jacks, ready to affix to the wall. Jess held them in place as Remi wiped her eyes, still bleary as she tried to concentrate on drilling in the masonry screws. Stifling a yawn, she got the last one in.

"Done," she said proudly, testing for movement. The cupboards were solid against the wall. No way they were falling down on her watch.

"Right, I'll be back. Just going to grab the big ladder off the ute," said Remi, grabbing her iced coffee from the bench and taking a big swig. Hopefully some caffeine would help her wake up.

She'd been up late last night looking over the final designs Sophie had put together for Flinders. They needed one last check before sending everything to Javier for ordering. Flinders had loved the initial ideas, and they'd been amazing to work with so far. Everything was off to a promising start. The best part? While they'd be busy, there were some things Remi wouldn't have to worry about anymore, like project managing certain aspects of the job or other trades. Flinders would be their one port of call, which should help streamline their work.

Ladder acquired, it was time to install the trim for the crown moulding along the very top of the overhead cupboards to the ceiling. Remi loved doing this part. It helped complete the entire room. Finishing details were everything. But first: measurements!

"Right, Jess, grab the end of the tape and hop up on that step ladder. I'll hop up on the big boy. Let's see what length we need." She shoved a pencil in her mouth and climbed. "Two and a half metres exactly, as it should be. Annnnd ten centimetres to the roof over here."

Remi handed the tape to Jess. "Let me know how high it is at your end."

"Eleven centimetres," replied Jess, climbing down.

Only a slight slope to contend with, not too bad for an old house. Remi made a couple of markings with her pencil and took a step to come down. Only her foot missed the ladder entirely.

She felt like a lost puppy in mid-air—limbs flailing, eyes bulging. She made a grab for the ladder, but it was too late. It toppled after her, adding insult to injury. An audible gasp rang out as time froze, and then she landed head over boots on the tiled floor with a crash so loud, she hoped she hadn't sent the ladder through the wall.

She blinked, her face now level with the cold tile floor. "Urgh," she groaned as she went to lift herself up. Scorching pain bolted through her arm and she crumpled back down. "Ow, fuck!" she yelped, cradling her right arm as she tried to scramble onto her knees.

Blonde hair was in her face. Hands landed on her shoulders, steadying her. Cobalt eyes pierced into her own. "Are you okay? Look at me. Did you hit your head?" Jess was frantic, taking in every inch of Remi for signs of harm.

"I think..." Remi couldn't think straight. Especially not when all she could smell was Jess. Remi smiled.

Jess gently shook her by the shoulders. "Remi, look at me." Remi snapped back to her again, trying to focus. "I think... I've hurt my arm." She was too scared to move; she didn't want a repeat of that pain.

"Can I?" Jess reached for it and Remi reflexively yanked it away. Pain lanced through her again.

"Argh." Why had she even done that? Jess was only trying to help. She sheepishly moved back to Jess, carefully moving her arm closer. Jess's touch was cautious and gentle as she looked it over. "Well, it doesn't look broken. Can you move your hand?"

They both watched as the tips of Remi's fingers flexed ever so slightly. "Ow!"

"Okay, they're moving, that's a good sign." Jess let out a breath, giving Remi a reassuring smile. "But pretty sure you hit your head too, so I'm going to take you to the hospital to get you checked out."

"Nah, I'll be fine." She had to be. She didn't have time for this, and she wasn't about to take any days off work. She could just—

The room spun as she slowly stood. Jess caught her elbow and gave her a serious look.

"Yeah, that's not up for discussion. I'm taking you. *Now*," Jess said with a fierceness Remi hadn't heard before.

Remi held in a giggle.

One: now was *not* the time to make inappropriate jokes, but GOD she wished she could. Two: she really needed to get her mind out of the gutter when it came to Jess and focus on getting to the car, because—*oh boy*—she did not feel good. Three: Jess was incredibly hot when she got bossy.

Jess mumbled to herself. "Got my car keys. Got the keys

for this house. Phone." She patted her work shorts. "Okay, lean on me. Let's go."

They made it out the front door, and Remi had just stepped off the patio when she lurched to the side and vomited straight into a bed of agapanthus. A car door slammed behind her, but she didn't have the energy to look. A warm hand started rubbing her back. Jess.

"Oh my god, Remi! What's going on?"

Right. Sophie was here.

"She's okay. Well, clearly, not great," Jess spoke up for her as Remi stayed still, not moving in case the nausea came back. Her vision tunnelled and she made every effort not to move.

"She fell off the ladder. Smacked her head, but I think her arm cushioned the fall somewhat."

"Oh, shit." A shadow entered her periphery as Sophie squatted beside her. "You good there, Bug?"

Wow. Sophie never used their childhood nicknames in public. Maybe it was worse than she thought? Remi cracked a smile, then winced as she accidentally went to move her hand and give a thumbs up. Oh, the stupidity.

She went to shake her head.

Nope. Double stupidity.

"Never better, Sis," Remi groaned.

"I'm taking her to the hospital. Here's the keys for the place. Sorry, I just locked everything up." Jess handed them to Sophie as she stood.

"Thank you."

"Of course. I'll send you an update as soon as we hear from the doc," Jess said, easing Remi up and getting her into the car.

"Are you sure you don't want me to take her?" Sophie asked, hesitating on the steps.

"And leave the apprentice on site? I'd be useless," Jess replied.

"Right. Makes sense. Well, look after her." She gave Remi one more worried look, before letting herself inside.

"Remi Pearce?" a new doctor asked, striding in and stopping at the end of her bed. They'd waited hours to be seen, before finally being taken to a bed in one of the public rooms. A nurse had taken Remi for an X-ray in the meantime, and they'd been waiting on results ever since. She wanted answers, and an all clear, so she could get out of here and sort out work. They'd already been so behind... Sophie had messaged to say she'd at least finished what they needed to on the laundry job today.

"That's me." Remi smiled brightly. The doctor seemed warm, but a straight-shooter type of guy.

"How are you feeling?" he checked, looking over his glasses.

"Better now I've had a rest. Just a little sore. Should be fine in a couple of days."

He frowned slightly. "You'll need a bit more time than that, I'm afraid. You've got quite the sprain, mainly your wrist. Nothing is fractured or broken, so you're very lucky, but you're going to need to give it time to heal and keep it strapped up."

Remi swallowed. "Um, how long?" She didn't want to know the answer.

"At least four weeks for a moderate sprain."

She could probably still use her drill *carefully* in a few days. It'd be fine. There was no way she'd be off the tools for four weeks, not when Flinders was due to start!

"As for the mild concussion, no screens for twenty-four hours and make sure you've got someone at home with you tonight, just in case. It's more of a safety measure; you'll probably be fine, but I take precautions with all my patients." He smiled.

"Of course." Again, she'd be fine. No need to worry Sophie. She'd order in and go to bed early tonight. Easy.

"I could stay with you," Jess offered.

Remi looked at her. She was serious. This was a bad idea. She wasn't sure she could handle Jess casually lounging around her home. Though, with everything Jess had been going through lately with Adam and her family... maybe it was a good thing? If only to keep her mind off things. Really, she'd be helping *her* out.

"What about, uh, Marie? And Hayley? Aren't you staying with them? I don't want to put you out."

Jess looked away, a flash of something unreadable crossing her face.

"I'll leave you two ladies to sort that out." The doctor patted the end of the bed frame. "And rest that arm," he warned with a pointed finger. "You're otherwise free to leave as soon as the nurse has been past to bandage it properly."

"Thank you," Remi and Jess said in unison as he left.

"Um, in answer to your question—I haven't been staying with the girls." Jess fiddled with her nails, still avoiding Remi's gaze.

"Where have you been then?" Remi sat up straighter, making sure not to move her arm.

"At home."

"What? With Adam?"

"Yeah. It hasn't been too bad," Jess rushed to say. "We've both been working, and we're in separate rooms when we're home. I'm in the guest bedroom. He still leaves his washing for me to do in the laundry though." Jess clenched her jaw, seeming less than impressed.

"No comment." Why Jess let Adam walk over her, she had no idea. "Well, ah, look. This is already way beyond your apprenticeship requirements," Remi joked. "You didn't need to sit here with me all day. Honestly, go home and chill out."

"Remi, you saw that doc's face. He was serious. You're not getting out of it that easily."

Ugh. She hated this. She was the self-sufficient one. She looked after everyone else, not the other way around. Looking at Jess, she knew she wasn't going to win the argument.

She hung her head. "Fine."

Her head snapped back up.

Ouch. Too fast.

She groaned, pausing a second. "What about my car—"

"Already messaged Sophie while you were having that little nap earlier. She and Tomás will pick it up and drop it off at your place."

"Gold star, Newbie. You've outdone yourself today."

"Calm down, Donatello. It was just a text message," Jess replied, smirking.

Remi smiled at the stupid nickname.

She couldn't wait to get out of the hospital, and she'd be lying if she said she wasn't relieved—*but only a little*—to have someone else at home to sort out dinner tonight. Oh, *Ninja*. He needed feeding too and a quick roam around. Having Jess around would give her time to work out what to do with their current projects and timetables. Her stomach dropped. Javier and Hadid wouldn't be happy. This could lose them the contract. She just needed to make sure their current work was still on track, and her arm was healed and ready to go on schedule. She could still do this.

A nurse popped her head around the curtain, holding up a bandage. "Remi Pearce? I'm here to strap your arm."

FIFTEEN

Jess

Remi passed the keys to Jess to unlock the door and let them in. A peek into Remi's bedroom showed clothes strewn everywhere; in the bathroom, a towel hung haphazardly on the rail, Remi's toothbrush lying on the edge of the sink. Once they reached the open kitchen and family room, Jess's eyes widened further. Papers were scattered around a laptop on the dining table, dishes and all sorts left on the bench. Everything was in complete disarray—a far cry from the tidy home she'd visited a month ago. Jess's hands were already itching just looking at the mess.

Remi looked sheepish, a hint of pink in her cheeks, as Jess dropped her bag on the floor.

"Sorry, I—uh, didn't expect to have anyone around and didn't get a chance to clean up this morning."

This wasn't one morning's mess, but Jess wasn't about to call her on it. It made her wonder how much work Remi had really been taking home.

"I know you've been here before," Remi continued,

"but that was hectic with my family and celebratory pizza, so let me give you the proper tour."

They'd only just walked in, and already Remi couldn't sit still. Jess narrowed her eyes. "Shouldn't you be resting right now instead of prancing around your house?"

Remi laughed. "You'd know if I was prancing. I'm being nice to my *guest* by showing you where the toilet and spare room are."

"Right," Jess drawled with a wry smile and squinted her eyes. "I'm keepin' my eyes on you."

That drew another chuckle out of Remi. "C'mon, at least let me show you to your room."

Jess hiked her bag onto her shoulder. "Lead the way."

Remi ended up giving Jess the full tour. There was no stopping the woman. The spare bedroom was, unsurprisingly, the neatest in the house. Jess threw her bag onto the foot of the bed.

"I'll let you get settled and go sit down," Remi said from the doorway.

"Thanks." Jess smiled.

They'd made a pit stop on the way back from the hospital to Jess's place, and she'd packed for a few nights, *just* in case. She was just thankful to get any space from Adam at this point. Aside from sleeping in different rooms, not much had changed. She'd still been cooking and cleaning, unable to help herself, the habit too ingrained. This physical boundary was necessary, a reminder that the end of their relationship meant Adam needed to start looking after himself. Jess wasn't always going to be there to pick up the pieces—a fact she needed to remind herself of whenever she had the automatic urge to step in.

A large window looked over the side garden where Remi had sunflowers growing. It was so cute and homey, the kind of space that made you smile. The rest of the room was fairly sparse, with a few house plants and two large art prints of silhouetted women.

They were back in the family room now, Remi resting on the couch while Jess sat at the other end with her legs tucked underneath her. The TV murmured in the background, something to fill the quiet while they chatted.

"How are you feeling?" Jess checked in.

"Better now the meds have kicked in. The aching's eased, and my head does feel a little clearer. Feels weird to be sitting down on a work day, though."

"You're not used to stopping, are you?"

"No."

"Or someone telling you what to do."

That pulled a smile from her. "Also no. Though you don't seem to have any trouble pushing that button."

"I like to push for the things that matter." Jess held her gaze. "If that's someone's wellbeing or something I truly believe in, then yeah, I'll get a little bossy."

"You know, I admire that about you," Remi replied, tilting her head to the side as she pulled her knees up.

"Yeah?"

"Yeah. Seeing the determination when you wanted to switch careers, despite your family's disapproval, that was pretty badass."

"It sure didn't feel badass at the time." *Still* didn't.

"But look at you now, swinging drills around like a pro."

"Oh, I've got a long way to go before I'll feel as good as you look wielding a drill."

An image flashed into Jess's mind, Remi drilling into a concrete wall the week before; sheer determination on her face as she used all of her force to get through a particularly hard section. Ever since her bloody birthday party, Jess had been more aware of Remi. Aware of... *everything* about her. It wasn't just attraction; it was attention, constant and sharp. She kept telling herself it was just the result of spending so much time together. But deep down, she knew better. Remi had been on her mind at work, in the shower, as she was falling asleep. Like a song stuck in her head that she couldn't, and didn't want to, shake.

Even sitting on the couch with her now felt intense, like a low-level hum of energy buzzing in the air. Yet, here they were just sitting and talking casually. Jess's fingers itched with the urge to reach out. It was ridiculous.

Remi idly played with her lip, brushing her finger back and forth as she stared into the middle distance. Jess almost groaned, only catching herself at the very last moment.

She hadn't slept with Adam in months. Maybe she was just starved for anything remotely attractive?

No. That wasn't it. Her gaze fell to Remi's lips.

A loud grumble made her jump.

Remi's stomach growled again. Her eyes slid to Jess.

"Hungry?" Jess smirked, thankful for the distraction.

"Starving, now I think about it."

"Leave it with me." Jess hopped off the couch and grabbed her phone, moving to the hallway where it was quieter. She knew exactly what to get.

"Limone Restaurant, how can I help?"

"Ellie? It's Jess."

"Jess! Oh my god, hi. How's things? We miss you!"

"Aww, I miss you too! Though, can't say I miss the job." Jess laughed.

"You don't have to tell me twice. Do you need to speak to Ricciardo?"

God, no. "Not tonight. Can you hook me up with two of Jimmy's lasagnes, delivered?"

"Of course."

Jess gave her Remi's address and hung up. She could already hear the Friday night crowd buzzing in the background. Lucky she'd ordered early, any later and they'd be waiting over an hour!

"Dinner should be here in about half an hour," Jess said as she walked back.

Remi was slumped on the couch, fast asleep. Jess smiled. She eyed the mess of paperwork on the table and set to work tidying while she waited on dinner.

Jess was cleaning the kitchen when the doorbell rang, startling Remi awake. She saw the wince as Remi sat up and squeezed her shoulder gently on her way past.

"Stay there. I'll get it."

Jess brought the food over and set it on the table. She looked at Remi. "I'd made space up here and set the table for us, but... looking at you now—wanna eat this on the couch instead?"

Remi looked torn, then nodded. "I think I might. What's in the bag?"

"Limone's lasagne."

Remi tipped her head back and groaned in delight.

"Yum. Wow, thank you, you're a lifesaver. That's my absolute favourite."

"I remember," Jess said with a grin, unpacking the containers and plating the food. "Now, want me to cut it up so you can eat it with your left hand?"

"Oh. Right. I hadn't thought of that. If you don't mind, that would be great."

The good thing about Jimmy's lasagne? The layers of pasta cut like butter, the bolognese sauce oozing out with every mouthful.

"You shouldn't have any trouble with that." Jess slid the plate onto Remi's lap and passed her a fork. Remi readjusted, sitting up a little straighter.

"How does it get better with every bite?" said Remi after a few mouthfuls.

"Jimmy is the man; he knows his stuff."

"Is Jimmy the chef at Limone?"

"Yep. Great guy. I'll always go back to that place for the food, regardless of how much I didn't enjoy working there towards the end."

"Can't argue with that," Remi replied.

A second later she scoffed out of nowhere.

"What?" Jess asked, confused.

"I've just realised what the date is. Typical."

"Still not followi—oh!"

"Friday the thirteenth!" they both said at the same time.

"Well, that explains my bad luck today," said Remi.

"And you didn't even walk *under* a ladder!" Jess chuckled. "Are you superstitious?"

"Mmm, not particularly. You?" Remi asked.

"Mildly? I will definitely avoid walking under a ladder if I can. And black cats. You can't trust 'em."

"What about turtles?" Remi asked, raising an eyebrow and looking toward the big tank in the room.

"Nothing against turtles, especially those who go by the name *Ninja*."

"Good, because Ninja needs to be given his dinner. And seeing as I'm still eating mine, would you mind dropping a couple of pellets into his tank? They're right there on top of the tank."

"Sure thing." Jess hopped up, moving over to the turtle, who was scratching at the corner of the glass, looking like he wanted to climb out. "Uh, is he trying to escape?"

"Both. He's hungry, and I usually let him out for a little run around."

"O-k-a-y," Jess dragged out, dropping in the pellets. He swam after them, eating them faster than she thought possible. "Woah, he *was* hungry."

"Don't let him fool you, he's just a pig who gets fed regularly. If you're comfortable, you're welcome to take him out and put him on the floor. Easiest way is to grab him either side with two hands."

Jess blew out a breath. "Here goes nothing," she mumbled, carefully picking the turtle up. He seemed very happy with the turn of events and thankfully didn't try to wiggle out of her hands. She placed him on the floor, and he took off.

"I thought turtles were meant to be slow."

"Not if they're *Ninja Turtles*."

"Ha-Ha," said Jess sarcastically.

He turned on the spot and started coming straight

towards her. "Ah!" Jess squealed, running around the couch and stopping behind Remi.

"Oh my god, don't make me laugh. It hurts," Remi said, holding herself still, trying to temper the chuckle. "Jess, he's not going to hurt you. He's just curious and he usually follows me around."

Jess did not believe her one bit. The turtle was ferocious and on the attack! He crept out from behind the couch, running towards her again.

"Stand still," Remi ordered.

Jess did as she was told.

Ninja slowed as he got to her feet, then stopped.

"Well, that was anticlimactic." Jess had been bracing for at least a little chomp. "Now he's just sitting there, not moving."

"He probably wants a pat."

"You can *pat* a turtle?" Jess asked, incredulous. She was learning a lot about reptiles tonight.

"It's not common, but Ninja is weird. If you bend down, just lightly scratch or pet the edges of his shell."

Remi hadn't led her astray yet, so she knelt down, reached out and—yep, she was scratching a turtle. *Not* how she'd pictured her night. "Remi, is he... no... is he *wiggling his butt?!*"

"Yep. He does that too."

"Wow. You have the coolest pet. Now I kinda want one."

"Well, you're welcome to come here and hang out with him anytime."

"I might just take you up on that. Wait—your tattoo,

didn't you say you got your pet turtle when you were, like, ten?"

"Nine," Remi corrected.

"But that would make him—"

"Almost thirty-two years old."

"Ho-ly shit. He's older than me." Jess sat back on her heels, wide-eyed at the cute creature. "Wow. I better respect my elders."

"Hey!" scolded Remi.

"I meant the turtle!" Jess replied, turning and giving her a look.

Remi sat with a wide grin. "I'm just messing with you. He's a Murray River turtle, so these guys can live to fifty."

"No wonder he's bonded to you. You've had a long time together."

"Yep. It's always been me and him. Hence the tattoo. I love having the reminder of one of my best buds with me."

"That's really sweet."

They let Ninja roam a little longer. He seemed content now he'd met the new person in the house.

Jess placed him back in the tank and turned to Remi. "You okay if I make a tea?"

Remi made a face that said, *you don't have to ask.* "Please. Make yourself at home. Tea bags are in the cupboard above the kettle."

"And mugs?" Jess checked.

"Right next to 'em. Can I have one too please? Splash of milk, no sugar."

"Hey, that's exactly how I like it. Adam hated tea, so I'm used to making the one mug for myself before bed. I find it calms me."

"Me too," Remi agreed, her head resting on the couch as she watched Jess potter in the kitchen. "This is nice. The company I mean. I wasn't sure how I'd feel having someone all..." she drifted off.

"Up in your space?" Jess finished for her.

"I guess."

"What about previous partners?"

"I'm not really the relationship type. I like being on my own. I've dated, here and there, but I'm so busy, it usually doesn't last. The girls I'd dated wanted to settle down pretty quick, and I'm just so wrapped up in work, driven by what I want to achieve... I guess I stopped trying after a while. Pretty sure it's been three years since I dated anyone."

So, Remi dated women. Jess tingled, filing away the new information as she threw a teabag into each mug.

"I don't think prioritising your business is a bad thing. As long as you're happy, that's what matters, right?"

"I guess? I haven't thought about it. Though, hitting that forty milestone last year and coming home to only Ninja, it does make me think *'what if?'* sometimes."

"Wait, does that mean you haven't slept with anyone for that long?" Jess wasn't sure if this line of enquiry was appropriate... but here she was.

"Nope," Remi replied, popping the "p".

"Not even one night?" Jess was also not going to think about her body's reaction to that question. It wasn't like *she* was asking Remi if she was interested in *her*.

Which she wasn't.

She just found Remi extremely attractive. That was all. The fact she looked so cute all bundled up on the couch in an old shirt and trackpants wasn't helping said—very objective—attraction. *Had the heat gone up in the room?* Maybe she was standing too close to the kettle?

Being attracted to a woman wasn't new to Jess.

Kate Gordon was the first girl she ever kissed, back in Year 12 in the girl's toilets. Not the most picturesque setting, but she certainly wasn't thinking about that when Kate had leaned in and captured her lips. They dated the rest of the school year, then went their separate ways when Kate moved to Sydney for a prestigious performing arts school. Since then, Jess had dated a few guys and girls through her early twenties before meeting Adam. She'd never really put a label on herself, preferring to just date whoever she wanted. She liked someone for who they were, not their gender.

Jess brought the two mugs over and set them on the coffee table.

"It's not like I haven't..." Remi pulled her lips in, cheeks flushing instantly. "You know..." She implored with her eyes.

"Masturbated? Touched yourself?" Jess finished for her directly, enjoying the way Remi squirmed. Boundaries be damned, this was way too entertaining.

Remi looked to the ceiling, then anywhere else to avoid Jess's gaze. "Yeah... that."

"You're cute when you're flushed." The line was crossed. That was a flirt if she'd ever heard one. She needed to stop. This was her *boss*. Who was also *injured* AND *had a mild concussion!*

"I didn't take you as someone to get embarrassed talking about their sex life."

"Shut up." Remi smirked, throwing a cushion at Jess

with her good hand. Jess caught it easily. "I've always been better with actions than with words," Remi finished.

While Remi's comment should've landed as more flirting, Jess sobered. "I'm going to have to disagree with you there. You've talked me through a lot of things over the past few months, and I'm thankful for every one of those conversations." She hugged the pillow closer, playing with one of the edges.

"Anytime. That's what friends are for," Remi replied, meeting Jess's eyes again.

At least she'd steered them back from dangerous waters. Though how long that would last before she tested the boundary again...

SIXTEEN

Remi

If Remi thought she'd hurt yesterday, she'd woken up this morning feeling very sorry for herself. Still, she'd pushed through the discomfort, showering and dressing, very, very slowly, opting for her stretchiest sports bra to manage everything one-handed. Now up and about she was feeling better. The pain meds were kicking in, dispersing the ache in her arm.

Whether it was a good thing or not, Jess had been on Remi's mind all night. She'd felt something shift between them. And it scared her. Needing to rely on someone like this. Needing *Jess* like this. This accident had brought down all her usual boundaries. Letting people in wasn't something Remi did. She was capable and reliant on herself. And yet, as much as she'd tried to fight it, she couldn't ignore how normal it felt to have Jess in her home, in her space.

"Do you want to give me a list of groceries, and I'll go do your shopping?"

"Jess, I can do that." Her arm might hurt, but she wasn't bedridden.

"I'm sure you could, but I'll be faster, and the doctor said you need to *rest*. I know it seems like you've never heard of that word in your life, but please—let me help you." Jess stared at her pointedly.

"You already have. You stayed over, my head feels better, I'm all good. Really." Because if Remi had to spend five more minutes in close proximity to Jess, in her pjs, with messy morning hair and those cute doe-eyed blue eyes staring at her... she was going to do something she couldn't take back.

Jess watched with a small smile as Remi tried to finish pulling a hoodie over her head, wincing as she one-armed it over her shoulder, accidentally jolting her arm.

"For god's sake, woman. You're incorrigible." Jess was in front of her in two strides, the air filled with her signature floral scent. Jess pulled the fabric out and over Remi's arm with precision, neatening the hem and adjusting the shoulders with a light finishing pat. "There," Jess breathed. Eyelashes flitted up to meet hers, and Remi sucked in a breath. Why were they standing so close? She couldn't look away. Jess had exceptionally nice eyebrows. Dark, matching the roots of her otherwise blonde hair. *Stop staring. And really? Her eyebrows?!*

Remi took a step back, breaking the proximity. "Fine. You can help with my groceries."

"Yes!" Jess fist-pumped the air. "It's helping me too. Otherwise, I'd just be hanging at home avoiding Adam, which, considering it's Valentine's Day, I really don't want to do..."

The vulnerability in Jess's voice made Remi's heart hurt. She kept forgetting Jess hadn't been able to stay with her friends. If it were her, she wouldn't want to be anywhere near an ex on this sickly-sweet holiday.

"Right. Well..."

She was going to regret this.

"Why don't, um, we do something?"

"For Valentine's Day?" Jess visibly swallowed.

"Yeah. We can do Galentine's Day."

"Right! That sounds nice," Jess replied, looking... relieved? Excited? Nervous? Remi wasn't sure.

"We can do a girls' night in. Maybe some food, drinks, a movie... something low-key?"

Why? Why had she not only suggested more time together, but something involving snuggling on the couch? Her brain wasn't doing a great job of fighting off *that* imagery either. She blamed the concussion. She clearly wasn't thinking straight.

"Perfect." Jess grinned. "Before I shop, I was also going to throw our work clothes in the wash. Do you mind if I do a load?"

"Um, sure." Remi still wasn't used to sharing her space, *let alone* them being so on the front foot. She showed Jess where everything was in the laundry, then stepped back into the kitchen. That's when it hit her: Jess would be handling her underwear. *Get it together, Pearce.* Heat raced up her neck regardless, blooming across her chest at the thought. The lines between them were blurring, even if Jess was just trying to help out around the house.

Ten minutes later, Jess reappeared in the kitchen with keys in hand. "Okay, see you when I get back. Please try not to move from that couch."

"Yes, *Mum*," Remi said. "I'll send through the list soon."

Jess's laugh floated down the hallway, and Remi never wanted it to end.

Remi had just sent off the list when her phone lit up with a call.

"JJ! What's happening?" It must be important, JJ was a notorious texter.

"A little birdy tells me you had a bit of a tumble."

"Little birdy Sophie needs to stop going around telling everyone," Remi said with a smile. "I'm fine, really. Just a sprain."

"Well, while I'm sure you are fine, I'm checking in anyway. Need anything? Food? Or a bit of company?"

Remi felt like she'd been sprung doing something naughty. "Actually, uh, Jess is staying with me at the moment."

"Your *apprentice*? That's asking a bit much, isn't it?"

"Hey! I tried to tell her to go home. She's a persistent one." Remi wasn't about to get into the details of Jess's recent breakup. At this rate, it felt like she was helping *Jess* too. At least, that was her excuse, and she was sticking to it.

"Sure, sure. I'm sure it's *terrible* for you with her around."

Remi lowered her voice, even though she was home alone. "Between you and me, it *is* terrible. She's incredibly thoughtful. She made my breakfast this morning, did our laundry and now she's out grabbing groceries. Not to mention we've been talking non-stop about everything and anything. She's become a close friend I didn't anticipate, and now the lines are blurring."

JJ full-on belly laughed right down the line. "Rem, you're fucked."

She scoffed. "Thanks for the pep talk, so helpful, *Jade*."

"Ooft. Low blow." JJ hated her first name.

"Sorry, it's just, I remember her from the restaurant. She's pretty sexy, Rem. So good luck trying to resist that. If she's the whole kit and kaboodle... and you guys have good chem too? Yikes."

"Still. Not. Helping! You're such a bad influence," Remi scolded, chuckling under her breath. "I think Sophie would kill me. It's so unprofessional. I don't even know why I'm talking like something will happen. It can't."

JJ softened. "You're an adult, Rem. You can make your own choices, your own decisions. Plus, I haven't seen you with someone in—I don't know how long. If she's as good as you say she is, well..."

"Thanks, JJ." Remi didn't need any further encouragement.

"Well, I'll leave you to it. Call me if you need anything, work or otherwise."

"Will do."

She dropped the phone onto her lap and exhaled.

Work.

She needed a miracle, because she had no idea how to handle the amount of projects they needed to finish. Or Flinders.

Or... Jess.

No. She knew exactly how she wanted to handle Jess. Flashes of her in PJs this morning came flooding back. Only this time, Jess was lying on her bed, blonde hair even messier, swollen pink lips, ice-blue eyes staring up from underneath her—Remi blew out another breath to clear her mind. And cool herself off.

In the words of JJ; maybe she was fucked.

"She can cook too."

Remi scooped another mouthful of creamy mustard chicken into her mouth. Absolute heaven.

They were sitting at the dining table tonight. Jess had even lit a candle she'd pulled off one of Remi's bookcases—with permission, of course—making their Galentine's dinner feel a little more special. If it wasn't for the chicken being pre-cut into little pieces on her plate, Remi could almost forget the dull ache in her wrist. Like a bad workout, she was feeling it more elsewhere today. Her body was sore, her shoulder and neck stiff from the impact. Having Jess around helped keep her mind off it and helped her do what she was told: rest. She couldn't remember the last time she'd just... sat. Laid up on the couch with the TV on. It felt weird. And she was already restless.

"I've always been the cook of the household," Jess explained. "First for myself when I moved out while at uni, then when I lived with Taylor—she can't cook for shit." Jess laughed. "Adam wasn't any better. By then, it had become routine. I enjoy it enough. It's not a chore—I like putting healthy, tasty food in my body. Makes me feel good."

"I don't think I've ever looked at cooking that way. For me, I just need to eat, and usually a lot, with the amount of energy I burn from our line of work. I need those calories. So, I just tick off the list; protein, veggies and throw on some carbs. This though," Remi said, pointing her fork at the plate, "is incredible."

"Well, you're welcome." Jess gave her a smile so wholesome, Remi didn't know how to react. This meal, this setting, this night... it felt like so much more than what it was. *It felt like a date.* All she could do was smile stupidly in return.

Jess raised her glass of non-alcoholic wine, nodding at Remi to do the same. She'd wanted Remi to still feel like they were celebrating tonight, even without alcohol. Always so thoughtful, always one step ahead. Remi loved that about her.

"Happy Galentine's Day." There was that smile again, Jess's eyes crinkling at the edges. "To good friends, good health, and good luck with the year ahead."

Remi clinked their glasses together. "Cheers to that."

Dinner was delicious, decadent even. Now they were back on the couch, wine glasses topped up. "Can't waste the bottle," Jess had said, jiggling it before pouring the last drops into Remi's waiting hand. The coffee table was now covered in all the movie snacks Jess had bought, complete with fresh buttered popcorn.

"Jess, that popcorn is bigger than my head. How are we going to eat all this? I feel like I'm at a disadvantage with only one good arm. I can either drink wine or snack. It's not fair." Remi stuck out her bottom lip.

"I can feed you snacks."

"What—Jess, no!" Remi tried to stop her, wide-eyed.

"Open up!" Jess threw a piece of popcorn at her from the other end of the couch. Remi was way too slow, and it bounced off her nose.

"No fair, I can hardly move!"

Jess's grin widened as another piece bounced off Remi's chin.

"Jess, I'm going to spill my wine!" Another hit her teeth mid-sentence. She let out a helpless burst of laughter, unable to do anything but succumb to being a clown at the sideshows. The next one landed right in her mouth as she laughed, making her cough as it hit the back of her throat.

"Ow!" she winced, accidentally moving her arm in her excitement. "What did I say about making me laugh or cough?" she scolded playfully.

"Sorry," said Jess, not looking remotely remorseful. She shoved a big handful of popcorn in her own mouth, then squeezed Remi's knee. "Fine, I'll be your waitress this evening." She took Remi's glass and swapped it with a bowl of Maltesers and popcorn. "Just let me know when you wanna swap back to your wine."

"Jeez, I need to hurt myself more often. Now this is the life!"

"Don't get too comfortable, lady. This is a special Galentine's Day only offer." Jess picked up the remote. "Now, what are we watching?"

SEVENTEEN

Jess

They'd just started the original Scream—Remi's choice—after her disbelief that Jess had never seen it. "Criminal," she'd said. Jess wasn't usually one for scary movies, though, as Remi had told her, this one was "less scares, more laughs." *We'd see about that.* The opening scene with Drew Barrymore already had Jess scooching closer to the centre of the couch. This was definitely a movie where she'd prefer a cuddle buddy. She loved reading a good murder mystery, but watching scary movies? She was an absolute wuss.

About a quarter of the way in, Jess had an idea. She'd been watching Remi fidget, rolling her head from side to side, trying to get comfortable. Jess paused the movie. "Hey, is your neck all right?"

Remi rolled her shoulders. "Just feeling a little stiff. I should be fine."

Jess patted the space in front of her. "Why don't you come sit in front of me on the carpet for a minute? I'll see if I can work some of that tension out. Can't guarantee I'm any good, but I once completed a five-dollar massage course

I bought off a coupon site. That's gotta count for something, right?"

Remi looked slightly incredulous at first, Jess sure hadn't done a great job on the convincing part, but then Remi slowly moved to the floor. "You know what, I'm just going with the flow tonight." She pulled a hair tie off her wrist with her teeth, then hesitated. "Uh, can you put my hair up?" Remi asked, passing Jess the tie as she wriggled to sit in between her legs.

Plunging her hands into Remi's hair was something else. It was thicker and longer than she'd imagined. She just wanted to grab handfuls of the stuff. And God, it smelled good. Like vanilla and sandalwood. Spicy.

"How do you tame this beast?" Jess laughed as she tried to wrangle the mass into some kind of messy top bun.

"I don't," Remi replied as Jess finally got it off her neck.

Jess resumed the movie. One dim kitchen light lit the curve of Remi's shoulders and neck in front of her, the only other light coming from the TV. Remi's loose grey camisole left a lot of skin exposed. Jess started at the base of her neck, working her way along the tops of her shoulders, then down along her spine and shoulder blades. She tried to keep her focus on the movie, but the groans Remi was eliciting at her touch made it extremely difficult.

Jess could feel her body reacting. Her legs were hot, the bare skin lightly brushing against Remi's arms breaking out in goosebumps all the way down to her ankles. She sat still, careful not to jostle Remi's sore arm.

Desire slid through her body, coiling tight in her stomach, sharp and unexpected. It shocked her. Usually, Jess needed time for things to build in the bedroom, she didn't react like this. The intensity was overwhelming. Did she need to extricate herself and cool things off? Her mind was reeling, but her hands couldn't stop touching. Roaming. She was losing control.

Her heartbeat began to pick up speed. Her breath, too. This touch was becoming wildly inappropriate from her side. She was in too far. Her thumbs pressed deep into Remi's shoulder blades, fingers lightly caressing along either side of Remi's neck and collarbones. Once or twice, she could've sworn Remi leaned into the touch.

Eyes on the movie, Jess. Focus.

Her legs almost quivered with the effort to keep still. Why had she suggested a massage in the first place? What was she doing?

She only realised her hands had stilled when Remi let out an almost pitiful mewl, nudging her hand with a shoulder bump. "So, I'm not terrible then?" Jess checked, trying her best to keep her voice light.

"You can honestly keep doing that all night, please."

So, she did.

Jess broadened her reach, working her way down Remi's back, along her sides. She swept her hands in sure, bold strokes and pinches, utilising all the techniques she'd picked up online.

"Hey, if I scooch to the back of the couch, do you want to sit in front of me? Might be more comfortable than the carpet, and I should be able to reach your lower back then too." Jess knew it was a dangerous offer, but she made it anyway.

"I feel really guilty, but it's too good to say no," Remi

replied as she shifted up. Now her arse was pushed up against her.

This was an extremely bad idea.

This was the worst, most terrible idea.

Jess had literally just pinned herself between Remi and the couch with nowhere to go.

"Okay?" Jess checked in again, her voice breaking slightly as her hands landed on Remi's lower back this time. She zeroed in on her fingers, following the touch. With the movie forgotten, her mind headed into fantasy overdrive.

"So good," Remi murmured.

This was killing her. This was self-torture. Wanting what she couldn't have, then putting it right in front of her. She was burning up at their proximity.

Before she knew it, the credits were rolling, neither of them making a move to get up. Jess's fingers lazily played at the nape of Remi's neck, then scratched down the length of her back, squeezing lightly at her hips.

She tried focusing on her breathing. It didn't help.

"Um." Jess couldn't think. "Do you want me to stop?" she almost whispered.

She waited a beat, her hands still moving.

Remi didn't respond at first. Didn't move for so long, Jess thought she hadn't heard her.

"No," Remi breathed out.

Maybe this wasn't one-sided.

Maybe Remi could feel what Jess was feeling in every stroke, every press. The thought of Remi being as turned on as she was right now? *God.* Jess tried to compose herself, her thighs wanting to squeeze together in an effort to stop the low ache that had built to breaking point in her centre. Having Remi between her legs wasn't helping.

Jess decided to test the waters, scraping and kneading at Remi's sides further around, lightly brushing the outer curves of her chest. Remi's breath caught, and Jess brushed a little harder on the next pass. This time Remi let out the smallest groan and Jess's clit pulsed in response.

Her heartbeat roared in her ears. She reached further around, this time trailing her fingers beneath Remi's bra, then tracing up her sides once more. She could see Remi breathing harder now, her chest rising and falling in sync with Jess's movements.

Leaning forward, her breasts pushed into Remi's back. Jess whispered for permission, "More?"

Remi swallowed, nodded, then shook her head.

"No?" Jess froze. Hands stilled, breath caught.

Had she read things wrong? Fuck.

Remi turned her head, eyes on Jess's lips. "We shouldn't do this."

Jess's heart thudded at Remi's mixed signals. She still didn't have an answer.

"I can stop." Jess swallowed, unable to look away from Remi's mouth, her control on a cliff's edge.

"We can't." Remi was an inch away, her wine-laced breath warm on Jess's face.

"Then get up and walk away right now. Or I'm going to kiss you."

Remi didn't move an inch.

So Jess did, closing the gap and crushing their lips together in a move that had them both groaning. The kiss was deep and messy, tongues clashing until they pulled back for air, panting. A beat passed, then Remi surged forward again. Goddamn, the woman could kiss. Of course she could. Skilled with tools *and* her mouth. Jess was impressed, though their angle was awkward as hell. Jess moved to the side to straighten things up, then pulled roughly on Remi's hair, unfurling the dark curls and allowing Jess to sink her fingers in. The kiss deepened, intense and consuming, like their lives depended on it—like this was it. The kiss to end all kisses.

Tongues explored. Groans escaped. Teeth nibbled.

"Ow!" Remi winced mid-kiss.

"Oh my god, did I hurt you?" Jess jerked away, but Remi caught her arm.

"No, that was all me—I was trying to slide my arm out of the sling."

"Maybe this isn't the best idea with an injury."

Remi carefully slid her arm free and moved it behind her on the couch. "There, problem solved. Now..." She pulled Jess back in, as Jess slid onto her lap.

Okay. This was happening. This was real.

Their chests pushed together, and Remi scratched down Jess's back with her good hand, pressing them even closer. Jess was all consumed by her taste, her feel, the fresh scent of her shampoo—

Loud music filled the room.

They sprang apart. Remi's eyes were wild, narrowing as she spotted the TV over Jess's shoulder.

"Fucking. Stupid—where's the remote?" cried Remi, hand fumbling along the couch. "Got it! Bloody auto-playing ads."

She silenced the room.

"Tell me about it. The amount of times that's scared the crap out of me when I've fallen asleep in front of the TV—"

Remi placed a finger on Jess's lips, eyes dark with focus. She dragged it slowly down her chin, her throat, and hooked it into the neckline of Jess's shirt. Remi moved lower, fingering the top of her breast against the edge of her bra.

Jess watched, mesmerised, her chest rising and falling with each breath. Remi's hooded eyes were fixed on her own hand as she slipped a finger deeper into Jess's bra and flicked Jess's already-taut nipple. It pressed against the fabric, begging to be released, the rhythm driving Jess mad. Each tweak pulsated straight to her core.

Unable to watch any longer, Jess crushed their mouths together again, palming at Remi's chest, but there were too many clothes between them and not enough skin. Breaking apart, she pulled Remi's hand away.

Confusion gave way to a knowing smile on Remi's face as Jess pulled her top off with ease, discarding it onto the floor. She unclasped her bra next, slowly easing down the straps either side before holding it out and dropping it onto her shirt.

"You are so beautiful," Remi murmured, caressing the curve of Jess's breast in a move that was so soft, so sensual. Remi's eyes followed the movement then flicked up to Jess as she licked her lips and leaned forward to take a nipple into her mouth. The heat from the movement made her suck in a breath as she arched her back into the touch. Remi kissed a path to the other one, making sure no side had more attention than the other. Structured. Precise. Just how she worked on site. Jess had no notes.

She moved up to claim Jess's mouth again, her tongue seeking entrance as her hands continued to roam. Their kiss grew hungrier by the minute, desire building, clit throbbing. Her pants were way too tight, adding friction where she needed release.

Remi must've sensed the change, sliding her hand down, cupping Jess through her pants. An uncontrolled moan escaped into Remi's mouth at the sudden contact, and she responded by pressing harder. Remi's hand moved to her waistband, but with Jess's legs spread wide, there wasn't enough room.

Remi growled. "Pants. Off. Now!"

Jess almost fell back as she scrambled to stand, her legs already wanting to cave beneath her. The pants hit the floor in an instant, stripped off in an ungainly way. She didn't care. Not with Remi looking at her like *that*. Face flushed, chest heaving. She was a tattooed goddess with dangerously dark eyes, pupils blown wide in the dim light.

"Fuck..." Remi murmured, drinking her in as she climbed back onto her lap. "You are... you are... wow."

Green eyes flicked to her mouth as Remi licked her lips and brought her hand up to caress along Jess's cheek. Fingers dived into Jess's hair next, grasping and pulling hard as Remi kissed her deeply. The pain and pleasure pulsated through her body, ending between her legs. Over and over, the waves becoming unbearable.

Remi's hand trailed down, agonisingly slow. Past her breasts that she pinched, pulled and twisted, eliciting louder moans with each touch.

Then her hand was gone. Jess whimpered, her eyes squeezed shut, hands still roaming Remi's body, squeezing and scratching what skin she had access to, willing Remi to touch her.

She was frustrated now. It had been too long. So long, since she'd been wanted like this. Kissed like this. She wanted to be touched, *god damn it*. She whined. The pitiful sound escaped her lips before she could stop it.

Remi's hand was at her entrance then. "You want this?" she whispered into Jess's mouth.

"Yes!" Jess all but panted.

One finger slipped in.

"More!" Jess commanded.

A fire lit under her as Remi added a second. Finally, she was filled with the touch she craved. Jess moved with Remi's rhythm, fucking herself on Remi's hand. Their sounds filled the room, and she loved every second of it.

They sped up, everything becoming messy and sloppy as they lost themselves completely in each other. Jess bounced desperately. Remi broke the kiss to watch her, her eyes were filled with so much heat, so much desire in that one look. Remi's lips were pink and swollen, dark hair spilled everywhere. She watched on as Jess rode her fingers with every stroke, gaze unwavering.

It was the hottest thing Jess had ever seen, and it was enough to tip her over the edge, the build-up coming out of nowhere as she screamed out, tightening around Remi's hand as wave after wave crashed through her. She jerked uncontrollably, riding the high of one of the biggest orgasms she'd ever experienced. She collapsed against Remi, panting into her neck as she came down. She planted soft kisses on Remi's warm skin, the taste of salt only adding to the heady experience.

Remi finally pulled her hand away, making Jess jerk once more as she sat up.

Wow. The last time Jess had slept with a woman, it hadn't been like this. She'd been young, drunk and explorative. The few female partners she'd had varied wildly in degrees of significance... and recollection. The memories were filled with a blur of reserved touches, awkward moments and holding back, getting lost in her head rather than in the moment.

Tonight was different, her emotions so heightened, she'd given herself over to Remi entirely. This was new. Unexpected. And so... intoxicating. What had she started?

Jess could see how much energy it had taken from Remi, though the hunger remained in her eyes.

"Bedroom?" Jess asked, tilting her head.

She wasn't finished yet.

EIGHTEEN

Remi

Remi couldn't pull her eyes away. Couldn't believe what they'd just done. No one had ever turned her on like this. Made her this *crazed*. God, it had been so long since she'd been with someone... never more evident than tonight. Jess was incredibly beautiful, soft curves and thighs she just wanted to grab, press and stroke. She wished she had the use of both hands, though it hadn't hampered her yet...

The pain in her arm was completely forgotten. Jess took her by the hand, pulling her up from the couch and leading her down the hallway to the bedroom. Remi's eyes trailed to her arse, catching on—

"Is that... a slice of pepperoni pizza?"

Jess sauntered into Remi's room, stopping at the side of her bed and turning around with a mischievous grin. "It is. Want a bite, *Donatello*?"

Remi took her in again, ready to devour. She raised an eyebrow, stepping into her space, squeezing the back of Jess's thigh where she'd spotted the tattoo.

"Why pepperoni pizza?" she whispered against Jess's lips as she claimed her mouth.

"Mmm," Jess hummed, breaking the kiss just enough to reply, "From my uni days. I survived on pizza, so Marie and I got our obsession immortalised with matching tattoos."

"Marie? From your birthday party?"

"Mmhmm," Jess hummed once more. "Except she got ham and pineapple."

"Blasphemy." Remi smiled into their kiss.

"Enough. Talking," Jess said between kisses, breaking contact to lift Remi's camisole and ease it over her head. She was thankful she'd worn loose clothing. Her sports bra was next, the removal awkward thanks to her arm. They managed to get it off with giggles and a little finagling.

"Finally," breathed Jess, pulling Remi close so they were skin-to-skin. Fingers hooked into her waistband, dragging her pants down as Jess trailed kisses down her chest, leaving a trail of goosebumps in her wake. Jess moved back up, breasts *dragging* against Remi's skin deliciously slow, driving her crazy.

Remi sucked in a slow breath, trying to ease the ache between her legs. Not having been touched in so long, and watching Jess ride her before, meant turned on didn't even begin to describe where she was at right now. She feared the lightest brush and she'd be—

Oh. Fuck.

She hissed as Jess's hand slipped between her folds. She was embarrassingly wet. Blue eyes held hers as Jess swiped her tongue along the bottom of Remi's lips, warm fingers gliding back and forth.

Her tongue swiped again, hot breath mingling.

Fingers gliding.

Tongue.

Fingers.

It was too much. Too good.

She groaned into Jess's mouth. Jess pressed harder, speeding up, and Remi fell *hard*.

It was beautiful. She swore she saw light behind her eyes as everything tensed in her body. It was overwhelming, then something bubbled up inside her... and she was laughing—uncontrollably—hanging onto Jess as she waited for the tingles to subside, and her giggling to calm.

Jess was laughing now too, unsure. She searched Remi's face. "Are you okay?"

"Yeah. I. Wow. Just. Jess—"

How did you describe the elation she'd just felt? So high on life and happiness that all she could do was laugh. Like there was no other way for the emotion to escape. A cathartic moment so profound. She was in awe. The last few weeks had played such an emotional, heavy toll on her. She didn't realise how much her body needed this release. A connection with someone she trusted enough to allow herself to let go and revel in a moment of pure joy.

All in the space of a few strokes.

"Jess, you're... that... was amazing." Her grin was ridiculous, and she didn't even care how embarrassingly quick she'd come beneath Jess's touch.

Jess grinned wickedly, pulling her to the bed. "I'm not done yet."

～

Remi felt the warm press against her skin, a hand splayed across her naked chest. Her arm ached from the position she must've fallen asleep in. She tried moving her fingers a little more. Sharp pain lanced through her. *Still*. She clenched her teeth, trying not to move. Blinking open her eyes, she focused on the golden hair and soft face of Jess asleep, curled up against her. Morning light shone through the Venetian blinds in her bedroom. She thought of last night and felt an ache of a completely different kind.

Wow.

That was a Valentine's—or *Galentine's*—Day she wouldn't forget anytime soon.

After the past week, it felt good to wake up without thinking about the million things she had to solve, fix, build or do. She'd forgotten how nice it was to be close with another person. To share herself completely, enjoying each other until passing out.

But now what? This shouldn't have happened. *She* shouldn't have let it happen. Taking advantage of Jess like that surely wasn't right. She was her apprentice for god's sake.

"*Fuck,*" she wordlessly mouthed to the ceiling.

Maybe it was a one-time thing. A rebound for Jess, a craving for human connection for her. Now, they'd done it. They'd got it out of their systems and that would be that. They could go on as friends, working alongside each other... Remi imagined Jess in those stupid pink safety boots and her little shorts just working away and, *ugh*. Why did she have to be so amazing? Why did she have to be such an attentive partner in bed? Probably one of the best Remi had ever had. Okay, pretty sure she'd set a new record for the amount of orgasms they'd shared last night. And all one handed none-the-less. Remi was impressed with that feat.

This would've been so much easier if Jess was still a waitress. Sans boyfriend, of course. No strings. It would've been fine. But this?

Jess stirred, fingers flexing, lazily moving over Remi's breast in slow strokes. Remi sucked in a breath, her body instantly awake with the contact. Jess brought her thigh up on top of Remi next, she felt Jess's centre pushing against her hip as she began pinching Remi's nipple to the rhythm she'd started.

Every fibre of her body lit up, ultra-sensitive to each touch from Jess. It was like a spark, constantly igniting her from the inside out. Jess's warm hand slid between Remi's thighs next. Remi bit down on her lip, writhing along with Jess's movements. It wasn't going to take much. Again.

Jess lifted her head off Remi's chest, eyes locking on to hers, a smirk on her lips.

"Good morning," Jess practically purred, hand continuing its languid strokes as she ground herself harder against Remi's hip. She could feel how wet Jess was, and—

"Fuck... morning..." Remi moaned in response, unable to form coherent sentences anymore. Jess slipped a finger in next, slowly pulling it out and stroking her clit. Back and forth she went, making Remi want to roll her eyes back. It was all too much. So many sensations.

Jess sped up, her hips bucking and thrashing in urgency, sounds from both of them bouncing around the room, until they both cried out and stilled. The only sound was a magpie outside the window, singing his merry tune or cheering them on, who knew. Remi was fucked. Every which way, she was thoroughly, thoroughly gone. And Jess was at the centre of it all.

God help her.

Later, dressed and full from breakfast and lazy kisses, Remi knew she needed to broach the topic of what this was between them, but in her hazy post-orgasm and slow Sunday morning state, that was a little harder than it had been when she'd first woken up.

Before Jess had blown all cohesive thought out the bedroom window. Honestly, it was impressive.

"We need to talk."

"Uh-oh. I feel like I'm in trouble." Jess gave a wry smile as she took another bite of her Vegemite toast.

"Wipe that smile off or I won't be able to keep this serious."

Jess's attempt at being serious looked ridiculous, making Remi chuckle anyway.

"You know this can't happen again, right? I'm your boss, Jess. I don't want to take advantage of you or blur the boundaries between work and—"

"The bedroom?" Jess finished for her.

"I mean it's more than that. I know we've been hanging out because we're both going through a lot right now, but I feel like I need to put some space here." She gestured between them with her spoon, then took a scoop of her cereal.

"Is that what you want? Or is that what you think we should do because of them?" Jess pointed to the front door. "Because of what others might think? I don't know about you, but last night was incredible. God. I'm not trying to climb a career ladder, I just feel this insane attraction to you, and last night it felt like there was no other choice but to sleep together."

"I don't know what I want. I didn't think last night could, or would, ever happen."

"So, you *were* thinking about it then."

"Jess, you just got out of a serious relationship two weeks ago."

"I'm not asking for a ring. Why don't we just... enjoy each other's company for now? Keep it between us?"

"Like friends with benefits?"

"Yeah."

Remi blew out a breath, mulling it over. She twirled the spoon in her hand and looked at Jess—glowing, relaxed, toast crumbs on her lips... She felt that pull in her chest again. The part of her that didn't want space, didn't want distance.

"This is a bad idea."

NINETEEN

Jess

Jess did not set out to get a fuck buddy today. Yet, here she was.

Remi had left half an hour ago when Sophie had picked her up for a family visit and playdate with Hudson. That left Jess alone with her thoughts, the turtle and instructions to feed him a couple of crickets. Easy peasy.

She'd spent the morning cleaning up after their movie-and-surprise-sex marathon. Somehow, popcorn had ended up *everywhere*. Adam had messaged, asking when she'd be back and if his clothes would be ready for Monday. She'd given him the hard task of either turning on the machine himself or taking it around the corner to his mum's. She knew what option he'd pick.

The space from him had been good. Necessary. Usually, she would've just done his laundry. Although it pained her to say, her first thought today had still been to quickly drive home and put a load on for him. Old Jess would have.

New Jess needed to introduce healthy boundaries with ex-boyfriends. She could still be his friend, still be there for him. But she didn't have to be his mother anymore. It wasn't like he had an injury like Remi. And boy, that did not set *her* back in the achievements department.

Last night had unlocked something in Jess. A raw, animalistic side she'd discovered; set free. She'd never been that wild in bed with Adam. Remi had awakened something within her, and all she wanted to do was explore it further. She understood why Remi thought they shouldn't continue. On so many levels. But denying herself, denying them more of what they'd shared last night? Unfathomable.

The question remained: Was last night so good because someone had wanted her so badly? Because Remi had desired her and simply made her feel good? Or was it that Jess's attraction ran deeper than first thought, and spending the night together only strengthened it?

Either way, it made her realise how much that connection had been lacking with Adam. How much her walls had gone up around him as time had gone on, until he was completely shut out. No wonder she'd been ready to walk away and into someone else's arms so soon. There was no physical attraction or connection left with him by the end.

Jess could tell she was fixated on Remi now. She'd had a taste, and it wasn't enough. She wanted more. Even with her gone for a couple of hours today felt weird, the house felt too quiet. She craved that closeness again. She picked up a photo frame of Remi and Sophie as kids. They looked to be on a beach holiday, matching red one-piece bathers, big grins and boogie boards. Jess smiled as she placed it back down on the bookshelf and turned to Ninja.

"Right, bud. Time for snacks and exercise." He was clawing at the corner of the tank again, so she lifted him out like Remi had taught her. Success! Once again, he turned to follow her. She headed to the kitchen cupboard where Remi had said the crickets were. Chirping alerted her to the right spot as soon as she opened the door.

"How the hell am I going to do this?" she muttered to herself, spying the pair of long handled tweezers behind the container as she picked it up. "Oh, thank god."

Ninja was already trying to climb his way up her tennis shoe, eyes on the crickets in her hand. She knelt down. "You hungry, huh?"

Carefully undoing the lid, she kept it on top of the container so they wouldn't escape. Ninja's neck was stretched out to the max trying to see the food.

Oops, the tweezers! She looked around and spotted them on the bench. *Aha!* She reached up to grab them, but they slipped from her fingers at the last second. Metal glinted in the air. She fumbled, smacking them with the back of her hand instead.

"Oh, for the love of—" They clattered behind her, so she stretched back to pick them up. "Woah, shit!" Eyes wide, she lost her balance, landing flat on her back with a thump.

Crickets.

Crickets were raining down on her.

She screamed as one landed on her nose, then jumped off behind her head. She sat up, hands swiping as crickets skittered and hopped across the kitchen floor.

Oh. My. God.

She swiped the container off the ground, capturing a few stragglers and slamming the lid back on. Ninja was in heaven, his eyes darting around not knowing which one to go after first. Jess set into action, trying to cup each one with her hands and get them back in one at a time. They wriggled, clawed and hopped within her hand.

Don't think about it. Don't think about it. Don't think about it. Her body let out an involuntary shudder. She was determined to get these little guys wrangled before Remi got back.

"Fuck. Fuck. Fuck," she uttered, scrounging around on her hands and knees as the bugs scattered.

Ten minutes later, at least half were wrangled. Hands on hips, she surveyed the room, spotting two in the hallway. "How'd you get over there?!"

Back on her hands and knees, she kept trying to cup the cricket in front of her who refused to sit still. Her hands smacked the wooden floorboard. *Hop.* To the left, smack! *Hop.* Right. *Hop.*

He stopped.

"Got you now, you little shit—"

"What are you doing?!"

Remi stood in the open doorway, key still in the lock, the weirdest expression on her face.

Jess turned for a proper look over her shoulder, mortified. Her butt was up in the air, both hands cupped— successfully, she might add—over the current insect-in-crime. She blew a piece of hair out of her face.

"Listen. It's all good," she said, slightly breathless. "There are maybe a couple of roaming crickets in your house, but I think I got most of them."

Remi shut the door, walking over to tower above her, a wry smile forming. "I see."

"I'm so sorry."

"Honestly, it doesn't look so bad from where I'm standing." Remi's eyes simmered, falling to Jess's butt as she bit her lip.

"Ha-ha," said Jess, concentrating back on the bug.

"All jokes aside, you think I haven't lost a cricket or two over the years? Only thing is, there's no way I'm catching them at the moment with this arm. I can help you spot them, though. Hey, where's Ninja?" Remi asked, looking over at the empty tank.

Fuck. She'd forgotten the bloody turtle.

In her haste to catch and return all the crickets, Ninja had been the last thing on her mind.

Act cool.

"He's, uh, out for a wander. Catching his own lunch."

"You have no idea where he is, do you?"

The captive cricket began hopping madly under Jess's hands in a last-ditch effort to escape. "At this very moment... no?" she squeaked out.

"Right. I'll find the little dude. You," she gestured vaguely with her good hand, "keep catching the hoppers."

"Yes, boss." She winked.

Work felt different today. Lighter.

Jess wasn't sure what to expect on site now that things had changed between them. She'd be lying if she said she wasn't a little nervous climbing into the car this morning. But then Remi had leaned across the console and kissed her. A kiss so soft, she'd melted instantly. A small, tender kiss

200

that lingered more deeply than anything they'd shared so far.

Of course, the sweetness didn't last. Even with Remi off the tools, there were more touches, heated looks and dirty words muttered under their breath. The effort it took to act normal at work made everything that much hotter. Jess was so turned on by smoko, it wasn't funny. They had to reign it in. She didn't want to stuff this up—not her job, not with Remi, not with Sophie, and definitely not with their clients.

The rest of her weekend had been the most glorious mix of eating, movies and ending up back in Remi's bed. Jess could've done without the escapee crickets, but all-in-all? A *great* weekend. When her alarm had woken them at the ungodly dark hour of six this morning, she hadn't wanted it to be over and had to drag herself into the shower.

Jess could tell Remi was struggling work wise. They were already behind last week and now, with Remi's injury? She had no idea how they were going to keep it all up. Remi had refused to stay home today, so instead of being on the tools, she was spending more time telling Jess what to do. Jess was loving the attention it brought, but the pressure on her to perform was a lot. As a first-year apprentice, everything was new, slow and she needed to be switched on. And while Remi was fun and flirty, she was serious when it came to both the business and the work.

"Set the level up to 870mm," suggested Remi.

Jess adjusted the laser level to Remi's tape measure height on the wall. "Wouldn't it be 720mm?" Jess countered.

"That's the base cabinet height only. You need to add in the kickboard height."

"*Right*," Jess stretched the word out as realisation dawned.

"Sophie, you finished those last two cabinets yet?" asked Remi.

"Trying," Sophie said, her face scrunched in concentration as she rotated a heavy base cabinet.

Level set, Jess moved to grab the drill she'd left near Remi, her breasts brushing up against Remi's arse as she did so. She caught the intake of breath and smiled to herself.

It was as if all her senses had been heightened. Five minutes later, she watched Remi's tongue flick out to wet her lip as she read an email on her phone, completely oblivious. Jess's muscles tensed, on high alert. She kept trying to focus on the work at hand, but with Remi going through each instruction in close proximity and nothing better to do, their games were becoming dangerous.

They were playing with fire.

TWENTY

Remi

Not being able to touch the tools was killing her. Not being able to touch Jess on site... also killing her. Remi was so thankful it was summer, because at least she *could* watch Jess in those shorts, a hint of her thigh tattoo poking out at just the right angle. Discovering *that* the other night was a treat.

Argh. This was already becoming a huge distraction she didn't need right now. A pleasant distraction, but a distraction nonetheless.

"Remi, why don't you order that benchtop for the Smith's? Gary finally made up his mind, so you might as well send it off while the couple are on the same page," Sophie said.

Remi knew what Sophie was doing. She was trying to get her out of the way. But goddamn it—surely she could help somehow? Just because one hand was out of action didn't mean she couldn't do anything. She could be ambidextrous. Saturday night had proved that. She thought back to Jess bouncing on her—

Sex daydreaming, really? Still not helping, Remi!

She tested out a drill with her left hand. A quick pull of the trigger still felt all right. This could work. She put the drill down and she picked up a couple of screws, trying to line one up into the bracket they were working on. She leaned over, drill back in hand—

"Remi! What are you doing?" Jess snapped, sounding exasperated.

She flinched, pressing on the trigger too hard, sending the screw flying and the drill into the bracket.

"I'm fine." Remi tried to defend herself, putting down the drill to pick up the screw again. This really did take much longer with one hand. She straightened and glanced at Jess, screw reacquired.

"What?" Remi asked as Jess stood there with her hands on her hips.

"Put the tools down. I may be an apprentice, but even I know this is stupid."

Sophie peeked out from behind her cabinet at the outburst, disapproval on her face and an agreement on her tongue. "Remi, that's enough. Just do what the doctor told you and *rest*, or you'll end up in the ER with your other hand next."

"What she said," Jess replied, picking up Remi's drill and putting it back in the toolbox. "I left you for two minutes to go to the toilet and you couldn't sit on your butt for that long?"

Remi opened her mouth to reply, but her phone started ringing. She dropped the screw and fished her phone out of her pocket instead.

"Cole, how's it going?"

"I wish I could say great. I was happy with your work, but Declan from Karkalla is telling me the tiles are cut wrong in the shower, and it's not going to drain properly."

Oh, for fu—she closed her eyes, took in a deep breath before responding.

"I see. I can assure you Cole, everything we do is to code. The way we've done it means cleaner lines and a better finish on the tiles, with proper drainage."

"I'm just unsure who to believe. It might be easier to get one team to finish off the job, and Karkalla has the bigger team..."

Of course, Declan would try to throw her under the bus on the Donaldsons' job. Why today? Of all days.

"Cole, I promise you—it's fine. Leave it with me and I'll call you back shortly."

She turned to Sophie, relaying the news. Her sister's cheeks were as red as her lipstick by the time she finished.

"At this point, I almost want to just give Declan the job, so we don't have to work with him anymore. Flinders is just around the corner. It could ease our workload," Sophie suggested.

Remi was so sick of letting people get away with tearing others down, pointing fingers where they didn't belong, of edging others out of the industry one accusation at a time. It wasn't right.

"I'm not letting that weasel-face go around telling our clients we're putting out sub-par work. But at this stage it's my word against theirs," Remi replied, kicking the screw across the floor. "Fuck." She rubbed at her temples, trying to think.

Her stomach dropped as memories came rushing back.

She didn't want to remember, didn't want to let those ghosts return; the screaming in her face when she'd done the wrong thing. The tools snatched from her hands while being told she'd never learn. It was never *"Hey, this is how it's meant to be done."* Instead, all she heard was, *"What? You still can't do that?" "How are you so bad at a simple cut?" "You stuffed it."*

Declan consistently dredged up old wounds, hitting her where it hurt most. She didn't want to second-guess herself anymore, didn't want to let doubt seep back in. How did you prove yourself in a man's world? Who was Cole more likely to trust? Sometimes, gender was enough to tip the scales. She scowled at the ground.

"Why don't you get a building inspection done?" asked Jess, pulling her from the dark spiral. Remi looked up as Jess drilled the bracket into place with precision. This amazing woman who, a few months ago, had pretty much never touched a tool in her life.

Remi had done this.

She'd helped someone gain self-confidence, in work and skill, without those imposter syndrome monsters lurking beneath the surface. Remi felt ashamed that she still carried her past pain with her as much as she did.

Jess continued on, oblivious to Remi's internal struggles. "That way it would be an unbiased third-party opinion, *and* it would buy you some time on the project to get other work completed."

Jess's advice was sound. Remi raised her eyebrows, considering. Cole couldn't oppose facts on paper.

"That is a cost I usually wouldn't want to shoulder. But... Soph—want to give Sandra a call? See if she'd do us a favour? This could actually work." She looked back at Jess. "How do you know about building inspections?"

"My friend Taylor made us get one on an old rental that had mould problems. They wouldn't take us seriously until we had the report in hand."

Another pair of women fighting to be heard. It didn't give her any solace to share that particular common ground.

"Well, there you go."

She eyed Sophie. "I think we pay Declan a quick visit. Can you drive?"

Ten minutes later, Sophie pulled onto the street. "Bingo," Remi murmured as the Karkalla Renovation vans came into view.

They were out of the car in an instant, Remi heading straight for the kitchen. "Declan. Can we have a word, mate?"

His eyes widened, narrowing once he realised who it was. He zeroed in on Remi's strapped arm, a small smile curling on his lips. Of course he'd revel in her pain. Such an arsehole.

"We can handle the rest here, girls." He stood tall, chest puffed, arms crossed, a satisfied smile in place. "We'll fix up the tiles and get it sorted for Cole. Wouldn't want you to hurt another finger." He nodded at her arm.

"Declan, there's nothing *to* fix. If you touch those tiles, you'll ruin the waterproofing layer, not to mention cause any other multitude of issues. I've already spoken with Cole. Stay away from our work and butt out," she spat, old hurt bubbling up in waves. At least these days she *did* have the confidence to stand up for herself.

He put his hands up in mock placation. "Hey, fine. But

don't come to me when the water starts running straight towards the toilet."

"I'm not hanging around to listen to your shit. Stay out of it!" she warned with more vehemence this time. She turned on her heel, Sophie jogging to catch up. She needed to get out of here before she said something she'd regret. She didn't want to stoop to his level. Ever.

"Hope your arm gets better!" he shouted down the hallway, zero sympathy in his words as the front door shut behind them.

Remi marched to their car, slamming the passenger door. She let out a cry of frustration as Sophie hopped into the driver's seat, delicately buckling her seatbelt and driving away. The radio murmured in the background, the soft click of the indicator the only other sound between them. Remi sat slumped in her seat, jaw clenched, staring out the window. Her sister knew to give her space when she got like this. It had been a long time since she'd been this triggered. And now she was frustrating herself for getting so worked up.

"Sorry," Remi said after a few minutes, offering Sophie an apologetic smile. "I swear, it's like I go from zero to a hundred whenever I have to deal with him."

Sophie patted her knee. "Hey," she soothed. "I get it. I *completely* get it. He knows how to poke the bear. And after the last few days? You didn't need this kind of crap on top of everything. It's okay to feel angry and let off some of that steam. God knows I'm feeling it too."

God, she loved her sister. So much.

"Has anyone told you, you're the best sister ever?"

Sophie gave her a brilliant smile. "You can tell me that as much as you like. Right back at you, Bug."

～

Jess drove Remi home. The tension that had built all day on site now palpable in the small confines of Jess's hatchback. Remi felt fidgety, the anticipation of possibly touching Jess again at an all-time high—and if Jess's heated looks were any indication, she wasn't the only one eager to get back. With the morning she'd had, Remi's anger had simmered into raw, hot desire. To touch and be touched. They hadn't talked about how long Jess was staying. The initial one-night requirement had now turned into three and counting. After the day she'd had, she was thankful to have someone else home with her tonight. The implications of that, having Jess stay in her space, she'd deal with later. Right now, she wasn't thinking with her head... or her heart.

Remi fumbled with the key at the front door, awkward in her left hand. Her fingers were almost shaking, which was ridiculous. Warm breath brushed across her ear just as the key slipped into the lock.

"If you don't hurry up and open that door..." Jess purred, squeezing her arse. "Your neighbours are going to be scarred for life." She licked Remi's ear lobe, making her groan as the door finally unlocked.

They tumbled into the hallway. Remi kicked the door shut with her boot and whirled on Jess, pushing her against the wall with her good hand, lips on hers in an instant. She wanted to devour her. That fruity scent went straight to her head. Remi pressed their bodies together, desperate for as much contact as physically possible. Their warm thighs touched, the heat already intense from riding in Jess's car, left sitting out in the sun all day. Jess's hands roamed, palming up and down Remi's back, arse and thighs as her tongue deepened their kiss. Remi felt wild, planning all the things she wanted to do to Jess after fantasising about it... All. Damn. Day.

Then Jess's hand slipped down the front of her pants. Coherent thoughts vanished. Jess kissed her neck, sliding her tongue up to nibble on Remi's ear lobe as her fingers slid between her folds.

Remi sucked in a breath, struggling to remain upright.

"You like that?" Jess whispered, her hot breath in Remi's ear sending her into overdrive.

All she could do was nod as Jess found a dangerous rhythm on her clit. Fuck. She was so close, her legs weakening under the touch, her hand against the wall the only thing keeping her upright. Jess kissed her again, tongue seeking out Remi's as her delicate fingers rubbed maddeningly back and forth, picking up pace. Remi squeezed her eyes shut, letting her body take over. The build-up hit out of nowhere, her whole body collapsing onto Jess.

Jess grinned devilishly.

"Wow," Remi panted, breathless.

She was in awe of this woman, her azure eyes now dancing with joy against the afternoon light filtering in through the windows.

"That was not part of my plan," Remi said with a hiss as Jess removed her hand. She was still *so* sensitive.

"No?" Jess questioned, biting her lip, head falling back against the wall, eyes darkening.

"Not at all," Remi replied, grabbing her by the hand and pulling her down the hallway.

They didn't make it far before landing on the couch. Then the carpet. Then finally—the bed. Four orgasms later, and Remi thought she had well and truly gone to heaven. Jess was a goddess. She'd never felt this off-the-charts chemistry before. Ever. She had no idea where all the energy had come from. Perhaps it was the frustration and anger from work finding its release? Her arm—even though she'd tried to keep it still or out of the way—was now starting to ache from all the movement. Jess straddled her, a sheen of sweat visible across her collarbones and chest. She bent down to kiss Remi, then reached over to the nightstand. It took everything in Remi to not suck in another nipple.

"What's the time?" asked Jess, grabbing her phone. "Shit, it's almost eight. We need to eat." She looked around the room. Their work clothes were strewn everywhere, scattered throughout the rest of the house. Now that they'd stopped, Remi realised how hungry she was. Jess ran a hand down Remi's chest, idly caressing her sides, making goosebumps spring up in her wake. "Want me to cook us some dinner?

Remi squeezed her hip. "I think we need it after all that, don't you?"

"I'm gonna need to eat double if you keep working me this hard at work *and* home."

Home.

The word landed deeper than Jess had probably intended. She'd originally come to take care of Remi, but even labelling them as friends-with-benefits felt too simplistic. It was starting to feel more and more like a domestic relationship. Remi felt uneasy with how serious they were getting so quickly, like it was the easiest thing in the world. Their lives slotting into place together.

It didn't feel right though, not like this, not hiding Jess away or feeling like she was using her as a release for pent up feelings and old frustrations. Though their time together felt mutual, something didn't sit right. The why behind it all. She felt torn, unsure how to talk about something she currently had no better solution for.

Jess gave her a playful wink, oblivious to Remi's inner turmoil. She lithely got off the bed, stretching her naked body from side to side and heading for the door. Remi watched on, unable to look away.

"I'm gonna grab a quick shower first, if you want to join?" Jess threw over her shoulder, a cheeky smile in place.

"If I do, we aren't going to eat," replied Remi, head falling back onto her pillow.

"Fine." Jess pouted as she walked out.

Remi glanced at the door and sighed. She could watch that butt all day.

The next morning, Remi woke to a cold bed. They'd agreed to sleep in separate rooms, knowing otherwise they wouldn't get much sleep. Remi needed it. She needed this time to think. Really think.

Outside, a light wind danced through the leaves of her ornamental pear tree, making them shimmer in the morning light. It was going to be another scorching day, and for once she was thankful she wouldn't be on the tools. Since her accident, things had been going so fast. So many changes in all areas of her life. She realised she hadn't given herself even five minutes of downtime to stop and collect her thoughts.

Half an hour later, she stared up at the ceiling knowing what she had to do and she didn't like it.

Not one little bit.

TWENTY-ONE

Jess

"Good morning! Wasn't sure if I would see you before I left. Very proud of you for *staying home* today, by the way." Jess smiled at Remi emerging from the bedroom as she loaded up the dishwasher with her brekkie dishes.

Remi didn't respond with the usual cheery attitude, and Jess knew straight away something was up. She still wasn't sure where they stood during the in-between-times of their *benefits* situation. Last night had felt pretty couple-y to her as they'd eaten dinner together and snuggled on the couch watching trash TV. This morning, though, gave very serious-boss-I-shouldn't-touch vibes that left Jess rooted to the spot, waiting to see what Remi did next.

Remi scratched her head—it was the messiest Jess had ever seen it, still completely mussed up from their adventurous evening the night before. It wasn't helping the urge Jess had to touch her all over again. Remi padded over and took a seat at the kitchen bench.

"I've been thinking..."

"You don't say," Jess said good-naturedly, earning a small smile.

"I like you a lot."

"This is sounding like a break-up. Just been there, remember?" Jess played with the edge of the kitchen bench-top, unsure how to stand or where to look, a sinking feeling starting to grow.

"Exactly. Which is why I wanted to talk to you." A pause. Remi bit at her lip as she met Jess's gaze. "I thought I could do friends-with-benefits, but it still doesn't feel right —to me. But don't get me wrong. Being with you these last few days has been out-of-this-world incredible. Like, Best Sex, Most Orgasms, all of the awards go to you."

Remi gave her a small smile. They were some pretty amazing accolades, but right now, they left Jess feeling empty. She didn't like where this was heading.

"I'm not denying I like you. But—and it's a very important but—if I'm going to be with you, I want to date you. And I... I can't give you that right now. I'm such a mess. Sleeping with you like I have still feels like I'm using you, even if only subconsciously." She looked at Jess seriously then.

"And that is the last thing I'd ever, *ever* want to do to you."

She held up a hand as Jess went to protest. "I love our friendship, and your workmanship, and I think continuing what we were doing with the baggage we currently have, isn't doing this for the right reasons. When I'm with you, I want to be able to give you my whole self, and I'm not just talking about when my arm is healed. I'm consumed by work being an absolute dumpster fire right now, and you haven't even had a minute to discover who this new, recently-thirty Jess is without someone at your side."

Jess's eyes shone at the earnest outpouring. As good as their time together had been, she'd had the same niggling feeling at the back of her mind. She didn't like it, but the last thing she wanted to do was stuff up what they had. Remi was one of the brightest lights in her life. In so many ways. Friend. Teacher. Lover. She'd taken all of it for granted, and if she lost all that, all of *her*, by jumping into this before they were ready... she'd never forgive herself.

"Goddamn, you have a way with words."

While she didn't want the outcome, she knew Remi's words to be true. "Argh. You're right though. Spending this time with you has been so nice, but we're both probably comfort-seeking right now, for different reasons. And while being close to you physically has made me indescribably happy—you're right. We need to figure out our shit. Properly. I should also head back to my place to give us some physical space, or, you know... my hand might slip." Jess gave an innocent shrug, trying to lighten the mood and let Remi know she understood.

It earned her a small chuckle, Remi's shoulders visibly relaxing. "And we wouldn't want that. I think staying at yours would be for the best. You're welcome to stay one more night, if only so I don't have to cook dinner again." Remi sighed wistfully, her eyes lingering on Jess. She felt it everywhere and wished she could go to her even now and wrap her up in a hug. Jess sure wanted the comfort.

"I really will miss your company," Remi finally said.

"Me too," Jess replied softly. "Okay. One more night, and I'll make sure dinner's sorted."

The car ride to work felt oddly quiet. Jess had become used to Remi's constant presence over the past few days. She'd usually fill any silence with anecdotes from past jobs, fielding calls for current ones or talking about proud aunty moments with Hudson. Jess was in awe of how Remi saw the world, always caring for those around her and able to juggle a million things at once. She wasn't sure she had the mental aptitude to do what Remi took on.

At smoko, Jess sat amongst the half-demolished kitchen with an iced coffee and a sausage roll. *Breakfast of champions,* she sniggered to herself as she bit into the flaky pastry. Her phone vibrated in her pocket. She answered it mid-bite.

"It hasn't even been three hours. You miss me?" Jess teased around a mouthful of food, earning a quizzical look from Sophie.

Reign in the flirting, Jess. They were meant to be friends *now.*

"You fancy yourself too much, Newbie," Remi played back. Jess was glad their banter was still alive and well. She'd been unsure how things would be since their morning discussion, but this was so effortless. She wasn't surprised they'd fallen straight back into their regular rhythm.

"I just called my friend, JJ."

"The painter?" Jess checked.

"Yep. A few weeks back she mentioned she was looking to rent out a room at her place, which is like five minutes away from me. Anyway, I checked, and it's still available. And as I know you're not a psycho, you're automatically vetted. You don't have to take it, but, uh... I know you weren't racing to get back under the same roof as your ex."

"Oh, wow." There went Remi again, sorting out everyone else's problems. "That's so thoughtful." If she was honest, she'd been dreading returning to her guest room. The awkwardness of seeing Adam again, being in each other's space, it wasn't what she wanted or needed right now. The fact Remi had even thought to look out for Jess like that, with everything else going on in her life... it sure tugged at the heart strings.

"Tell her I'm interested, and I'd be happy to get in touch."

JJ responded almost immediately, and by the end of smoko, it looked like Jess had a new place lined up after all.

That afternoon, she and Sophie had completely demolished the kitchen and bathroom. Now they just had to clean up the debris. Jess filled buckets with tile and rubble, hauling them out to throw in the skip. Even though she'd only been an apprentice for a month, she could feel the changes in her body from all the physical work, especially in her legs. Her arms were already fairly strong from slinging plates of pasta to patrons over the years, but the physical demands of building were a whole other level.

"Has Remi seemed okay?" Sophie asked as Jess placed the empty buckets in front of her to fill.

"Okay, how?" Jess checked.

Sophie stood and leaned on the shovel. "I mean, how do you think she's doing? Has she been acting any differently that you've noticed?"

Jess's brain helpfully supplied the image of her on top

of Remi on the couch, her incredibly talented hand curling just—

"No," she replied quickly, shaking her head for added effect. Completely unnecessary. She felt herself heating. Thank god she had a dust mask and safety glasses on; she was already red-faced from exertion. She didn't need Sophie noticing the guilt currently manifesting under her gear.

"I'm worried about her."

Oh. *Right*.

Work related.

Not suspecting they were sleeping together. She tried to switch gears and think back over the last few days. Had she noticed anything up with Remi?

"I mean, she works a lot at home. She's always on the laptop, sorting emails and orders, or on the phone chatting with suppliers and clients. But she hasn't said anything to me specifically."

"Oh, she'd never say anything. Remi's too proud for that. I just worry she's taken on too much." Sophie paused. "Please keep this between us. But you've seen the mistakes she's made recently, and now with her accident... I just wish I could fast-forward time. Get these last few projects out, start Flinders and have Remi back on board with her arm as good as new."

"We'll get there. Look at us today." Jess gestured to the bomb site that had been a dated, old bathroom just that morning. "We've made so much progress. As for Remi, why don't we try planning a team meeting? Under the guise of a new initiative now that the team's grown? We could set it as a monthly thing, to check in with the progress of each project, share goals or ideas we have for the business moving forward and talk through any issues. Together."

"Well, that sounds very logical and easy. Why didn't I think of that?"

"Because you're both incredibly busy women, with a family, a business to run, projects to complete—the list goes on. Neither of you is stopping to take a breather. Even standing here like this for five minutes isn't done enough. It's no wonder the business has probably felt like it's swallowing you both whole."

Sophie nodded, getting more animated as she thought it over. "Leave it with me." She picked up the shovel. "I'll make it happen."

After work that night, Jess swung past her place to pick up a change of clothes and check in on things. Adam had still been messaging her quite frequently, anything from asking where the dishwashing tablets lived to asking whether there was more toilet paper stashed somewhere. He was slowly learning.

The place was a mess, dishes gathered *around* the sink, a work shirt slung over a dining chair. She stifled the urge to clean again, heading straight for the bedroom. It wasn't her problem anymore. The front door thudded shut just as she zipped up her duffle bag. Adam appeared in the doorway.

"You're back," he said, the slightest hint of hopefulness slipping through. He stood with bloodshot eyes, a five o'clock shadow and a gaze that made her heart hurt. She noticed the crumpled shirt next, half untucked. God, he looked like shit.

She cleared her throat, realising she'd been staring at his

scruffy transformation. "Uh, yeah, just to grab some more clothes."

"Oh." He dropped his head.

"I'm moving out. I've found a new place to stay. I should be out by the end of the week."

His head shot back up. "So, this is really it?" He hung on to the last bit of hope like a lifeline, still seeking her clarification.

"This is it." Jess hefted her bag over her shoulder. She needed to get out of here, needed space. Every time she looked at him, she still felt like helping. She couldn't stop herself.

"I don't want you to be without a place, so have a think about what you want to do. We can chat to the landlord, and I'm happy to cover my portion of the rent until you're sorted."

He nodded along, scratching at his stubble. "Heath did offer to move out of Mum and Dad's place and in with me, but I wasn't sure if you might've wanted to come back." He looked at her again, as if to double check she really was serious.

"Heath moving in is a great idea. I know he started his new job this year, so at least you know he'd be right to pay rent," Jess encouraged him. "I'm not coming back, Adam. I've made my decision."

He nodded again, shifting on the spot as he sniffed, his eyes shining as he looked to the ceiling. Her heart broke to see how much he was hurting, knowing she was the cause and knowing she wasn't the one to fix it this time. He had to do this on his own. He remained frozen as she moved past him.

"I'm sorry," she muttered on the way out. It wasn't much consolation, but it was all she could give right now.

Jess let herself into Remi's house with the spare key, ambling down the hallway with dinner dangling in her hands. She'd picked up Indian, keen to see if Remi liked her picks. She could never resist a good cheesy garlic naan with a spicy beef madras.

She stopped short at the end of the hallway. Remi sat at the dining table, head in hand with her laptop in front of her. Jess's heart picked up speed.

"Remi?" she asked, slowly moving towards her and placing the dinner on the table. "What's going on?"

Remi stared at the screen, unmoving. "Everything is fucked."

Jess moved beside her, carefully touching her shoulder. "Hey," she whispered. "Talk to me. I'm sure we can—"

"Flinders have cancelled our contract," she spat, still facing the screen.

"What?!" Jess reeled back. "Why?"

"Not fit for the project." She let out a bitter laugh. "Dickhead-*fucking*-Declan. He ratted me out to Javier, about my accident, about being behind on our work and the complaint about the tile work at the Donaldsons. Fuck. I should've done better. Should've known better. *Why* did I let him see me injured?"

"Remi..."

"No," she said harshly. "I did this to us. I've run this business into the ground."

"Hey, that's not true—" Jess bent down to her level, trying to make eye contact, to connect in some way. Jess wanted to reach out and offer comfort, but after the boundaries put up this morning, she held herself back. Everything in her protested. She gripped the back of Remi's chair instead.

"I hedged everything on Flinders, Jess." Remi finally turned to face her, eyes red. Looking, but unseeing. Lost in her own head. "Nothing else is booked in. I can't believe I put you both at risk like this." A gut-wrenching sob burst from her lips as she turned away. "I can't do this anymore. It's too much," she mumbled through sobs, shoulders shaking.

Jess pulled Remi up off the chair and into her arms. Fuck their talk, she couldn't sit here and do nothing—it went against every grain of her being.

"Come here," she spoke softly, and Remi acquiesced as Jess wrapped her arms around her as carefully as she could. Right now, she wished she was taller, to be the bigger spoon and offer that comfort, but Remi still managed to rest her head on Jess's shoulder and let it all out.

Jess stood in silence, playing with Remi's hair and rubbing her back. She was so thankful Remi hadn't been alone tonight to bear this all by herself.

Once Remi had calmed down, Jess held her at arm's length. "Feel better?" she checked in, searching Remi's face, wet and puffy from crying. Jess had never seen her so lost and vulnerable, fear and hopelessness haunting her eyes. Jess would do anything to take that away. Seeing Remi's confidence stripped like this was unnerving, so raw.

Remi gave a nod, trying to compose herself as she wiped her nose with the back of her hand. "God, I'm a mess." She choked out a laugh. "And I've snotted, like, all over you. I'm the worst boss."

"Please," Jess replied, fixing her with a look. "Don't even. I want you to sit down, and tonight, as your *friend*, I'm going to grab you some tissues and heat up our dinner."

She picked up the bag, moving to the kitchen and grabbing some plates. "Then, I'm going to tell you about my awesome day of demolition and officially having a new place to live with JJ—thanks to you, no less. Let's not even think about Flinders for the next hour."

Remi gave a sullen nod, sitting back down and closing the laptop, shoving it away.

"Give yourself a break, Rem. You're doing the best you can, always with others in mind. This is just an unexpected roadblock we need to figure out how to get around."

"That's not your job, to have any part of this on you. At all. We could—"

"Uh-uh. No shop talk. Starting now. I want you thinking about rainbows. Turtles. Crabbing. Anything you love—Hudson! But no more trying to solve problems, okay?" Jess moved around the bench, placing a box of tissues in front of Remi. "Switch off that brain of yours." Jess patted her head lightly, earning her a small smile.

"Always so bossy..." Remi muttered under her breath, making Jess feel she was perhaps easing the hurt, even if only a little.

Jess did her best to entertain Remi through dinner, recounting how Sophie had given her a shot on the demo hammer. How she'd screeched when it first vibrated against the wall, but she'd managed to take off a few of the old splashback tiles in the kitchen and was so proud of herself for that fact. She tried to keep the conversation upbeat and happy, but Remi still looked dejected, closing in on herself and moving back to the laptop by the end of the meal.

"Of course they appointed Karkalla Renovations as the replacement." Remi scoffed, re-reading the email out loud to Jess.

"Have you told Sophie?"

"I didn't want to worry her."

"She'd want to know. And you'd want her to tell you if the roles were reversed." While Jess didn't want to overstep, intuition told her Sophie might be able to step in as more of a support than she could. This was how Jess could help while maintaining their boundaries.

"If I could just..." she trailed off. "You're probably right. I'll call her later." Remi remained staring at the screen. "This is not the year I envisioned for The Lady Builders."

"I'm sure there's something we can do; there's always a way. Or, if I remember correctly 'everything is a possibility.'" Jess pointed to Remi's tattoo on her upper arm, trying to inject some sort of positivity—some tiny semblance of hope. "Plus, it's only February, and this is just one day. We've got the whole year ahead of us."

"Jess, this is bad. I took you on with the Flinders work lined up. Without that..."

Jess stared at her, blinking slowly.

"What?"

She hadn't understood, hadn't even considered there might be repercussions involving her. Jess frowned, waiting for Remi to say more.

Remi looked pained as she met her eyes.

"I won't be able to keep you on the team."

Jess felt the moment her stomach dropped, her breath catching in her throat.

"Oh."

What else was there to say? She'd never considered that both of their dreams would be crushed tonight. She couldn't possibly fathom the fallout of Flinders would mean no more Remi in her future. No more apprenticeship. Her heart thudded harder at the true ripple effect of this situation, white noise rushing her ears. Remi's fear now reflected in her own eyes. Her mum and Adam flashed into her mind, nodding solemnly at this inevitable outcome.

Her chest physically hurt. She wrapped her arms around herself.

"You'd be able to get a transfer," Remi offered, trying to help Jess. Always helping others instead of herself.

Jess dropped her arms, squaring her shoulders. "I refuse to believe this is it," she said, defiant. "I believe in The Lady Builders, and I thought you did too."

There *had* to be a way.

But... if Remi truly believed this was it... maybe she was right.

"Jess, what else can I do? It's out of my hands. Literally, thanks to this stupid accident." She gestured to her sprained arm.

"That's not forever."

"But it may have cost us forever." Remi tore her eyes away, scowling. She was as bad as Taylor now, shooting herself with the second arrow, compounding the pain when they were already down.

"Remi—" Jess could feel her slipping, shutting down,

pulling away. Everything was too fresh for Remi to see any other outcome.

"I think I need to be alone tonight."

The statement stung, but Jess understood.

Things between them were complicated, and the last thing Remi needed right now was more complication. But Jess didn't want her to be alone tonight. Jess stared at her feet and nodded. "I get it. Just don't give up on this. Keep talking. Let us help you—as a team. This is not all on you Remi, no matter how much you think it is. And tonight, don't try to solve everything with your emotions in overdrive. Go get some sleep, get some rest and tackle it fresh in the morning."

Jess stood awkwardly, unsure if she should hug Remi goodbye or just leave.

Fuck it.

She stepped into Remi's space, hearing her shuddering breath as Jess enveloped her. "Good night, Remi."

She wanted to say more. So much more. But Remi was already overloaded, so she kept it simple, squeezing her shoulder as she pulled away. Remi's eyes were closed, a long exhale escaping her lips.

"Goodnight, Jess."

Later that night, Jess lay on her back staring up at the ceiling in the guest bedroom of her own house, wondering how she'd gotten here. Her heart refused to calm down, Remi's words echoing in her mind:

I won't be able to keep you on the team.

Had she completely blown up her own life?

Maybe her mum and Adam were right. Maybe she had rushed things?

Maybe this whole cabinet-making dream had been one huge, monumental mistake. And now, she'd possibly lost that too.

Here she was, thirty years old and starting over. Single. Her friends were busy living their lives. Her apprenticeship now on the line and, *oh god,* if she couldn't find a transfer, she wouldn't be able to afford the rent for JJ's place. She'd have to move back in with her parents.

Or go back to Limone...

No.

She refused. She refused for that to even be a possibility.

She would fix this.

She had to.

TWENTY-TWO
Remi

Remi hadn't moved. She sat watching the front door. The house was silent apart from the fridge's low hum and the steady tick of the kitchen clock, both in rhythm with her pounding heartbeat. She took deep, grounding breaths, blowing them out slowly and shakily as her mind raced. Traces of Jess were scattered everywhere. Her perfume still lingered in Remi's hair. The kitchen bench was spotless, cleaned so Remi wouldn't have to worry about the dishes. A pink hair tie left on the coffee table from their weekend together.

Telling Jess she couldn't stay had crushed her.

She hadn't expected the hug that followed either. She'd expected distance. She *needed* distance. She felt so frayed, so fragile. She couldn't handle herself a minute longer around Jess without completely losing it. All she wanted was Jess to tell her it would all be okay, to take her to bed and sooth her soul. But sweet nothings didn't fix the huge pit she'd dug herself into. This was one of the biggest fuckups of her life.

She didn't deserve kindness right now. She'd done this, and she needed to fix it.

Her actions, her choices, had now actively harmed the people she loved most.

Liked.

She *liked* Jess. There was a difference there, a blurry, blurry difference. Why were feelings so messy?

Her phone blasted in the silence, making her jump.

Sophie.

She watched it vibrate in a slow circle on the dining table, Sophie's name yelling at her to answer. She stared, waiting... it stopped, the screen going dark.

Then it lit up again.

"Argh, *fine*," she huffed, swiping up the phone.

"Hi," she answered, trying for neutrality.

"What's going on, Bug?" Sophie's voice was laced with concern. "Jess said I should reach out. Talk to me."

Remi chewed at the inside of her lip, eyes watering again at the sound of her sister's voice. The sound of comfort. She wanted to protect Sophie, to fix this herself. But, Sophie was also her business partner. She had a right to know.

Heat rose up Remi's neck, spreading like a slow fire.

"We lost the Flinders job," she admitted. She had failed her sister, failed her family.

"What! Remi, when were you going to tell me?"

"I didn't want you to worry!" she cried, emotions pouring out.

"This is *our* business. We're in this together." Sophie was sounding like Jess now. "I know you take care of the admin side, but this is bigger than an order mishap, Remi. This isn't yours to carry alone."

"But it's my fault." Shame snaked its way around her body, constricting her breath. Her clothes felt too tight, too claustrophobic. She pulled at the neck of her shirt.

"How is it your fault?" Sophie was patient, like she was with Hudson, encouraging and waiting for Remi to open up.

"Declan told them about my arm. That we're behind on jobs. That our work isn't up to code. Javier doesn't trust we have the manpower to uphold the project scope, so they're going with Karkalla."

"Remi, you need to stop blaming yourself. Your accident was just that—an accident. We'll work something out."

"God, between you and Jess with your positivity."

"What other option do we have? Pack up shop and let them win? Is that what you really want?"

Remi let out a long exhale.

"No," she said after a beat.

"You know what I think?"

"You're going to tell me anyway." Her sister was always right. She always listened to her.

"You're overwhelmed. You've taken on too much, trying to do it all to keep everything running. And then, it all came crashing down. You—*literally*—came crashing down, Remi. You need a break, Bug. And you need to share the load. You've got to open up more about what's going on with the business. That's what I'm here for. That's what Jess is there for. We're a team, and we need to help each other."

Remi let the words sink in, her next breath coming a little easier. She warbled as she tried to reply. "I think... I think you might be right." She sniffed, wiping under her eyes.

"Listen. This isn't the end of the world. Even if it feels like it right now. Remember where you came from. Who you used to work for. It could be worse. Remember where you're going, and who The Lady Builders stand for. I love you. Now go get some sleep. And don't read any more emails tonight," Sophie warned.

"Love you. I will."

The following morning, Remi did feel better. Talking to both Jess and Sophie the night before had kept her grounded. She felt lighter, thankful for the support she had around her. She'd managed to sleep right through the night, and now it was time to face the facts, see what could be done, and create a new plan.

She'd start with an easy win.

"Sandra? Hi, it's Remi. I'm calling to confirm the building inspection for the Donaldson's this Friday?"

Sophie had the forethought to schedule it for the only day Declan wouldn't be on site; the one advantage they still had over him at this stage. Sandra had everything booked and ready to go, so Remi happily struck the first job off her to-do list.

Javier's name glared at her next.

"Time to bite the bullet." She winced as she hit the call button, bringing the phone to her ear. She was thankful for a clear head and less emotion clouding her judgement, but her stomach churned nonetheless as she listened to the dial tone.

"Remi."

"Javier, I got your email. Look—is there any way we can make this work?"

Because at this point she'd do whatever he asked.

"You know this can't work, Remi. As much as I want The Lady Builders, right now we need reliability. We need numbers. Karkalla Renovations have both. I'm sorry. It's not personal, it's business. At the end of the day, the projects need to be done on time to the highest standard. A three-person team was already cutting it fine, but I wanted to give you a go. Hearing you were behind in work, out with an injury, and Declan's accusations about your work standards—you have to understand, it doesn't instil me with confidence."

Remi closed her eyes. Deep down she knew he was right. He was making the best decision he could with the information in front of him.

That didn't make it hurt any less.

"I do understand. I do. I just... wish there was a way."

"So do I, Remi. All the best."

Her phone clattered onto the table. This was real. Flinders was gone, and there was no coming back from it. How did she get here? She scrubbed her face with her hand and ran it through her hair. "Fuck," she muttered under her breath. She'd known the chances were slim to none with Javier, but she had to ask.

Remi spent the rest of the morning looking up suitable businesses with apprenticeship openings for a possible transfer. Losing Jess was the last thing she wanted, but without the work lined up, she couldn't afford to keep her on.

By the afternoon she'd reached out to every contact she had, trying to drum up new business. Her left hand ached from all the extra use—typing emails, taking calls, hell... even just feeding herself and cleaning up the dishes. It made her realise how much Jess had been helping around the house. Helping *her*. As much as Remi stood by her decision to create space, she missed her.

A thunderstorm grumbled outside, the air hot and muggy as thick rain pelted down, adding to her mood. Her stomach churned, worsening with each clap of thunder. She stared into space, willing some kind of answer, some next action she could take to make herself feel better. Restless, she took Ninja out for a quick walkabout to help take her mind off things. Remi hadn't been this unsure about where her business was heading since she and Sophie first started. She'd have to dig deep, summon up every ounce of resolve she had left.

They'd made it work before; she just had to believe they could again.

TWENTY-THREE

Jess

It was moving day.

Jess couldn't wait to feel settled in her new home. JJ had been so accommodating and friendly over the phone. She hadn't seen the house in person yet, but the video tour had been enough to get her excited. It was a super cute two-bedroom Art Deco place styled with a mix of eccentric and stylish mid-century furniture. It felt homey and fun—the kind of space she could bask in.

She'd wanted to hire a truck, but Remi had insisted Jess use her ute. Which was how Jess found herself back at Remi's place early Saturday morning. She hadn't seen her since she'd walked out three days ago. Remi had been deep in "project fix-all-the-things" mode while Sophie and Jess balanced the remaining on-site work. She hoped things wouldn't be weird between them and that she hadn't over-stepped on Wednesday. She'd been replaying everything she'd said and done, spiralling and driving herself crazy. Not even books or meditation could stop her thoughts floating back to Remi every five minutes.

"Thanks again," said Jess as Remi handed her the keys. Remi looked better today; dressed and showered, eyes bright and a warm smile directed straight at her. *Ooft*.

Jess resisted the urge to hug her, opting to play it safe with an awkward wave instead as she walked off and hopped in the driver's seat. She adjusted the mirrors just as the passenger door opened and Remi hopped in.

Jess looked at her confused. "What are you doing?"

"Uh, coming with you?" replied Remi, looking just as perplexed as she awkwardly clicked her seatbelt in with her left hand.

"Oh." This was a surprise. "I just assumed I was borrowing the car for the day."

"Oh. Well, I just assumed you meant me too."

They stared at each other for a beat, then cracked up laughing.

"Remi, you're so shit at resting that arm. How are you even going to help?"

"Excuse me, I can still lift things. I've had no complaints about my left hand."

Jess stifled a smile, thankful to get back to their usual banter and break the ice. She started the car, thrilled at the new turn of events.

"Yeah, can't argue there," she agreed, her thoughts racing straight back to their first night together on the couch. Remi blushed, and warmth bloomed in Jess's chest. It was good to see her looking lighter and more relaxed. She could empathise with Remi wanting to get out after being house bound and trying to sort everything out for the business. Though, she didn't dare bring up the topic and bring down the mood now.

Jess had to admit, Remi ended up being more help than she expected, carting odds and ends to neatly pack in the ute's tray. Jess wasn't bringing a huge amount with her, in the end, coming to an agreement with Adam to keep most of the existing furniture. He'd swung her a bit of cash for the difference. She was already planning an IKEA trip before the day was out.

JJ was out the front watering the garden as they arrived at Jess's new home.

"Didn't expect to see Rem's car pull up in the drive today," JJ said, greeting them both with a hug and a wide grin. An eyebrow raised at Remi.

Remi shrugged. "Figured it was easier for her than hiring a truck, and I'm happy to be out of the house today."

"Yeah, man, I'm sorry to hear about Flinders Homes. I'm keeping an eye out for you though. Any inkling of reno work and I'm sending it your way. Now Jess—you want your official house tour?"

It felt like Christmas morning.

"Yes, please!"

The house was even better in person. Loads of natural light filled the place, and her new room was huge.

"Just dump everything in the corner for now," she said to both women. "I'll set it up when we get back."

"Get back from where?" Remi questioned.

"Quick trip to IKEA, if you're up for it?"

"Give the girl a ute, and IKEA will be added to the travel plans," JJ joked.

"Maybe Bunnings as well, for a couple of bits," Jess added.

"A girl after my own heart. But wait—you getting a snag too?" JJ asked.

"Only if we're not full from IKEA hot dogs," replied Jess.

"I'm sure we could fit in both," Remi added with a grin.

"The amount I eat nowadays, I wouldn't be surprised. I've been an eating machine since working with you." Jess tapped her stomach.

"You gotta keep up the appetite; the amount of calories you burn on the tools is no joke," Remi replied.

"I don't care where you guys go as long as one of you brings me back some form of sausage for lunch," said JJ, walking off to grab more gear from the ute.

IKEA was packed like an ant hill, with people milling about everywhere. At least Jess knew all the shortcuts to get to where they needed to be—fast.

"I forgot how busy this place gets on the weekend," Jess mumbled as they made their way up the escalator. One downside of working Monday to Friday: no more off-peak shopping.

"Do you know what you want?" Remi asked, glancing sideways at her as they passed through the lounge displays.

"I mean, a bed would be nice for tonight, that's going to be this afternoon's project. Aside from that, a lamp for reading my books, and a cute plant."

"Cute plant. Got it." Remi smirked.

"Hey! It cleans the air and everything."

Remi chuckled, bumping Jess gently. "I know, I'm just giving you shit."

They stopped in front of the bed section.

"You want this one?" Remi asked, patting the spot next to her on a single kid's mattress with a stupid grin.

Jess shook her head and lay down on a nearby queen bed. She closed her eyes, feeling the bed dip next to her.

Remi groaned. "Oh, that's good. Think I'm just going to stay here. You can bring me meatballs and hot dogs. Yep, that sounds good."

Jess rolled onto her side, ready to shoot off a quip, until the smile slipped from her lips. Remi was much closer than she thought, her black hair in a wave around the pillow. All Jess could do was stare. Remi had this one group of freckles she absolutely adored. They formed a little triangle, just under her eye. It reminded her of the kind of face markings she'd give her characters in the video games she used to play with Taylor.

Remi turned to face her, close enough to feel each other's breath.

"What?" Remi asked quietly, her eyes dipping to Jess's lips.

"I don't mean to alarm you," Jess whispered, "but there's a small boy staring at us from the end of our bed."

Moment broken, they turned their heads, laughing as the boy kept staring while playing with his paper measuring tape until a parent came to guide him off to the next section.

That was close. Jess couldn't mess this up on top of everything else. She needed to be more aware of the space between them, keep her distance before she did something she'd regret.

Remi bounced on the bed, making Jess chuckle as they sat up, breaking the tension.

"So, is this the one?" Remi asked.

"I think so. It's comfy." Plus, it would now forever remind her of lying there, staring at the one person she couldn't have right now, made worse by knowing exactly how good it felt to be with her. Though... perhaps not in the middle of a furniture store.

Hot dogs and furniture acquired, they pushed the last box into the ute tray.

"This baby is riding up front with us," Jess said, tucking the monstera plant she'd bought under her arm.

"Wouldn't dream of leaving it in the tray. It would be wrecked before we got home." Remi smiled, shutting the tailgate.

That afternoon, Remi stuck around to help, so Jess appointed her to TA duties. Remi currently sat on the floor, head buried in an instruction booklet, sorting the parts Jess needed for the bed. They worked effortlessly together, and the bed frame was up in no time.

"Can you believe a few months ago you didn't even know the difference between screwdrivers?" Remi asked as Jess tightened a bolt with her drill.

"Who even is that girl? I hardly remember her at this point. Having a good teacher helps." Jess winked, then scolded herself for being too flirty again. It was too easy around Remi.

"Right. Time to unpack this mattress and lift it on."

They cut the cable ties and rolled it out together, both flopping onto the finished bed immediately.

"Thank god I have a bed to sleep in tonight. Teamwork!" Jess cheered, raising her hand for a high five. For the second time that day, Jess found herself too close, watching Remi lying on her back. Her gaze fell to Remi's mouth.

"Thanks, for today. You didn't have to do all that," Jess added quietly.

Remi rolled onto her side to reply.

Mistake.

Warning bells went off—this was beyond dangerous territory.

"I was happy to." Remi closed her eyes, placing the sweetest of kisses on Jess's lips.

Remi's eyes flew open, shock registering on her face as she froze.

"You realise that 'just friends' means no kissing right?" Jess smirked. Remi's hair fell over her shoulders in soft waves, and Jess tried with everything in her to keep her hands to herself. One of them had to keep these boundaries in place. Her lips tingled, taunting her.

Remi closed her eyes, giving a small nod. When she opened them again, they locked onto Jess. "I don't think that was a conscious choice," she whispered.

"You guys want a beer—oh, my bad. You—never mind," JJ stuttered, turning on her heel and legging it out of the room.

They sprang apart, sitting up. Jess smoothed down her hair and looked at Remi, who was as red as a tomato.

Jess laughed awkwardly, unsure what to say. She felt embarrassed having been caught well... *almost* kissing. JJ was Remi's friend *and* Jess's landlord now. She did *not* want to fuck this up. Her job was already up in the air; she didn't need her new home taken from her too. "We can pretend that didn't happen—"

"But we probably need to go talk to JJ," Remi finished, scooting off the bed.

Remi didn't look nearly as panicked as Jess had expected. Curious. Very curious. She followed Remi to the kitchen, glad to have someone else taking the lead on this conversation.

JJ was about to put two beers back in the fridge.

"We'll have those, I think," said Remi. JJ paused and reversed course.

"Jess?"

"Yes, please." Anything to make this a little less awkward and give her something to do with her hands.

"Sure thing." JJ twisted off the tops and slid the bottles across the benchtop. "My lips are sealed, by the way." She mimed zipping her lips and leaned back against the kitchen cabinets, grinning. She was enjoying this way too much.

Jess picked at the label on her beer, avoiding her eyes.

"I'm happy for you both," she continued, nodding to Remi.

"We're not together actually. Just friends."

"You don't have to hide it from me." JJ shrugged, looking between the two of them for more.

"Remi's right. We're not," Jess clarified. Though, with each day spent together, Jess was starting to ask why.

"Okay, well, for the record, I don't care if you are." She pushed away from the cupboard. "Now, want to show me your room setup?"

Well, that ended up being less painful than Jess imagined. She silently let out the breath she'd been holding and took a swig of her beer, the crisp bubbles a welcome balm after the day's work. It was kind of nice having JJ know about them... not that there was anything going on. But it made her appreciate it, nonetheless.

Later that night, Jess had dropped Remi home and was now back at JJ's, having just finished their first dinner together.

"Thanks for cooking tonight. It was an extra special treat after the week I've had. You've been so welcoming." Jess sat back in her chair, content and enjoying JJ's company.

"I bet," she replied, clearing the table.

Jess had filled her in on the apprenticeship, Remi's accident, the Declan drama and losing the Flinders job. JJ was very easy to talk to, and looking around at the spotless house, Jess could tell they'd get along living together as well. It was great to be housemates with someone who cleaned up after themselves! Especially after Adam... While she'd still done a lot of work while staying at Remi's, it hit differently when someone couldn't look after themselves versus simply choosing not to.

"I keep meaning to thank you for the referral for Marie and Hayley, by the way. They're booked in next month."

"Oh, you're welcome. Happy to help."

It was a good reminder for Jess to reach back out to her friends. Find out what was happening with Brooke, and why she was back all of a sudden. With everything going on in her own life, she'd completely dropped the ball on checking in.

"So, what's the story with you and Remi?" JJ asked, blindsiding her. She sat back down across from Jess with a fresh beer, scooting an extra over.

Jess shook her head with a laugh. What was the story, indeed? She'd like answers too, because today, they'd cut things way too fine. "We're friends who, at another time, may have been more. She's helped me so much since I first met you at the restaurant. More than I ever could've imagined."

Everything made so much sense the more she played everything back in her head. The magnetism she'd felt from the first moment she laid eyes on Remi was unforgettable.

JJ nodded. "That's Remi for you. She's always going out of her way to help. I don't think I've ever seen her sit still, and I've known the Pearce sisters since they first went into the industry together. We met at one of the quarterly tradeswomen dinners, like the one where we met you."

"Oh, I didn't realise that's what the dinner was for," replied Jess.

"Yep. I'm sure they'll haul you along to the next one. It's great chatting with the other girls, everyone's always so welcoming and helpful, no matter what trade you're from or how long you've been in the industry. It's like we all just *get it*, you know?"

"Wow, I can only imagine." Meeting other women, other apprentices... She'd love to hear their stories, swap notes and make more friends. Having more people in her corner who understood what she was going through sounded pretty good.

"Anyway, I don't want to butt in where I don't belong, but when it comes to Rem, she has a habit of pushing people away. She loves to say she can do it all herself, but you've seen her, even when she's at her lowest, she still doesn't let up on letting people in. Not even her own sister. When she told me she'd let you stay at her place to help..." JJ let out a low whistle. "Honestly, I was shocked. So I don't know what you said or did but keep doing what you're doing. It's good for her. I can see she's happy, and I can see how much she likes you, even though—I know," she made quote marks with her fingers, "you're 'just friends'."

"Thank you."

And Jess meant it. It still wasn't the right time for her and Remi, but when the stars aligned, she'd be ready. And she'd be pushing for what she wanted.

TWENTY-FOUR

Remi

Acceptance. Remi had come to that conclusion over the weekend. She'd accepted they'd lost the Flinders work, and she was ready to forge a new path.

Spending the weekend with friends had been the remedy she didn't know she needed. Instead of stressing out about trying to fix everything, she'd stayed in the moment, being a little silly, and yeah, maybe getting a little caught up in a certain beautiful blonde. She blamed Jess's lips. They were too kissable. Too soft. Too plump. Too damn close. She shouldn't have kissed her. Remi knew that much, but it had been an automatic response, like it was the most natural thing in the world. Like—there was no other option.

Remi needed to stop sending mixed signals. Especially since *she* was the one to put the rules up in the first place.

It didn't help that this morning, while she was trying to focus on her emails, she kept daydreaming about Jess instead. She rubbed her eyes, took another sip of coffee and stretched with a half-hearted yawn. She'd left her sling off this morning, testing to see how her arm felt. It was still sore and weak, but she could move her fingers easier, and she had more movement without fear of rippling pain. She hoped to be able to do some light work in another week or two, but in the meantime, desk duty it was.

The groundwork she'd put in last week was beginning to pay off. A few people had reached out for quotes, something she at least *could* do while healing. It was nice to feel useful, to not just be sitting around doing nothing. Sophie had called a team meeting for tonight, and Remi was looking forward to telling them about the potential new work. She'd also heard back from two companies who were willing to look at Jess for an apprenticeship transfer. Her stomach dropped at the thought, but knowing Jess would be looked after and could continue her study was what mattered most.

The doorbell rang repeatedly. Must be six o'clock. Jess was here, and somehow the workday was already over in a flash.

"Coming!" Remi yelled, padding down the hallway to the incessant ringing. She should've let Jess keep her bloody spare key. She threw the door open to a grinning Jess who pushed the bell once more.

"Jeez, ease up on the injured one, ey?" Remi held the door for her to enter.

Jess breezed past, ignoring the jibe, a mischievous glint in her eye and her arms full of paperwork. She practically skipped down the hallway. *Honestly, this woman.*

Remi shut the door, following her to the dining table.

"You look pretty chipper for a Monday," Remi commented.

"That's because I am," replied Jess, giving nothing away. She sat at the table, hands folded on the stack of paper. "How's the arm? No sling today, I see."

Remi flexed it a little. "Feeling better. Nice to have a little more freedom with it. Doesn't hurt as much to get dressed, which is nice."

They both turned at the sound of the front door slamming shut.

"Here!" Sophie called, boots clomping down the hall. "Sorry, I'm late. I wanted to make sure the boys had dinner sorted before I left. Tomás is making Hudson's favourite— Toad in the Hole."

"Aww, I used to love that as a kid," said Jess.

They all sat around the dining table as Sophie kicked off the meeting. Remi was eager to hear how work had been progressing. She'd tried her best to give Sophie space, resisting the urge to check in, but she didn't want to micromanage.

"Jess and I made more progress than we thought today. We finished the kitchen install for the Richards, completed the bathroom grouting at the Smiths, *and* we got all the base cabinets put together for the Millers. Oh, and the benchtops are getting delivered early, so we'll be able to complete the Miller job tomorrow."

Jess was nodding along with the updates, both of them proud of their achievements. The substantial amount they'd been able to complete without her took Remi by surprise. Perhaps she'd given herself too much credit for how essential she was on site? Something to reflect on later.

Remi updated them on the new potential jobs and slid two forms across to Jess. "I heard back from these two companies who are willing to take on a transfer. They're both large but well regarded in the industry."

Jess slouched down the more Remi spoke, sighing as she picked up the papers to glance over them. "You know this isn't what I want. But I'll apply to both, because I do want to complete my apprenticeship, and there's no way I'm going back to hospitality. If you say they're good companies, then I trust you."

Remi looked away from the hurt and resignation on Jess's face. This was the hardest part of her job, but she knew she was doing the right thing.

"I do have a counter offer, though."

Remi's head whipped back to her, Sophie's snapping up just as quickly.

"What do you mean, a counter offer?" Remi asked, confused.

"Last week I did some digging." Jess's mouth twitched. "I had an idea, but I needed more information before bringing it to you both. I also needed a plan, to know if these had any chance of becoming reality."

Remi was confused and looked at Sophie who shrugged. What was going on? This wasn't on the agenda. Why would Jess need a plan? If she wasn't transferring, the only counter offer she could think of was—quitting.

No. Surely not. But Jess's sassy smile told her it was something else entirely...

Jess flipped over the paperwork she'd brought.

"My first proposal—"

"Proposal?" Now Remi was *really* confused.

"When did our apprentice turn so business-y and professional?" Sophie leaned over to ask Remi.

"Oh, she's always been a bossy one," Remi replied, the side of her mouth tugging into a smile.

Jess gave them a pointed stare, unimpressed with the interruption. "My first proposal," she repeated, "is for us to apply for a government grant for my apprenticeship. I believe you're eligible, and we meet all the requirements for you to start receiving payments to help keep me on. It's not a huge amount, but it would help."

"I thought those were only for certain trades, like plumbing or electrical?" Sophie asked.

"Nope." Jess gave them the listed criteria, where cabinet-makers were highlighted in pink. She'd really done her homework.

It warmed Remi, knowing how much Jess wanted to stay. That she was *fighting* to stay with them. Then she saw the amount.

"Wow. Jess, this is great. Truly. And so thoughtful of you to put all this together, but you're right, the amount wouldn't be what we'd need to keep you on. I'm sorry."

She could see Jess was trying hard, and it pained Remi to know it still wasn't enough. Remi was expecting Jess to be deflated. Instead she pulled out a second, thicker folder.

"It's okay. I expected as much. That was only the start. Now I'd like to go through proposal number two."

Blue eyes locked onto hers.

What was Jess planning? Those eyes didn't hold an ounce of uncertainty. They burned with pure fire again, charged with energy as they held her gaze. Remi's breath stopped as she waited for what else Jess had up her sleeve, hanging on to every word.

"Remi. You once told me you got your queen bee tattoo

for a reason—to remind you of who you are and to lead your business."

Remi looked at her tattoos. She'd hardly given them a glance since her accident. Half of them were hidden under her bandages. The bee's wings "opened" as she extended her arm. A timely reminder.

"Losing Flinders was not on the cards, and I know—in your mind—they were your ticket to expand the business. But you know what else a queen bee stands for? Resilience. And I refuse to believe that losing the Flinders contract means going back to only the two of you. Which is why I want us to submit a proposal for funding. And I'm not just talking about a few thousand like the Government grant. I'm talking up to two *hundred* thousand dollars."

Jess flipped over the pages to show the fund overview and requirements. Funding hadn't even crossed Remi's mind. That kind of money would be... game changing. A hand flew over Sophie's mouth, her sister just as shocked as she was at the opportunity being laid out in front of them.

"This... is the Fearless Women Fund," Jess continued. "Submissions are still open for the first quarter, but the kicker is, cut-offs are in two days for EOI submissions. I've highlighted here where they mention they give precedence to companies within the building and construction industry, with a focus on growth initiatives, *and* those led by LGBTIQA+ identifying women with at least fifty-percent ownership of the company."

"Wow. You really have been doing your homework," said Sophie, flicking through the pages in more detail.

"There's more. As part of the submission, you need to show how we'd use the money, so I've come up with this."

Another piece of paper was placed in front of them, full of Jess's curly handwritten notes.

Remi tried not to swoon, but hot damn if she didn't find a determined, empowered woman extremely sexy. Especially one trying to save her business from the rut they'd found themselves in.

Sophie slid her eyes to Remi, looking just as impressed with Jess as she was.

But Jess wasn't done yet.

"Obviously, there's no guarantees, but this would be enough to fund my apprenticeship *and* take on up to two more full time employees. We could expand The Lady Builders to a five-person team. With more people on site, Remi, you'd have more time to work *on* the business rather than drowning *in* it. You could finally start running those workshops you told me about and working with more women in the industry. It's just a draft... Anyway, what do you think?"

Jess's hands were clasped together, gripped tight. Now that Remi was looking, she could see Jess was brimming with nervous anticipation, eyes wide, probably wondering if she'd pushed too far and crossed a line.

"I'd think..." Remi paused, unable to hold back a smile. "I'd think you've rendered me completely speechless right now." Her throat closed up as tears sprang to her eyes at the effort this woman had gone to for her, for their business, and to save her own job. Hell, with the potential to expand the whole damn team if this worked out. Yeah. Speechless was about right. Though nothing was guaranteed, the odds of them actually getting the money...

Jess must've noticed the change in Remi.

"All you can do is apply," Jess encouraged. "It says here we should hear back within two weeks, which isn't too long. The hardest part will be putting our heads together for the proposal, and if we share the load we could do it."

"That simple, hey?" asked Sophie.

"What have we got to lose? ...Well, besides me," replied Jess with a self-deprecating smile.

"If we only have two days, I'll get to work on this tonight." Remi stood, moving to the lounge to grab her laptop.

Sophie picked up her handbag to leave. "I need to get back home. This isn't my field of expertise anyway. Remi, I trust you completely, you know how to get this business to the next stage; and Jess, you've clearly done your research, so you know what's needed for the proposal. You two work on this together. Remi," she fixed her sister with a pointed look, "share the workload with Jess."

Remi opened up her laptop. "Fine. Not going to win this argument with you two anyway."

"And there's no way I'm *not* helping. My butt's on the line here!" Jess added.

TWENTY-FIVE

Jess

Jess opened the kitchen cupboard. Then a drawer, then another. "Where's your snacks, Donatello?"

"When do I get a better nickname?" Remi replied, ignoring her question entirely.

"I call my best friend 'loser'; sure you want a new one?" Jess threw back.

"Donatello is great," Remi acquiesced.

Jess scrounged through a few more cupboards. No one stayed up working late without snacks. She spotted a tin of Milo. They were off to a good start. Then a half-opened packet of Tim Tams. Oh, and party mix lollies. Even better. Remi raised an eyebrow as she dumped everything onto the table.

"Really? I want to be able to sleep tonight," said Remi, eyeing all the sugar-based snacks with concern.

"And? There's no caffeine in it," Jess fired back.

"No, we'll just be bouncing off the walls like Hudson."

"Well, snacks make me smile, and smiling makes me

happy. And, they say a positive mindset opens up your creative ideas—hence, lollies." Jess bit the head off a raspberry snake and offered the bag to Remi. Lips pursed, she still looked skeptical but reached in and took a black cat. Jess recoiled.

"Don't tell me you like *liquorice*?" Jess shuddered.

Remi grinned, popping one in her mouth. "Yep," she said simply.

Jess pretended to gag, picking the rest out of the bag. "They. Are. All. Yours," she said, placing four more in front of Remi, who chuckled.

"See? You're laughing already. Let the creative ideas flow!"

Remi read through the fund requirements in more detail, while Jess jotted down notes as they brainstormed. Once Remi was up to speed, Jess got out a fresh piece of paper to start on a more solid proposal. She was so excited Remi had let them work on it together, even if slightly under sufferance. But she wanted this to work—for the both of them. Jess could see the cogs ticking over as Remi delved further into the proposal. Ideas began to pour out one after the other, the black cats slowly disappearing in front of her.

Jess loved watching Remi in business mode like this. The confident, mesmerising woman she'd first met was creeping back, a fire simmering behind her eyes with each flash of insight about the future possibilities for The Lady Builders.

"I love the idea of taking on two full-time tradeswomen. The growth would be twofold then..." Remi trailed off, tapping a pen to her mouth. "Hire the full timers... then each could take on an apprentice. Oh, this could be good. Really good."

Jess scribbled down the ideas as they flowed.

"If that's the case," Jess pitched in, "why don't we say as a direct influence from the funding it wouldn't just provide the initial jobs, but the flow on effect of two to three more women within a five-year time frame."

"Yes!" Remi cried, eyes lighting up as she pointed her pen at Jess.

Thinking big picture, this proposal would shine in front of the judging panel. At least, Jess hoped so. Her stomach twisted at the thought of any other outcome. Or maybe she needed to stop eating all the lollies. She pushed the bag away.

Remi picked up the proposal questions. "Okay, next we need to provide proof of work or proof of concept..."

"You have previous business income you can provide, and as for future work..." Jess trailed off.

"Without Flinders..."

They both looked at each other, willing the answers to come.

"You had enough work to take on Jackie previously, right?" Jess asked.

Remi nodded along.

"I know you cancelled the other jobs for Flinders, but that's just where the business is at *now*. With the funding, you'd have more dedicated time for marketing to drum up new business. I'm sure if we outline those new marketing initiatives, that could help get us across the line."

Jess was already scribbling. "If you've previously relied on word of mouth, let's branch out. Limone used to do monthly letterbox drops in different suburbs, for example. And I'm good with social media, so I could do video content on our latest projects..."

An hour later, they had an entire list of marketing ideas. Jess could see the relief in Remi's eyes. Even if they didn't get the funding, the exercise alone was already helping Remi plot next steps, without relying purely on existing clients. *And* Jess had managed to get her to allow someone else in on the ideas, without the pressure of needing everything to be perfect *right now*. For Remi, this plan was only a potential future, but Jess could see the ideas taking root already.

It was close to midnight when Jess glanced at the time. "Oh god, I gotta get home and get to bed. Your apprentice needs to be up at six tomorrow."

They'd miraculously completed the entire proposal in a single night. Well, the bones of it. Remi would pull together the presentation and tidy it up ready to send tomorrow. Jess was thankful, but tired.

So tired.

Tired physically from work, mentally from the massive last-minute proposal and emotionally, because, well, working alongside Remi all night was bliss and agony all rolled into one. There were sideways glances, the accidental brush of a knee, each moment sending electricity straight through her body.

"Just crash here," Remi offered as Jess stifled a yawn.

Jess gave her a pointed look.

"In the guest room," Remi clarified.

At this point, Jess was too worn out to argue. She

nodded mid-yawn, her eyes watering as she rested her head on her arm.

"Come on," Remi encouraged, standing up and cracking her neck. "We both need to go to bed before we fall asleep at the table. I've got a spare toothbrush you can use."

They meandered to the bathroom, switching off the lights as they went. Remi grabbed her toothbrush and handed Jess her extra.

Brushing teeth was such a simple, mindless action, but when shared with another... it felt so—*intimate*. The domesticity between them returned, and Jess was trying her best to concentrate on the taps, the vanity... anywhere but at the beautiful woman in the mirror. Sage eyes caught on hers in the reflection. It seemed Remi didn't have the same problem, watching Jess unabashedly with a lazy smile. It made Jess self-conscious. How could Remi look at her like that so freely? She'd have a meltdown if she gazed at Remi the same way. She certainly wouldn't be able to march herself into the guest bedroom. She'd have Remi up against the sink so fast—

Her toothbrush slipped, leaving a smear of white across her cheek.

Remi chuckled, almost choking on the foamy tooth-paste as she leaned over to rinse her mouth out.

Jess tried to scowl and explain herself, but she couldn't talk either. She rinsed her mouth next, wiping the back of her hand across her face and giving Remi a sparkling grin.

"You distracted me," she explained, cheeks heating as they walked out the bathroom together.

"Uh-huh," replied Remi, humouring her, "I managed to brush mine just fine, even *with* my bandaged hand."

Jess ignored her quips. At the guest room door, she stopped. "Goodnight, Remi."

Remi looked like she might say something. Instead, she stopped and looked at her feet, leaning on her doorframe with a small smile. "Thank you. For everything today. Even if we don't get the funding, you've lit a fire under me to make this work."

The sincerity landed low in Jess's gut, warming her from the inside out.

Remi glanced back down again. "I don't want to lose you," she added quietly.

"Hey," Jess replied, making Remi meet her eyes. "We won't let that happen."

She willed her words to be true, even though she knew there were no guarantees. What she wouldn't give for another cloud of dancing morning bugs to wish upon.

Remi gave her a final smile, though it didn't quite reach her eyes.

"Goodnight, Jess," she replied, then turned and slipped into her room.

Jess woke with a start in the semi-familiar room, briefly forgetting she hadn't gone home. She'd flicked a message to JJ the night before about working late with Remi. JJ's only response: *suuuure*, with a winky face.

Jess wished it had been something other than work, but somehow working side-by-side with Remi last night had been just as satisfying.

As a new hire, it was nice to feel seen. *Heard*. No idea

was shot down; she wasn't told she was silly... Remi believed in her and her words every step of the way. They built upon each other's knowledge like blocks until they had a wall so strong, their combined ideas shone on the page.

It was surprising how many times Jess's past experiences came in handy, or could be utilised in a way that clicked with Remi's deeper industry knowledge to create something stronger. Perhaps that was exactly what Remi needed: a push in a new direction, fresh ideas from someone not infused so closely to the work yet, to enable Remi to see things from a different perspective and add in those unique layers to their proposal that would hopefully see them across the line.

And save Jess's job.

The kitchen was still dark when Jess padded into the lounge to say good morning to Ninja. He was still tucked into his shell, stirring slowly under the dim glow of his UVB light.

"Morning buddy," she whispered, holding her hand up to the tank. He was the strangest little pet she'd ever seen, especially with his quirks of chasey and butt rubs, but he was growing on her—even if she was scarred from feeding him crickets. She'd stick to the pellets from now on. That was, if she ever ended up looking after him again.

Moving into the kitchen, she made a quick breakfast and chomped down mindlessly on some cereal, washing it down with a strong coffee. She reflected on just how much her life had changed in the last year. Thirty was feeling vastly different from twenty-nine, and she was feeling the age difference, in a good way. The last few years felt like she'd been coasting through life, one thing leading to the next, everything happening to her. Now? She felt like she'd grabbed the wheel, steering her ship on the course she wanted.

Well, for most things, anyway.

There were some things... some *people*, who were so close, yet still so far out of reach.

She gazed down the hallway at Remi's closed door and sighed into her next mouthful of cereal.

The strangest change of all? She felt *younger*.

Not that she was old by any stretch. But lately, she was full of energy. So much so, she hadn't realised how much it had waned over time. Life had become so mundane, so stagnant; the daily habits dug so deep, she'd forgotten to question them, accepting each new day without a flicker of desire to change it. Until it had all become too much. When the mundane morphed into something else. The habitual grooves wearing down so hard they started to squeak, to grind and to itch, until finally the irritation became so unbearable, change felt not only necessary, but inevitable. The only solution.

Recalling her disagreement with Ricciardo, she wondered what would've happened if Remi never saw the altercation. If she hadn't been offered the job. If she'd never got to spend time with *her*? The thought made her ache. Remi was so much a part of her life now, she couldn't imagine it any other way.

If they'd never met, she certainly wouldn't be here now, sipping coffee in Remi's kitchen, feeling alive, brimming with energy at the thought of the work ahead, and the potential for the changes they were about to make for the business.

Something good was building.

She could feel it.

TWENTY-SIX

Remi

It was eight o'clock by the time Remi got up. She'd completely forgotten to set her alarm, and the glaring sun streaming into her eyes was the first clue something was off. The guest bedroom was empty, the bed made. Not a trace left that Jess had ever been there. The thought made her sad. She'd hoped to have breakfast with her, chat about the day ahead and see her off for work—

She stopped. What was wrong with her? She was thinking about Jess like they were partners. Her brain clearly didn't care about the boundaries she'd set. It didn't care about boss-slash-employee relationships. It didn't care about the baggage they were still wading through. Her thoughts were simple, uncomplicated: Remi wanted Jess.

Dressed and ready for the day, she hoped a hot shower would clear her mind.

Walking into the kitchen, Jess had laid everything out for her breakfast, right down to her instant coffee with one sugar in her favourite mug. All she had to do was switch on the kettle. Why was she so damn thoughtful?

Then she saw the note:

Have a great day!
Proud of what we did last night. X

Proud of what *we* did.

Because they were a team.

She'd wanted to scowl at Sophie when she'd suggested for Jess to stay back and help. Remi hadn't thought she'd get anything done with Jess just so... there... again. But she wasn't the playful or caring Jess from the weekend before. This was determined, on-a-mission Jess. She was the note-taking queen, firing off ideas left, right and centre. She didn't stop. She pushed and pushed, leading the entire night until they'd collated everything and whipped it into some sort of order. Remi was impressed. And turned on. So inconveniently turned on.

And so, her thoughts returned to Jess. To the ongoing debacle that were her *feelings* for her. They were getting worse, and she couldn't switch them off. If Jess did have to transfer, at least it would give them space. Maybe then she could entertain the idea of a date.

A buzzing pulled her from her thoughts, and she ran over to the dining table.

Sandra.

Her heart thudded in her chest. While Sandra was a friend, she was a ruthless—but fair—building inspector. If their bathroom renovation wasn't up to code...

She swallowed.

"Good morning, Sandra."

"Remi. I've got your report." The woman gave nothing away.

"And?" Remi encouraged her.

If there was bad news, she wanted it out on the table. Get it over and done with. Add it to the list of dumpster fires she was already sorting through. What if the slopes in the bathroom were out by a few millimetres? What if they had to redo the entire thing? *"Don't worry unless there's something to worry about."* Sophie would say.

"The bathroom is fine. Great job by the way, it really was stunning work, but," she pressed on, giving Remi no time to bask in the good news. "I can't say the same about the kitchen extension."

Oh no, what had they done. Wait—

"What?" Remi said out loud.

They hadn't worked on the kitchen extension...

Declan.

"I've seen some bad sites in my day, but this was like a can of worms. One thing leading to another. It started when I spotted a small wet patch in a corner. Cole Donaldson was on site with me and cut a piece of gyprock out to investigate. Turns out, they'd pierced a water pipe during installation. Looked like it had been leaking slowly for a while. Once we cut a bigger hole to access the damage, we realised there was essentially no insulation in the walls either."

Remi frowned. She thought she'd seen them putting it in. "None at all?"

Sandra chuckled. "If you count an odd section here and there. It amounted to only a bag, if that. Two tops. For the entire extension."

Those dodgy bastards. She'd known Declan was a jerk, but hadn't realised it flowed all the way down to bad work ethics as well.

"I could go on, but I won't bore you with the details. The report has been sent through to you and Cole, so you can have a read in your own time. Long story short, I'm reporting them to the building association. I certainly wouldn't want them working on any further jobs, not with the corners they've cut. I'm so glad you called."

So was Remi. *Of all the possible outcomes...* "Wow." She was rendered speechless, standing by the table shaking her head. "Thanks for the heads up, and all your work. It's always appreciated."

Remi spent the rest of the morning in higher spirits. The fact Declan would—hopefully—be fined or forced to fix all damages pro bono after what he'd done to her? Well. Karma sure was in full swing today. She called Sophie with the news. The relief was evident in Sophie's wild laughter, taking a full minute to control herself before apologising. "Sorry. I really hate that schmuck," she said. "That is the best news we've had all week!"

By the afternoon, Remi had finalised the proposal and sent it to Sophie to review tonight so they could submit it before cut-offs tomorrow. She'd even carefully used her hand a little today to help type a few things up, and now it was starting to ache again from pushing it a little far.

Jess's voice was loud in her head— *Will you just rest!*

"Fine!" she argued with the non-existent Jess.

So that's how Remi found herself bored on the couch at 4pm.

"Beers?" came the one-word text from JJ.

She called her, not having the quickest dexterity to type a reply.

"Yes," Remi said as soon as JJ picked up.

"Where do you want to go?"

"Either pick me up and we can head to The Wharf, or come here and stay over because I'm lazy and my arm is sore."

"Boo. We're not staying inside on a day like today," JJ replied with a light chuckle. "I'll come pick you up. Get you out of the house."

Did this count as resting? Remi took another sip of her beer as she sat across from JJ, doing the same. She counted it as resting—it definitely wasn't work. Remi let out a relaxed sigh.

"Why don't we do this more often?" JJ asked, leaning back in her chair as she looked out toward the ocean.

"Because we're usually both busting our arses?" Remi answered in question.

"And why do we bust our arses so hard?"

Remi chuckled, though the question landed heavily on her chest, sobering her mood. She'd had this niggling thought recently. Well, since Jess had asked her those offhand questions: *Who was she without work?* and *where did she want to be in five years?* The questions hadn't stopped swirling. Around and around, chasing each other in her thoughts and even in her dreams. Since her accident, the extra time away from the tools had meant more time alone, and more time in her head. At some point, her work had become her life. She told herself she did it for her family, and for other women in the industry.

When she first started The Lady Builders, it was an escape from her previous misogynistic workplace. She'd blocked out that time, focusing on building up business and supporting herself and Sophie. Once they were stable, she started looking outwards, taking on more work, and, as a result, more tradeswomen. But slowing down had made her realise she'd forgotten to ask herself what she wanted, beyond her career. Then Jess had come stomping into her life, all pink safety boots and wide smiles, upending everything in ways she could never have imagined.

She still wanted the same things she'd told Jess that night on the rocks, but now... she wanted more. A tiny bit more time. She wanted to spend the odd evening having beers like this with a friend by the beach, to get a boat and take fishing seriously as a hobby—she could already see it clearly: baiting up a rod for Hudson, having an aunty-nephew day out on the water. And maybe—just maybe—she wanted to slow things down enough to consider a relationship. To have time dedicated not only to herself and her work. Maybe she was ready for that.

"I think it could be time to pull the foot off the pedal a bit," she finally responded.

JJ pretended to faint. "Okay, you really did knock your head. What have you done with Remi?"

Remi chuckled, taking another pull of her beer. "I mean, yeah, it's partly because of that. I've been thinking."

"Uh-oh."

Remi threw a scrunched-up napkin at her, but JJ was too quick, catching mid-air with a full belly laugh.

"Nah, I'm just messin' with you," JJ said. "I've been thinking too." She nursed her beer and played with a piece of varnish flaking off the weathered outdoor table. "I realised I'm thirty-five and I've never really travelled. I've just been head down, grinding away at the business to get the house, then grinding away again to renovate and pay off said house..." They watched a group of cyclists pass by on the bike track before JJ looked back to Remi. "You know, I've never even been to Kangaroo Island."

"Aww JJ, you gotta go to KI. It's beautiful."

"See? Even you've been. And you never take holidays either."

It was true, Remi couldn't remember the last time she'd taken a trip away. Time off, yes, but she didn't usually leave Adelaide. She'd last been to KI as a family vacation, so even that was long ago.

"Well, looks like we need to make some changes."

Remi held up her glass. "To more travelling, then."

JJ clinked her beer to Remi's. "And more down-time."

"I don't mean a crazy amount either, just—"

"More balance?" JJ offered.

"Yeah. Try and figure out who Remi is when I haven't got a tool in hand."

With the funding proposal still fresh in her mind, Remi realised how much she wanted this now. She could see the changes she'd implement in the business clear as day. They just needed the cash boost to make it happen.

TWENTY-SEVEN

Jess

They'd submitted their proposal to the Fearless Women Fund and now they were in limbo, waiting each day to hear something... anything. They'd at least had an automated reply confirming their application had been received successfully, but the waiting game continued. While Jess felt positive, she didn't want to rely on the funding coming through, so she'd gone ahead and applied to both companies Remi had suggested for a transfer. One had already responded with an offer for placement and had given her a week to get back to them with an answer.

She'd had a phone interview with the HR manager, who'd seemed friendly enough, and the company sounded good, taking on work all over Adelaide. She'd be working on larger jobs with a bigger team, and he'd confirmed she'd be the only female on the team. While unsurprising, it left her feeling a little unsettled at the unknown of who she'd be working alongside. The last thing she wanted was to end up under someone like Declan. That thought alone gave her shivers. She'd seen firsthand how much he riled up

Remi, and with some things she'd mentioned about her past, she wanted to make sure she was moving to a good place.

Almost another week had passed with no news on the funding, and tomorrow Jess needed to confirm if she was going to take the new position. Everyone she'd met at her in-person interview had been friendly and polite, with no red flags thrown up during the process, so she'd made up her mind to go ahead with the transfer. There was a melancholy feel on site, the air heavy with the possible changes to come should Jess accept the offer.

Remi was working with them today, light duties only. It was great to have her back. While Jess got on well with Sophie, she'd missed the extra sassy banter she shared with Remi when they were together. Their texting had increased a lot with the distance, more than probably necessary, but they couldn't seem to stop messaging each other. It was incessant. A quick check-in would turn into a three-page-long text essay about new tattoo ideas Remi had, or the latest theory Jess was debating about her current murder mystery read. Jess did everything she could to keep things friendly, carefully crafting each text so it could in no way come across as flirting. Though, there were a lot of close calls.

"Hey, can you pass my circular saw?" Remi asked Jess, sticking a pencil behind her ear as she measured an end panel to cut.

"Nope. But you can ask me to cut something for you."

Remi's arm was now in a compression bandage, but she had most of her movement back with hardly any pain.

"Jess, it's been three weeks," Remi whined.

"And the doctor said a *minimum* of four weeks off the tools."

"Honestly, I forget who's the boss around here sometimes," Remi said to Sophie.

Sophie snorted, outlining a sink cutout for the benchtop.

"Fine. I'll go set up the sawhorses out the front," said Remi, heading outside.

"I swear it's like babysitting a big kid. Every time you let Remi out of your sight, she's trying to lift something, drill something... bloody hammer something... the list goes on," Jess joked.

"This is the longest she's been on office duty since we started working together. It must be getting to her pretty bad. I'd be itching to be back on site if it were me," Sophie said, glancing towards the doorway. "I'm glad you're around to tell her off. She doesn't listen to me. Only if it's super serious and I have to pull out my mum voice."

Jess laughed. "I just give her shit. That seems to work."

"I see that," replied Sophie, chuckling.

Remi slid into the doorway, gasping for breath. Jess and Sophie looked up, bewildered.

"Wha—"

"WE'RE FUCKING THROUGH TO STAGE TWO!"

Sophie screamed and covered her mouth. Jess dropped what she was doing and jumped into the air as Remi barrelled into her for a hug.

This was huge. This was everything. One step closer, a *giant* step closer, to that funding. Jess breathed in, Remi's hair blurring her vision as she inhaled a mixture of fresh shampoo and sawdust, her hands sinking into Remi's back. She allowed herself to relax into this moment, to revel in this beautiful, amazing woman. Why did they have to fit together so perfectly?

"Thank you," Remi said in her ear, squeezing the air out of her lungs.

"Careful of your arm," Jess tried to say, as Remi crushed their lips together. And then they were kissing, the elation of the moment building on their momentum.

Her lips were warm and soft. So soft. A contrast to the urgency of the kiss. Jess melted, right there on the spot. Her cheeks hurt from smiling and trying to kiss at the same time, the stupidity of it all. It felt like coming home, her hands threading into Remi's hair.

Jess was done fighting. Herself, the world? It didn't matter. Remi mattered. This kiss mattered. Each brush of their lips filled her with happiness until her entire body tingled. She stood on steel-capped tippy toes to bring herself closer to Remi, her hands—

Sophie cleared her throat.

Remi's eyes went comically wide as they pulled apart. Remi clutched at Jess, holding her at arm's length, frozen.

Jess's mind had left Earth. She was on a completely different planet, short-circuiting from the amount of dopamine and adrenaline pumping through her body. Hopefully, it wasn't about to all come crashing down.

She turned to Sophie.

What had they just done?!

Sophie was hunched over, and for a moment Jess thought she was crying, until she realised she was howling... with laughter.

"I fucking *knew* it!" Sophie pointed between them as she straightened.

"Finally!" She threw her hands in the air, laughing again. "My god. I thought I was going to have to have a cold shower if I was around you two any longer."

Jess blinked slowly, her mind trying to keep up with everything that had just happened. She was still clutching Remi's wrists, her eyes darting between the sisters. Her shoulders eased with Sophie's reaction, but when she looked back to Remi, she frowned.

Remi was shaking her head. She broke the contact, stepping away from Jess. "We shouldn't. I'm sorry."

Jess felt the space immediately and willed her to come back. Sophie didn't sound angry, though?

"Why?" asked Sophie, confused, her arms dropping.

Remi searched Sophie's face for an answer. "It's unprofessional. I didn't think you'd want us to."

Jess knew the last thing Remi wanted was to let her sister down. The disappointment hit as quickly as the high had come. She'd had a glimmer of hope that maybe, just maybe, that kiss meant something had shifted between them.

Then Sophie spoke up. "Look at what she's done for the business, Remi. Look at what she's done to help *you* these last few weeks. That's not some young thing looking for a hook-up or a rebound. She cares for you. She cares for us and our future. Don't be an idiot. Ask the woman out already."

Jess's smile spread wide, hope blooming again as she waited for Remi's response. And okay... so maybe they had hooked up for a fraction of the time, *but* it was an exceptionally mutual hook-up. And god how she missed that touch. Thinking back, it never felt like "just" anything. It was deeper, always *more* with Remi. The timing just hadn't been right.

She knew they were adults and didn't need permission to date, but this endorsement had to mean a lot to Remi. Not only because it was coming from her sister, but from her business partner too. If Sophie didn't care, Jess certainly didn't. Still, with Remi's initial reaction to Sophie, she wondered if she'd choose to still keep those boundaries in place.

Remi turned back to Jess, a grin curling at the edges as she took her in. Jess held her breath.

"Well then, guess I better ask you out on a date before my sister here organises one for us. We'd end up at the theatre watching the ballet."

Jess scrunched up her face. "Ew. No offense Sophie, but yeah, the theatre is not for me."

The mood lightened, and Jess let the last of the tension go. She couldn't believe this was happening. Remi had officially asked her out on a date. She didn't even care where they went or what they did.

"And Jess?" Remi asked, a glint in her eye. "Cancel that transfer. We've got work to do."

"Oh?" Did this mean what she thought it did?

"I get that the second stage of funding still isn't one hundred percent guaranteed, but it's pretty damn close." Remi paused, looking between both of them. "We've officially beat out almost two thousand applicants in the first stage of EOI submissions."

Sophie's hand flew to her mouth. "Holy shit!"

Remi nodded. "I know. Crazy. Now, it's essentially crossing off boxes and proving we're serious that our ideas will work. They want business financials, a video pitch and a business plan with everything laid out on how we'll implement it all in detail—timelines, budgets, the lot."

"Well, what are you doing standing around here? You've got a date to plan and a business to save!"

Remi looked torn for a second, unsure whether to stay on site.

"Go!" Sophie and Jess yelled in unison.

Beaming, Remi practically skipped out of the room. Sophie turned to her, eyes sharp.

"So, you want to date my sister?"

Jess gulped. Oh no. She wasn't prepared for this talk. She'd barely come to terms with the fact Remi had just asked her out on a date. The adrenaline from all the news had well and truly worn off, and now Jess stood there awkwardly not knowing what to do.

"Uhh..."

A smile crept onto Sophie's face.

"I'm totally kidding." She chuckled, moving back to work on the cutout. "Your face though. Ha! Priceless." She paused, pencil back in hand. "I guess it goes without saying —treat her right, don't hurt her, yadda yadda... or I'll... have you sweeping sites for the next three years."

Relief flooded through her.

"Noted." Grinning, she left to cut the end panel.

She had a date. With Remi. And her job was looking like it was saved.

It was a good day, a good day indeed.

TWENTY-EIGHT

Remi

Maybe Remi should've let Sophie organise this date. She combed her hair for what felt like the fifth time, trying to get her dark curls to fall just right. She growled, running her hands through it next to try and reset the look until she was happy. She leaned on the sink.

"What's wrong with you?" she asked herself in the mirror. "You've already seen her naked. You spend most days together enjoying her company. What are you so nervous about?"

Her reflection stared back wide-eyed, a deer in headlights. Fake it til you make it.

She straightened herself up, re-tucking the long-sleeved shirt she'd picked out. It was the same one she'd worn to Jess's birthday, sans the suspenders. Her sleeves were rolled up to put her tattoos on show, and she turned to check her black jeans from the back. She looked *good*. She slipped on her boots and double checked everything in the mirror. "That'll do." She nodded to her reflection and walked out.

Time to impress.

Ten minutes early, Remi rang the doorbell and waited, listening to a cricket chirp in a nearby bush. She had flashbacks to Jess opening the door at her birthday, and the outfit that had made her tongue hit the floor like a cartoon.

The door swung open.

Oh.

"Don't look so disappointed," JJ said, holding it open for her to come in. "She's in her room getting ready."

"Thanks."

She didn't stop for idle chit-chat, feeling like she couldn't stand still until she saw Jess. As she moved to go past, JJ smacked her on her shoulder.

"About time, by the way." The genuine smile on JJ's face made her crack into a matching grin, helping her relax as she made her way to Jess's room and knocked.

"Coming!"

And there she was.

Remi couldn't stop the tug of her lips into a lopsided smile. "Hi."

Jess had straightened her hair, shiny pink lip gloss making them look fuller than usual... and way more kissable. She was stunning. Perfect. All of the words to describe someone of Jess's calibre. And she was Remi's date tonight. She'd never felt so lucky.

"Um..." Remi stood in the doorway, lost for words and not knowing how they should greet each other now. Shit. She hadn't planned this part. The indecision must have shown on her face as Jess took a step forward, lifting up on her toes to plant a kiss straight on her mouth. The look Jess gave her as she stepped back, assessing Remi up and down, made her chest flush. Yeah, okay, that was how you greeted someone.

Remi grinned stupidly at Jess. "Hi."

"You already said that." Jess's smile widened as she rocked back on her heels, hands shoved into the back of her jeans.

"Right!" Remi laughed lightly. Why was she so bad at this? Act normal! She went to lean on the door jamb, missing it completely and stumbled on the spot. A laugh down the hallway caught her attention, JJ peeking around the corner.

"Oi, back in the kitchen—you! And give us some privacy," said Remi, shaking her head as JJ disappeared.

Then to Jess: "I don't know why I'm so nervous. I'm making such an idiot of myself right now." She wiped her hands on her pants for no reason at all, the clamminess making her fidget. It had been so long since she'd taken someone on a proper date. She didn't want to stuff this up. She wanted it to be perfect for Jess; she wanted her to be adored, surprised; for the night to be something they talked about for years down the track. Okay, now she was getting ahead of herself.

Jess came up and slid her hand into Remi's, locking onto her eyes.

"How about... you take me on this date?

All Remi could do was nod at those baby blues.

"You're being very cute right now. I haven't seen this nervous side of Remi yet. Confident? Yes. Flirty. Sad. Angry. Hurt. But nervous? Never. I like that I make you nervous." She leaned into her ear. "Surprising though, when I've already been between your legs."

Remi groaned, catching herself as she remembered JJ was probably still listening. "We're taking this slow, especially since this is our first date," Remi replied, narrowing her eyes at Jess in light-hearted warning as she pulled her down the hallway.

Dinner was perfect. Remi had taken Jess to a Thai restaurant for more spicy food, with an array of aromatic plates including curries and her absolute favourite—the stir-fried lemongrass duck breast. Being their first date, Remi made sure to keep work talk off the table. Instead, they dove into childhood stories of both growing up by the beach, family holidays over the Christmas break and what it was like growing up with Sophie for a sister versus Jess being an only child.

"I thought we were heading home?" Jess asked as Remi drove them toward the city.

"Nope," Remi replied, giving nothing away. "The dinner was just the beginning."

They arrived out the front of an old, dilapidated warehouse.

"Is this the part where I find out you're a psycho murderer?" Jess asked, unimpressed with their surroundings.

"Look up." Remi pointed as they got out of the car.

"The Smash Up?" Jess read aloud, still confused.

Remi held out her arm. "This way."

She led Jess into the building and up to the counter, where a woman scanned tickets from Remi's phone.

"Someone's organised," Jess mumbled as the lady took them down a long corridor and around a corner. They stopped outside a large room filled with smashed-up rubbish. The woman handed them two sets of blue overalls and protective glasses, ran through the safety rules and left them to it.

"I've never heard of a smash room." Jess stared wide-eyed at the crap in front of them. "Oh wow, look at all the tools."

Remi smiled gleefully. "Yep. Golf club, baseball bat, metal pipe. Pick your weapon of choice and smash the crap out of whatever you want for the next hour. With the amount of changes we've had this year, it could be good for our mental health to just let this stuff have it!"

Only one of them could go in at a time, so Remi waited outside as Jess went in and picked up the biggest wrench Remi had ever seen.

"Oh, there'll be a few people I'll be picturing while I smash these," Jess said, picking up a wine bottle and placing it on the stand.

Jess hadn't done much demolition yet in the business, and Remi couldn't wait to see how she handled it.

Her first swing clipped the top of the bottle as she shied away from the impact, turning to Remi and giving her a big *whoops* face.

"Come on, you can do better than that!" Remi cheered her on from behind the glass. "Smack it!"

Jess nodded, picked up a lamp, widened her stance, gripped the wrench and took a big breath. Remi watched the exact moment Jess's eyes narrowed, seeing and yet unseeing the item in front of her. She swung hard. The lamp shattered with a spectacular spray of glass over the entire room. Jess turned, her jaw dropping at the impact of the hit. Then she laughed, deep and guttural, until she let out, "Woo! God, that felt good! Okay, I'm seeing the appeal."

Next came a bottle, then a few glasses. She tried to smack a big plate but the sledgehammer she chose was too heavy. Shrugging, she picked up the plate and slung it at the wall like a frisbee, creating another shower of ceramic confetti. The maniacal laugh that followed had both of them grinning like idiots.

"You're enjoying this even more than I thought," Remi commented as Jess exited, huffing from the exertion with sweat pouring down her bright red face.

"I didn't realise how much I needed that. Thank you." She kissed Remi again, then pulled back quickly. "I'm sorry."

"Why?"

"I'm so sweaty!"

"Pfft, come here." Remi pulled her in for a proper kiss, building on the adrenaline in the air. Remi didn't care one bit about how messed up Jess looked. Their kiss grew in intensity, and Remi was thankful they were the only ones at the centre, because this was getting indecent. Sorry to whatever security detail were watching the cameras; they were getting a show.

Jess pulled away, placing a hand on Remi's chest over the blue overalls. "We need to stop or we'll run out of time, and you haven't even had a go yet. And don't think I won't be keeping an eye on you. I know the doctor cleared you, but that doesn't mean swinging that sledgehammer in there. Got it?"

"It's still so hot when you're bossy," Remi replied, ignoring her completely. "But yes, I'll be careful. Left hand only, promise. And you can laugh at how unco I look while doing it."

"Oh, I am getting this on video!" replied Jess, holding up her phone.

Remi entered the room; the smell of dust hung in the air. It reminded her of being on a demo site with tile rubble surrounding her. She picked up a beer bottle and a baseball bat.

"Here goes nothing!" she called before thwacking it into the back wall.

A plate smashed next and, "Why does this feel so good?" she cried, throwing a mug to the ground. After five minutes, she was breathless. She was surprised at how much energy it took out of her. She realised she hadn't been this active since her accident. It felt so good to use her muscles. She screamed as she threw a heavy wine bottle at the wall, jumping in victory when it exploded on impact. She was laughing next, sounding just as crazed as Jess had.

By the time her session ended, her safety glasses were completely fogged up from the work out. "Okay, that was amazing."

Jess nodded profusely. "So therapeutic."

"Well, the night's not over yet!" said Remi as she climbed out of the awful overalls.

"No?" Jess's eyebrows raised.

Their final stop was a small ice cream parlour on the main strip of Karkalla Beach, just up from The Wharf. Being the end of summer, the nights were still long, and the sun was still setting. Cones in hand, they made their way to the jetty.

Remi grabbed Jess's hand, her fingers sliding over soft skin, their palms clasping together like they'd done this a hundred times before. Jess's hand was smaller, and Remi loved the way it fit into her palm. They reached the shoreline and began strolling along the water's edge.

They were quiet at first, content just walking along in silence as the last of the sun slid slowly into the horizon.

"You know," Jess said softly, "I think today's the first time in a long while that I've looked out at the ocean, thought of my friends on their boat, living their life... and I haven't felt jealous."

"I didn't know you felt that way."

"It's easy to compare your life to others when nothing feels right in your own. I think tonight in that smash room, I released the last of that built-up anger. Those tangles of jealousy, comparison and wishing I was living some alternate life. I left it all in that room, a million pieces scattered on the floor."

"Wow." Remi had expected her to enjoy it, but she didn't realise the profound effect it could have on her.

Jess squeezed her hand, looking at Remi with the sweetest of smiles, so relaxed and content. "I have you to thank for that."

"I didn't do anything." And it was true. "All I did was take a chance on a waitress I thought might want to work with me. The rest? That was all you. You took a chance, changed your career, left a relationship that no longer served you, moved house... I mean that's one hell of a way to turn your life around."

"Last year I promised myself this would be a new life. Entering my thirties, I didn't imagine that would mean starting over in every aspect like I have. But I wouldn't have it any other way. I'm excited to take these next steps with you, whatever the future holds."

They stopped to face the water, ice cream cones long gone.

"I like you," Jess confessed.

Remi smiled, thinking to the time when she'd stood here, confessing the weight of liking girls to her sister. She still liked girls, and she definitely liked Jess.

"I like you, too." Remi grinned.

"So, where to from here, with us?" Jess's face was full of hope, a touch of uncertainty around the edges as her eyes searched Remi's. What was in store for their future? That was the big question, wasn't it? They still had things to work out, each day becoming a little less complicated, a little more hopeful, but for now...

"I think... let's take it slow. I know there's a lot for you that's still relatively fresh to unpack, and even if you had checked out of that relationship, these things still take time. I care for you a lot, and I'm not going anywhere."

Jess nodded, seemingly satisfied with Remi's answer. "Slow is good. We already know we can do fast." She bumped into Remi's shoulder with a smirk.

"Can I still kiss you now, Donatello?"

Remi laughed. "Yes, Jess. You can kiss me now."

TWENTY-NINE

Jess

Jess watched Remi as she concentrated on the cabinet layout of their current kitchen project. The little frown on her face was extremely cute. She was biting her bottom lip, teasing it with her teeth as she scanned the design plans. The movement was so sensual, Jess wanted to kiss her all over again. And now, she could, if she wanted to. The thought made her smile so wide it hurt her cheeks.

Even though they were dating now, they'd put boundaries in place to minimise PDA and keep things friendly on site. They had jobs to do, cupboards to build and—

Remi's lip released from her teeth, looking so plump and irresistible. Maybe just a little peck...

Stop it.

Jess shook her head, refocusing on the cabinet she was constructing.

"Keep it in your pants, Jess." Her head whipped around to see Sophie standing there, hands on her hips, clearly suppressing a smile. Remi looked up at them, eyes questioning.

"Jess was sitting on the floor drooling over you," Sophie said to Remi.

Remi came over and leaned across the cupboard in Jess's face, her chest at eye level. Jess swallowed, flicking her eyes up as Remi ran a tongue across her bottom lip.

"Like what you see?" She raised an eyebrow.

"Oh, get out!" Jess slapped her on the shoulder, then turned to Sophie. "You saw that. It's not my fault I keep getting distracted. Your sister is hot."

"I think I liked you both better when you weren't dating," Sophie replied, humouring them as she picked up one of the cabinets to line up against the wall.

The air felt lighter lately, especially since they'd made it through to the second round of funding. The money hadn't landed in the business account yet, but they could see the end in sight. They were so close. Remi had shifted to half-days, splitting her time between being on the tools and prepping all the business materials for the fund. Once stage two was approved, they'd get the green light on the money, and they could truly celebrate.

Jess was beyond relieved that her left-field idea had saved her job. She'd withdrawn her applications and turned down the transfer offer. She was officially staying with The Lady Builders. On Remi's orders—and Jess wasn't going to argue with the boss. Not about that, anyway.

Knowing more women would be joining the team soon had Jess so excited. Each new addition meant more learning, more growth, more confidence.

That was one surprising benefit from her date night; smashing everything in that room had given her more confidence on the bigger tools like the demo hammer. She'd taken up floor tiles in a bathroom earlier in the week, getting into a rhythm and popping up multiple tiles at a time. She loved it, getting a thrill every time another line of tiles came up.

It was finally Friday night, and Jess couldn't have been more thankful. The week had been gruelling, *but*, thankfully, she wasn't working until almost midnight; slinging pasta plates and pouring wine, cleaning up after kids and adults alike. Instead, Jess had just taken the longest and most luxurious bath of her life. JJ's oversized bathroom still felt like an Airbnb she somehow hadn't been kicked out of yet. It was incredibly decedent, all of her muscles relaxing almost immediately. She slipped on her fluffy pink robe and shuffled across to her room. She flicked on the light and... nothing. Flicking it several times had no change. Darkness.

Huh.

Jess found JJ watching TV in the lounge. "Hey, you got a step ladder?"

"Uh, yeah, why?"

Jess hooked a thumb over her shoulder. "Lightbulb's blown."

"Right," said JJ hopping up and pulling a ladder out of the laundry. "Here you go. I'll bring a torch."

With JJ holding the light, Jess climbed the ladder, Remi's words playing in her head. "*Lefty loosie*" she said to herself as she reached overhead.

"How many women does it take to change a lightbulb?" JJ asked, laughing at her terrible joke and making the light bounce all over the room.

"Ha-ha. Watch it you. I don't want a repeat of Remi and end up on my butt!"

"Good point," replied JJ, standing still once more with the torch.

Jess took a breath and unscrewed the bulb, popping it out easily. She handed it to JJ. "Got a spare?"

JJ looked at the end. "Screw bulb. Yep. Give me a sec."

She returned a minute later, taking a new one out of the box. Jess screwed it back in and walked over to the switch, flicking the light on.

"And that... is how you change a lightbulb," she said proudly.

And she didn't even electrocute herself!

"I've had an epiphany."

Jess sat out the back of JJ's, appreciating her immaculate garden. The big jacaranda tree shadowed overhead interlaced with an overgrown pergola covered in grapevines. It was the epitome of cosy vibes. The dappled light played on the outdoor table as she nursed her mug of tea. The sun was shining, and the bees were buzzing. Jess stretched her legs out along the cushioned bench seat.

"Oh?" came Remi's voice through the phone. Jess could picture the raised eyebrow, the twitch of her mouth. It was Saturday morning, and they were meeting for lunch in a few hours, but Jess couldn't hold in her idea. It had arrived red-hot and bursting to be shared. Remi was the first person on her mind, and the only one she wanted to share it with. She'd hit dial without a second thought.

"Is there room in the business plan for an adjustment?"

"Mmm, maybe?" Remi hummed.

"I was thinking about your idea to host workshops, and I think I'd like to run one of my own. Not for tradeswomen specifically, but for all the Jesses out there who were like me six months ago."

"Like how?" Remi asked, sounding a little unsure.

"The version of me who wanted things done around the house, but didn't know how. Didn't know where to begin, overwhelmed with how difficult she assumed it was and so tired of asking someone else for help. I want to empower women, help them to believe in themselves and teach them. A Handy Women's Workshop. Perfect for any age. The girl who's just moved out, the woman with a husband who works away a lot, the widow who seeks resilience in looking after herself, or the person who just wants to know how to change their own damn lightbulb."

"Jess..." Remi trailed off. The silence left Jess on edge.

"I know it has nothing to do with apprenticeships or cabinet-making..." Jess prattled on, not knowing what else to say or how to define her idea further.

"Stop."

Jess stilled on the bench, almost sloshing her tea all over herself.

"It's amazing."

Oh. Thank god.

"Truly amazing, Jess." She could hear the smile in Remi's voice, feel the adoration, and it thrilled Jess all the way down to her toes.

Remi continued, "I think it would make the perfect addition to our business plans. It's a completely different offering, but it opens us up to a new demographic. At the end of the day, we're still helping women—all women, from all walks of life."

Jess felt the energy building on her idea as she listened to Remi.

"I've seen the way you look when you finish a job you're proud of," Remi added. "That's one of the most rewarding parts of my job—seeing your growth. And I mean that as your boss, not just as your girlfriend."

Jess sucked in a breath. They hadn't talked about labels. Though, the grin currently burying itself into her cheeks and getting wider by the second, told her this was exactly what she wanted. The only thing stopping her from agreeing to the relationship was outside opinions—and assumptions at that. Why would Jess get into a relationship so fast after leaving Adam? Why would Jess get into a relationship with her *boss*? Why was Jess in a relationship with a woman now? These were the questions persistently on her mind since they first talked about their mutual attraction. But she'd figured out the answer to every single one of them.

Who. Fucking. Cares.

Listening to herself and taking her career seriously had been the best decision Jess had ever made. Was it hard? Yes. Did she have doubts? Almost every bloody day. But she'd pushed through and believed in herself every step of the way.

It was time to listen to herself again, because no one else was Jess, and no one else knew how she felt.

"Shit—sorry. I know we haven't talked—"

"Yes." It was Jess's turn to cut off the rambling. "Girlfriend."

Better English would help the situation; her brain was still scrambling to come to terms with the decision.

"That is, yes." A pause. "I would love to be your girlfriend, Remi."

"Can you get over here already?" Remi chuckled down the line.

Jess couldn't drive fast enough, her tea left on the table, growing cold.

"So, what? No sex?" Marie asked sweet as pie, earning another slap from Hayley.

"You're so tactless sometimes, woman!" Hayley scolded, kissing her wife on the cheek as Marie pinched her nose in retaliation.

Jess burned under the spotlight, all eyes landing on her. Why she'd agreed to come to games night knowing she'd be grilled the entire evening, she'd never know... though she couldn't blame her friends. She'd hardly seen them with all the life changes, and wasn't sure she'd even come tonight. Jess only agreed after Marie called to say she'd told Adam and Heath it was a girls-only night, twisting her arm. Sam and Taylor were on the big TV screen, tuning in from their boat in Broome.

"Um... yeah, but no?" Jess confessed, feeling as bright as a beetroot. She wasn't as open to talking about bedroom shenanigans as Marie was.

"What does that even mean?" Marie pressed.

"We kind of slept together for a short time, then agreed it was better to be friends. That didn't really work, as much as we tried, so now we're trying to date properly, without making things too messy. Taking it slow," Jess explained.

"Glad it's you and not me," Taylor piped in, eyes only for Sam. They were so sickly sweet, and Jess loved it. This time, she was revelling in their love rather than wishing she had it too. "Nah, I'm really happy for you, Jess," Taylor continued. "We could all see the tension between you and Adam. I think you made the right call."

"Agreed." Marie and Hayley nodded along.

"Thanks, guys. I mean, you could've told me," she half-joked.

"I think you needed to come to that decision on your own terms," Sam added.

Jess sighed, letting her head fall back on her favourite blue velvet couch. "I know. You're right." She popped a Malteser in her mouth.

This downtime was just what she needed. Board games laid out, snacks aplenty and laughter shared as they updated each other on life.

"So, you know how we said we didn't want a flashy wedding?" Taylor was saying.

"I think we're going to elope!" Sam squealed, making Belle bark in the background. The dog jumped onto the screen and into Sam's lap, drowning her in kisses. "Sorry, Bell Bell, didn't mean to excite you. C'mon, lie down," Sam instructed, settling the dog down. Jess's heart squeezed in that moment. She missed the cute pup who used to live with her when Taylor was her housemate.

"She still loving the water?" Jess asked.

Taylor gave her a pointed look. "At this point, she's half fish, half dog."

Everyone laughed as Belle barked in agreement.

"And she's stealing the show again!" Sam added playfully.

"Right, tell us about this elopement already!" cried Marie on the edge of her seat.

Taylor started, "Do you know how many things you need to organise for a regular wedding? *All* the things. And anyone decent is booked out, like, a year or more in advance. It's crazy!"

"As we found out while we were back in Adelaide. The more we looked, the more we thought..."

"Yeah, nah," Taylor finished with a smile. "Not sure if it's boat life and living all minimalist but seeing the extravagance and showmanship of weddings these days... it's getting ridiculous! I also can't picture half the boaties—who we'd want at the wedding—showing up in suits."

"So... we're sailing across to Indonesia!" Sam revealed.

"That is an epic wedding idea!" Hayley added.

"What's with all the noise?"

Jess turned to see a woman descending the stairs, sleek and straight; blonde hair cascading down. She was almost as tall as Hayley; but wore a scowl Jess would never see on her friend. "Brookie?" Jess stared, wide-eyed at the girl she hadn't seen in almost a decade.

"It's just Brooke now," she corrected, hand on hip as she stood at the bottom of the stairs.

"Right..." Jess stumbled, not recognising the new, older *Brooke* that stood before her.

"Hey Brooke!" Taylor said from the screen. "Sorry for disturbing you, you know how game nights go," she added, trying to lighten the mood.

"Right. Forgot that was on." Brooke adjusted the handbag on her shoulder. "I'm heading out," she said flatly to Hayley.

"No worries." Hayley's smile was tight.

If this was anything like what they'd seen between her and Adam, how had she not seen it sooner? The tension in the room stretched taut like a rubber band, and Jess wasn't sure who was going to snap first.

Brooke stormed across the room, not bothering with any further pleasantries. The front door shut with a thump that made the girls jump.

Jess sat wide-eyed, unsure what to say.

"Well..." Taylor trailed off. "She seems happy."

Hayley and Marie shared a look.

"She's been pissed twenty-four-seven since she got back, giving us the sullen or silent treatment. We thought we were helping by letting her stay with us, but she's been so difficult. Hasn't opened up at all. All I know is she sure doesn't want to be back in Adelaide." Hayley looked toward the hallway, eyebrows pinching.

"And we've got the painter starting next week. It's been a lot," Marie confessed.

"JJ is great," said Jess, hoping to cheer the girls up with a new topic. "Honestly, the best housemate."

"Hey!" Taylor cried.

Jess held up a finger. "*Second*-best housemate. Sorry Taylor! I think you'll love JJ, and I can't wait to see this place transformed."

"Housemates and painting aside, I want to hear more about Remi! We're so behind on all this gossip!" Taylor had moved right up on the screen, leaning closer.

At this rate, they were never going to get any games started tonight, let alone finished.

THIRTY

Remi

"Remi? Hi, I'm calling to officially welcome you to the Fearless Women's Foundation. Congratulations. The Lady Builders have been accepted."

They'd done it. They'd won.

Tears sprang to her eyes, and she swallowed a lump in her throat, unable to speak as emotion overwhelmed her.

"Wow," she warbled into the phone, trying to at least say something while she contained herself. "Wow," she repeated, the woman on the other end laughing lightly.

"Your proposal and plans were some of the best we've seen, and we're so excited to see you bring your ideas to life."

Remi was thankful for the added time to calm down. "Th-thank you," she stammered. "This means so much to me. So much to the women out there. Thank you. Wow."

As far as speeches went, it wasn't much, but it was all she had right now.

"We'll be in touch with next steps, and everything will be emailed through within the next twenty-four hours."

She thanked her again, rather lamely, and hung up. She stood out the front of a bakery, a pie and an iced coffee still hanging from her hand.

She couldn't wait to share the news, but first... she walked straight back into the shop for a celebratory chocolate doughnut.

With sprinkles.

Remi was pretty sure she had permanent hearing loss from the screams Jess and Sophie let out at the news. *Worse than two demo hammers going, they were!* With hugs and silly dances, there were lots of reasons to celebrate on site.

Now that everything was official, the serious work began. It was time to deploy all the new marketing tactics, to build up the workload, and start job listings for two fully qualified tradeswomen. The Lady Builders were growing, and Remi's dream was coming to fruition.

That night, Remi and Jess strolled along the beach hand-in-hand. It had become one of their date night rituals —time by the water to unwind, unload and slow down with each other, watching the sunset and enjoying the weather. Though it was meant to be the middle of autumn, summer still clung to the air, not wanting to let go.

"Did you ever think you'd be here?" Jess wondered.

"Business-wise, yes. Though I never expected it to happen so quickly. It was my five-year plan, remember?" She chuckled. "I could never have anticipated the path to get here." Remi squeezed Jess's hand, unable to look away from her in the soft light. "Couldn't have anticipated *you*."

Jess's megawatt smile hit her right in the gut, pure happiness radiating from her eyes as they crinkled at the edge.

She couldn't deny her feelings at this point.

She was hopelessly in love with Jessica Greaves.

The words sat quietly on the tip of her tongue. She couldn't say it yet; she wanted to respect that Jess had only recently left a serious relationship. She didn't want to scare her off. Allowing herself the knowledge it was love was enough for now. She said it in other ways instead.

In how she held Jess's hand, her thumb gently caressing the back of it.

In how she listened to everything Jess had to say, making sure she felt heard and cared for.

Or right now, when she allowed her eyes to express what she couldn't say aloud, planting the softest of kisses on Jess's forehead as she pulled her in for a hug. Remi wrapped her arms around her tight, head leaning against Jess's as they stood for a moment. Remi inhaled, hit with everything so quintessentially Jess—her fruity perfume and soapy clean skin mixed with the salty sea air.

Soon.

Jess's hand rested on Remi's thigh as she drove them to work, tapping out a lazy beat to the radio. The small touch grounded her.

Since they'd openly begun dating, Remi found their relationship was less of a distraction at work than she'd initially thought it would be. Jess had integrated into her life so seamlessly, Remi questioned why she'd ever thought she didn't have time to date in the first place. Perhaps it was the person. She hadn't wanted to change for anyone else, or let anyone else in. Though with Jess, it hadn't been so much of a choice in the end. Jess was just... there. Part of her life. And Remi didn't want her to leave it.

She interlaced their fingers, hanging on tight, her other elbow resting out the window as they coasted along the beachfront.

It was time to head back to the Donaldsons' today and her feelings were a mix of anticipation and curiosity.

Cole had called the day before to let them know everything had been delivered so they could make a start on the laundry. He was extremely apologetic about the Declan saga and for doubting Remi's word, but thankful at the same time that she'd helped to uncover their dodgy workmanship. She didn't press the issue and had no idea if the boys had rectified the problems in the kitchen. At the end of the day, she just wanted to focus on their own work and complete Cole's project to the best of their abilities. She was, however, looking forward to finishing this particular job and moving on, hopefully never working alongside Declan and Karkalla Renovations again.

They hadn't been on site since she'd given Declan a piece of her mind, and the last thing she wanted was to see that wanker again.

Pulling up to the house, there were no cars out the front and the house seemed locked up.

"Weird," she muttered, eyes scanning the yard.

"What's up?" Jess asked from the passenger seat. They'd been carpooling all week, using the drive as a mini-date to spend time together before work started... and maybe throw in a sneaky kiss—or two.

"There's no one here. It's only Wednesday, so I thought

Declan's boys might've been here to finish or at least rectify the kitchen."

Remi let them into the house. "Hello?" she called into the silence.

Nothing.

Oh well, not something to complain about.

Walking past the kitchen, she saw the piece of gyprock from the inspection, still on the floor. Everything left unfinished, untouched. It looked like they hadn't been back at all. Bringing her toolbox into the laundry, they laid the drop sheets down and started on the benchtops.

Halfway through the day, there was a knock at the door.

Maybe the boys were doing an afternoon shift?

They should have a key, but knowing them, they'd probably misplaced it. She made her way to the front and swung open the door.

Javier stood there, full suit and all, with a smile that was slightly reserved. He looked so out of place, away from his sleek office, she thought she was seeing things. Wait—ah, he was probably here to see Declan.

"Declan's not on site, sorry," she apologised.

"Actually, I'm here to see you. May I come in?"

Her face ran through a range of emotions, settling on perplexed. "Sure?"

Why the hell was he here to see her? Had Declan said something else? They'd already lost the work, what else could it be?

Her mind swam as they moved to the empty kitchen extension. With no seats around, they stood awkwardly,

Javier taking particular interest in the kitchen details before turning to Remi, hands clasped behind his back. He smiled again, but it didn't reach his eyes. He almost seemed... nervous? It was so unlike him, it threw her off.

"Look," he started, pacing slowly around the room. He let out a short laugh.

Okay, he really *did* sound nervous. Her eyebrows furrowed trying to concentrate harder on where this was going. "I don't know how to say this, so I'll just say it. Would you—" he cleared his throat, "would you consider working with us again?"

His eyes flashed to her, edgy but hopeful.

"What?" The word flew out her mouth, disbelieving. "What about Karkalla?"

"Karkalla Renovations have had their building licence suspended, effective immediately. As you can imagine, this has left us in an extremely tight position."

"Oh."

That explained the empty house and untouched kitchen extension. Remi wondered what else the building association had dug up with their investigation. Handing down a suspension was a serious decision. How many other people had Declan been ripping off or leaving with such defective work? She stood, stunned.

"Yes. It's definitely taken us by surprise. I wanted to apologise for what we did to you and your business for cancelling the work in the first place. I can only imagine the impact it would've had on your bottom line."

"Actually," Remi interrupted. "I have to thank you for dropping the contract."

Javier's head snapped up. "What?"

"You were right."

"I was?" he replied, eyebrows flying to his hairline.

"We weren't in the best position, running behind on work and trying to squeeze everything in. If I'm honest, we would've been burned out by the time we started your work. My accident was a blessing, forcing us to rethink—everything. Rebuild from the ground up."

Javier listened intently as Remi explained, "Three people would've been too tight for your workload, but getting the opportunity to work with you, I believed I could make it work. Hurting my arm forced me to see the reality. If one of us was out, the whole wheel broke."

It felt so good to get this off her chest, the weight lifting with each word.

"When you told us we'd lost the job, I was in a bad place. But my team gathered around me to work out how we could come back from losing your business. You have to understand, we had nothing else in the pipeline. We were banking everything on the Flinders contract." He frowned as she held up a hand. "Which is on me—not you."

She continued, "Thanks to our teamwork, we've recently won funding to expand the business. So, in terms of divine timing, this couldn't be more fitting. I'm currently in the process of hiring two more qualified women, which should be a much healthier team size for your work, while allowing us to keep other jobs going in between."

She'd learned her lesson about promising staff before she had them. This time, it was the honest truth. Take it or leave it.

Javier blew out a breath, shaking his head as he looked at the ground. When he finally looked up, he was smiling.

"I think we could make this work, Remi. Perhaps, as you say, everything worked out exactly the way it was meant to."

"I think you're right." Remi grinned, then a thought struck her. "Wait, how did you know we were here?"

She'd never given him the address, and they hadn't spoken since last time.

"Cole and I are friends from way back. He let me know you were on site today, something about being an arse for not listening to you in the first place."

"Ah," replied Remi with a smirk.

"He tipped me off to Declan's investigation initially, warning me to be careful as soon as he had the report—which was a great idea, by the way. It seems we were both duped by his smooth talking."

"Yeah, he really dug himself into a hole with that one, doubting *our* work. If he'd kept to his own projects, the report would've never been made."

"Things sometimes have a way of working themselves out though, don't they?" Javier tilted his head, his smile saying more than words.

"That they do," Remi agreed with a chuckle.

With promises to speak further, Remi walked Javier out and came back into the house, shocked.

Had that really just happened?

"You girls hear all that?" Remi called out, grinning wide as Sophie and Jess poked their heads out of the laundry like two chipmunks.

"Does this mean what I think it means?" Sophie asked, eyes alight.

"I *really* need to find those new tradeswomen. It's gonna be a busy year."

Epilogue

JESS

One month later...

Every single seat was filled. Every single one.

It was Jess's first Handy Women's Workshop, held at the local Karkalla Beach hardware store, and she'd sold out.

Women of all ages streamed into the venue. Jess greeted a few of the early attendees, then put her head down organising everything she'd brought for the night ahead. When she looked back up, fifty sets of eyes were on her.

Wow, this was happening.

Jess stood at the front, beginning her introductions and going through what they'd be learning. Halfway through the drawer and hinge adjustments section she squinted, eyes catching on copper-blonde hair at the back. She was probably mistaken.

She continued the workshop, the energy building with each segment. She'd call up a helper for each one, so she had someone to teach directly. It made the experience much more enjoyable, and even more rewarding, every time she saw the gears click into place as the helper did it themselves.

"Well done, Ashley!" she said to a particularly shy young girl, who couldn't have been older than fifteen. She'd just learned how to pull apart a door handle, picking up every instruction with ease. Though her cheeks were red from being up front, her smile was joyful. Jess couldn't help but revel in it.

The entire night went off without a hitch—better than she could've ever imagined. With all the demonstrations complete, it was time to open up the floor to Q&A.

Hands flew up immediately. There were no crickets in this room. She smirked—*thank god for that!*

"Will you be holding more of these sessions?" the first woman asked.

"Yes!" There was no doubt in her mind this was a success.

"What toolkit do you recommend at home when you're just getting started?" another queried.

Jess pulled up a bag from under the table. "You'll all be going home tonight with more than just knowledge. We've included a booklet on everything you've learned today, and the hardware store has also kindly put together a starter toolkit. So, you should all be ready to start tinkering on those squeaky doors and broken handles in no time!"

Everyone clapped at the news, and Jess grinned so much her cheeks were well and truly aching. She'd almost gone through every participant when the copper-blonde woman at the back raised her hand.

"What do you love most about being a cabinet-maker?" her mother asked.

Because that was definitely her mum. Jess would recognise her voice anywhere. Her mum leaned to the side, face coming into view with the question.

Jess couldn't remember the last time her mum had asked her something like this. An open-ended question, free of judgement or presumption. Wanting and waiting for Jess to answer.

She was momentarily stunned but recovered quickly as dozens of other ladies waited on her response.

"I love how happy it makes me, and I love how proud I am of myself each day. Do I make mistakes? All. The. Time." She rolled her eyes good-naturedly. "But! It's all part of learning. So, when I try for the fifth time and I finally get it, I know that's another skill I've just acquired for life."

She smiled. And her mum smiled back, a warmth passing between them that had been missing for some time. She hadn't seen her parents since their disastrous dinner, giving herself space to grow and heal on her own without the pressure to do or be anything else for her mother. She'd kept her mum up to date by text or short phone calls instead, maintaining the distance. For her to come here tonight, this was an olive branch in itself, buying her own ticket to come in support of her daughter.

It meant so much to Jess. Perhaps this was the beginning of change in her mum, the beginning of her road to accepting Jess living life on her own terms.

Arms wrapped around Jess as she flipped a pancake.

"These smell so good," Remi murmured in her ear, her breath warm on Jess's neck.

"Mmm, and you *feel* so good." Jess pushed herself back into Remi, who nuzzled in closer, swaying her on the spot.

"Give me one more minute and I'm yours," said Jess, waiting for her last pancake to brown.

"Are they your famous ones?"

"Sure are. Apple and banana, baby!" Jess said, flipping the last one onto the stack and switching off the stove. She turned into Remi's arms, eyeing the dining table over her shoulder. Remi had already set it for the two of them, their mugs out ready for coffee.

A flashback surfaced—Adam asking her, or at least insinuating, to make them breakfast. The two moments couldn't have been more different. Though they weren't living together full-time, everything just flowed at Remi's. If one was cooking, the other was cleaning. If Jess cleaned up after Remi, it didn't bother her in the slightest, because there was no doubt Remi had helped in some other way that day—whether it was a foot massage on the couch or listening to a particular problem she'd been trying to sort out at work. They were always there for each other. Building each other up. In big ways and little ways. In all the ways that mattered. They were a team.

"What?" Remi asked as Jess stared at her girlfriend.

Jess brought her lips to Remi's, intending a small, soft kiss of affection. Remi had other ideas, deepening the kiss before spinning them on the spot and lifting Jess onto the bench with ease. Jess squealed, holding on tight to the toned muscle beneath her touch. She ran her hands through Remi's hair, then down her back and under her shirt, enjoying the feel of warm skin. *Mmm, no bra.* Jess brought a hand to the front, cupping Remi's breast and rolling a nipple between her fingers. Remi hissed into their kiss, squeezing Jess's arse in retaliation. In under a minute, Jess was already in overdrive, her body flushed and needy.

Remi broke the kiss.

"Bedroom?" She nipped at her ear.

Jess couldn't nod fast enough, wrapping her arms and legs around Remi as she carried her easily down the hall. Jess was so happy Remi was back to full health.

Pancakes forgotten, they fell back onto the bed in a huff, pillows softening Jess's landing. Remi towered over her, strong arms either side of her face, a curtain of dark hair spilling down. Jess brushed some aside, trailing her hand over Remi's tattoos in the process. Remi watched the affectionate touch, catching Jess's hand in a kiss as she reached her shoulder. Jess slowly traced along Remi's jaw then and across her lips. She stopped.

Remi sucked in a finger, running her tongue along its length before Jess's breath hitched at the sight. Then Remi sucked on two. Jess gasped, the warmth hitting straight at her core.

Releasing her hand, Jess slid it between Remi's waist-band, teasing at her edges before pulling it out with a snap of the elastic.

"Tease," Remi growled, going in for a kiss.

Jess smiled, enjoying being on the bottom now Remi's arm was healed.

Such a good view. Made even better if she was naked.

As if reading her mind, Remi sat them up and pulled Jess's top off in one fell swoop. Remi's followed a second later, with Jess sucking in a nipple before the shirt had even hit the floor. Remi threw her head back in pleasure, hands reaching out to squeeze and knead Jess's breasts while Jess sucked and nipped at Remi. Sitting up together like this felt wild. Each touch, each flick, building each other up layer by layer.

Jess could feel how close she was. Sitting up didn't give her anywhere near as much room to touch Remi how she'd like. She pulled them back down on the bed, Remi rolling to the side. Jess kicked off her sleep shorts and underwear, done with the amount of clothes they still had on. Remi followed suit, eyes never leaving Jess's and a smile so wicked she wanted to giggle with delight. How did she get here? With this absolute tradie goddess in front of her. All t-shirt tan and long legs, looking at Jess like she was the best damn thing on earth.

Remi's mouth was on her then, deep kisses that lit her on fire. A hand pinched and flicked at her nipple, and Jess writhed under her touch. She slid her hand down Remi's chest, over her stomach and down to her thighs. Remi lifted her leg in response, her hand mirroring Jess's, lowering until it circled around where Jess wanted it most.

They loved this dance, ratcheting each other up to the point of crazed desire, on the precipice of losing control and wanting to take control all at once. As their kiss continued, both hands explored, every edge, every crease, driving themselves wild.

Jess couldn't take it anymore. She slipped a finger into Remi's folds, groaning at how wet and warm she was. *For her.* The thought alone made her dizzy. Remi followed suit, the sensation of her fingers sliding over Jess's clit had her arching off the bed. *So sensitive*. Remi knew just the right amount of pressure to apply. Long, languid strokes, mixed with the feel of her tongue, made Jess's own hand stutter.

They were a tangle of limbs, moving, writhing as one.

Remi's finger dipped into her next. Jess repeated the motion until they were both desperately pumping, their kiss slipping, losing control. Their sounds filled the room. It was as if they'd become one. Jess wasn't sure where she ended and Remi began. Lost in the touch, and being touched. This is what it felt like to be whole, to be complete.

Her build was slower this time, maddening when her body screamed for release *now*. Overloaded on sensation, on emotion, on... *everything*.

As the familiar tension climbed, higher and higher, she felt Remi's hips grinding, her face pinching. Jess's body echoed her movements, hips lifting off the bed.

Then the dam broke, both crying out at once. Waves rolled through her, every colour of the rainbow bursting behind her eyes. It was magic.

Ecstasy.

Euphoria.

And every other E-word she could think of.

Her heart pounded. Her grin stretched wide, toes tingling.

Yeah, this was her person.

Jess held Remi's hand under the table as they listened to JJ giving a speech about her journey from apprentice to starting her own business. It was Jess's first tradeswomen's dinner, and looking at all the smiling faces, she knew these were her people. She'd yet to spot Ricciardo, but was thankful to be on the other side of the restaurant tonight at Limone, relaxing with her girlfriend by her side.

"Hi, I'm Freya, and I'll be your waitress this evening." Jess didn't recognise the new girl as she handed out the menus to everybody.

"Don't even think about offering her a job," Jess joked as the waitress gave the last menu out.

"Wouldn't dream of it." Remi's eyes didn't stray from Jess as she leaned in for a chaste kiss. "Plus, I think the five of us is enough, don't you?"

Jess grinned at the two women sitting across from them. Both fully qualified tradeswomen, they were the latest recruits to The Lady Builders, thanks to the funding that had come through. Michelle was a cabinet-maker. Lara was a tiler by trade and also halfway through a cabinet-making apprenticeship—making her a double win for the business. Jess got on great with both women, but Lara already had her excited to dabble in tiling down the track. Remi had hired well, as she knew she would.

To create boundaries between work and life, Remi had assigned Jess to work under Michelle from now on, so Remi wouldn't technically be her direct boss anymore. They were both happy with the pressure it took off of their relationship. Plus, it gave them much more to talk about when they were together, both raving about different projects they were working on or ideas they'd had for the business.

They'd just completed their first week on the job for

Flinders Homes, with everyone working at a much more comfortable pace. Jess could see Remi was happier, more relaxed and had kept to her promise of working less. She now spent two days a week at home working on the business. And with the new marketing strategies implemented, they'd drummed up enough work to be booked out three months ahead, with more quotes still rolling in. Maybe they *would* need more help...

"Actually, six really would round things out..." Jess trailed off.

They shared a look, Remi lifting her arm in the air before she could argue. "Excuse me, Freya?"

"Yes, what do you need?" The young woman strolled over, face open and friendly.

"Any chance you'd want to be an apprentice?" Remi asked boldly. Jess admired the confident woman sitting back in her chair, eyebrow raised. Her signature look. No wonder she'd fallen for her charms—how could you say no to that?

God, she loved this woman.

The realisation hit her so hard she flinched. Here Jess was, staring at Remi all starry-eyed and full of adoration, how could it not be love?

The waitress chuckled, taking Remi's remark as a joke and walking off.

"Well, I tried." Remi turned to Jess and paused, searching her face. "You okay?"

"Yeah. Yep." She was going to burst. And she really hadn't planned on doing this at a work event.

"What?" Remi pressed, bright green eyes peering at her through long lashes.

She bit down on her tongue, trying to hold it in just a little longer. Her smile betraying her, becoming too big, too much—

"I love you." There. It was out. And *oh, god* the relief. So much pressure on those first three words. Why?

She realised she'd started gripping Remi's hand too tight and eased off slightly.

Remi was staring at her, eyes in wonder, jaw slack, before curling into a wide grin.

"I love you, too," she replied, squeezing her hand under the table as she did. It was said so simply, like she'd spoken the words a million times before.

Jess's heart burst at the declaration.

This woman.

They'd already been through so much together, and yet as Jess sat there, it felt like it was only the beginning. She leaned into Remi, eyes never wavering. "I'm so glad I jumped onto that other train."

Remi's eyebrows furrowed, perplexed. "Okay, not the next words I expected out of your mouth."

Jess waved her off. "You know, the life analogy I told you about. Jumping from one running train to another. Taking a chance on a new journey. New me."

Remi relaxed, eyes crinkling at the edges. "Right. I'm with you."

"I sure hope you're with me." Jess nudged her shoulder in jest. "Because I am so excited for what the future holds for us, and it finally feels like we're on the right path."

Remi grinned. "Me too, Jess. Me too."

Acknowledgments

You know I had thoughts—very naive thoughts—that writing my second book would be easier. I mean, I'd already done it... right? But writing book one, my intention was: *can* I write a book? Writing book two: can I write a *better* book? And for that answer, dear reader, you'll have to tell me.

Swept Up In You was such an intrinsic journey for me, whereas On The Right Path was the first time I had manuscript feedback (thanks to editors Kathryn and Alex) where I could really dig into the world of the Tradie Lady Series. Wow, these amazing women really helped to push me as a writer.

I also have to thank the women who were part of the inspiration behind this idea, No. 1 Lady Tradie. These girls are so inspirational in what they do day-to-day, and for other tradeswomen in the industry. Getting to chat with them gave me the spark for: what if Jess was offered an apprenticeship?

For all the other amazing tradies who have helped along the journey. Shout out to Leanne from Tradie Lady Elechick for her knowledge on doing a trade apprenticeship and to Aimee from Zadie Workwear who is an inspiration doing so many fantastic things for women in trades.

Shout out to the BETA crew, you all helped craft this

into the best book it can be, and I'm forever thankful for your feedback and thoughts.

Thanks to Mum and Dad, you got us into this mess of renovating our house for the last couple of years and spurring us on to doing everything we could. I went into it as naive as I did in writing this book, and I wouldn't have it any other way.

Finally, to my wife. Words aren't enough, but you know I'll make you a damn good coffee. Thanks for being the best TA, and painting the tallest wall in the house, even when it was scary. I love that we push each other to do the hard things. Even when we fail, we fail happily.

Rian x

About the Author

Rian Birch writes fun and witty sapphic rom-coms for fans of low-angst romance who love a splash of emotional growth with their happily ever after. The perfect balance of sweet and spicy with a good dash of Aussie humour.

She lives in Adelaide with her wife where she likes to potter in her backyard food forest and cycle to new cafes around the city. Every one of her childhood stories ended with her characters coming home and having a cup of tea. She promises to write new endings for her adult novels.

Also by Rian Pirch

Swept Up In You

Tradie Lady Series Book 1

Swept Up In You is a fun and spicy lesbian romance that will have you laughing, crying and craving puppy cuddles.

Perfect for fans of low angst romance, who love a splash of emotional growth with their happily ever after.

Samantha Garner dreams of sailing away. If only her family business didn't have her completely anchored down. A conversation has her plotting new paths that may just get her out to sea, *if* she can avoid hurting the people she loves most.

Taylor Scott knows what she wants. To build up her maintenance business, forget about her ex, and to not—*definitely not*—get into another relationship. Discovering a new boat shop by accident lands her a client she didn't expect and can't take her eyes off.

As their friendship grows, a games night leads to a spark they can't ignore. While Sam questions everything she knows, Taylor must decide whether to keep her heart safe... or dive into the unknown.

Will they find common ground and sail off into the sunset, or will their relationship sink to the bottom before it even begins?

—

Anywhere But Here

Tradie Lady Series Book 3

A sapphic road trip rom-com with one bed and forced proximity that's not just a slow burn: It's a slow tease. From Rian Birch, author of *Swept Up In You* and *On The Right Path*, comes the next instalment of the unapologetically Aussie *Tradie Lady Series*.

Brooke Mayfield is back in the last place she wants to be: Adelaide. A place she hasn't called home in over ten years. She didn't see herself here at twenty-nine: broke, feeling lost and alone yet surrounded by family with their oh-so-perfect lives. Everything she does just feels like she's in the way with nowhere to go.

Jade "JJ" Johnson longs for a break. She's got the house and the business, but never carved out time for herself. She's ready to travel, starting in her home state of South Australia. Her only problem? Perfectionism is keeping her rooted to the spot, unable to make a decision on where to go and what to see.

When a chance encounter with JJ allows Brooke an opportunity to travel again, Brooke finds herself agreeing to go more out of spite than excitement. There's *no way* her boring state of South Australia could ever win her heart, and she'd be happy to prove JJ wrong. She's seen the world from every different viewpoint after all. Though maybe travel isn't all about where you're going, but who you're with...

Opposites definitely attract in this outback adventure that begs the question: Will their trip bring them closer together, or send one of them packing?

This can be read as a standalone but does feature characters introduced earlier in the series.